CW01221303

SAM CRESCENT

EVERNIGHT PUBLISHING ®

www.evernightpublishing.com

DAMAGED QUEEN

Copyright© 2019

Sam Crescent

Editor: Karyn White

Cover Art: Jay Aheer

Proofreader: Laurie White

ISBN: 978-1-77339-910-2

ALL RIGHTS RESERVED

WARNING: The unauthorized reproduction or distribution of this copyrighted work is illegal. No part of this book may be used or reproduced electronically or in print without written permission, except in the case of brief quotations embodied in reviews.

This is a work of fiction. All names, characters, and places are fictitious. Any resemblance to actual events, locales, organizations, or persons, living or dead, is entirely coincidental.

SAM CRESCENT

DEDICATION

To my amazing readers for giving me a chance. I hope you guys love this conclusion to my duet as much as I did writing it. You guys are the freaking BEST!

SAM CRESCENT

DAMAGED QUEEN

Darkness Within Duet, 2

Sam Crescent

Copyright © 2019

Prologue

Ten years later from The Initiation

Draven was precise as he slid his blade across the man's throat. No one in this world would ever be allowed to betray him. Not again.

Anyone who even thought it, or if there was even a hint of a rumor, he was going to slit the person's throat. No one would live to tell the tale of their betrayal, of how they made a fucking mockery of him.

"Are you done?" Axel asked, taking a long drag on his smoke.

"I'll be done when I'm fucking ready."

Axel held his hands up. "You're right. You're the judge, jury, and executioner. You're not going to find her."

Draven ignored his friend.

Oh, he heard every single word, but he wasn't paying attention.

Not today.

Not any fucking day.

"I'm not looking for her."

He'd given up on finding Harper years ago. She'd gone from Stonewall, left without a backward glance. His father had kept tabs on her, always dangling that shit in front of him as if it was some kind of fucking victory card. Whenever he went to find her, she was gone, moved on, and his father always knew. Part of him wondered if his father expected him to keep him alive based on his knowledge of *her*. He had the biggest fucking surprise of his life then.

So much had changed since Harper left. The town wasn't the same.

When the war started, it turned the streets red with blood. His father, Alan, had been planning to rid the world of everyone who opposed him, from Axel's father to the politicians who were threatening to turn their secrets in, as they were tired of being blackmailed.

Draven had been the one to make the final hit to Axel's father, to land the blow that would put his father out on top.

Even now, he still remembered the proud look on Alan's face, how he'd been so happy to finally have his son be something.

Alan never expected him to turn the gun on him.

There was only one outcome with an all-out war, and that was for him to rid the world of monsters. The only problem? During the process, Draven knew the beast within him had finally been set free. The darkness hadn't even been touched during this. From the moment he set about killing, about putting Alan as the leader, as the king, he'd been setting about his own father's destruction. As if he'd allow a world where Alan ruled.

Not on his watch.

Cleaning off Jett's knife, he pocketed the blade and stared over at Axel.

"You've been looking for her since the day she left."

"Are you fucking deaf? I'm not looking for her."

"Then why do you still have guys on the lookout for her? Looking for any possible crumb she may have left behind?" Axel asked. "She's gone, and she's not coming back. You just can't handle the fact you've been played. You were played ten years ago."

"I've got men out there looking for her because when I find her, and I will, I'm going to make sure she pays for everything we've lost. Everything she caused."

"Draven, let her go."

"No. I'm not letting her go. I gave her everything, and she threw it in my face as if I was fucking trash. Not going to happen."

Axel looked down at the dead bodies.

Draven stared at the blood and found a sense of calm in all of the chaos. This was his world now.

He watched as Axel pulled another cigarette from his pocket and lit it up. The scent filling the small room. The apartment block was rundown, filled with junkies and crack whores. Some of the women even tried to get him to buy them, to put them up for auction. They were used pussies, and his auctions only ever had virgins on them, especially now. He knew how much they fetched. The money was a more welcome price, and well, the bitches always stayed intact when he held them.

"Call the cleaning crew. I'm out of here."

"When is all of this going to stop, Draven? You've won. You own everything. You're the king! You've got everything your father ever wanted.

Stonewall is all yours, all of this is yours. You own the cities, the MCs, it's all yours."

Draven smiled. For a twenty-eight-year-old man, he certainly had a lot of power at his fingertips. He'd shown the world just how bad he could be, and some didn't like it. They tried to bring him down, and others, well, they wanted to kill him, to own him.

No one had ever won.

He was evil.

He heard the rumors. Men and women liked spreading rumors about him. Some said he was sired by the devil himself and they'd cast him out of hell as he was too bad even for that place. Others thought he was the boogeyman. Women were both excited by and afraid of him.

He never corrected anyone, never made excuses. He was what he was, and no one could change him.

Why hide it when people already thought the worst of him?

"I'll stop when I get what I want."

"What is it you want?" Axel asked. "Do you even know what you want?"

He stared at his friend, waiting.

Axel opened up his wallet and pulled out a picture.

Draven didn't need for him to open it to see.

It was the picture of the five of them together, taken during the night they stayed in the woods.

Him, Harper, Axel, Buck, and Jett.

All of them together.

When he made plans for a future that would never see the light of day.

"Do you still want to kill her?" Axel asked. "Give up. Let her live her life, wherever it is, because she's not worth your time or effort to drag this out."

Draven took the picture from him and stared down at her smiling face. Her head was pressed against his chest. Even though this had been ten years ago, he still felt her head as if it was only yesterday, leaning against him. The citrus scent of her. The smile that had called to him. The sweet cry of his name on her lips as she came. He'd truly believed she belonged to him. All of her, his.

It hadn't been the case.

Taking out his lighter, he put the flame to the picture and watched as it went up.

"Draven, what the hell?"

He didn't give it back to Axel even as he reached for it.

The only place this deserved to be was up in smoke like all of his plans and dreams. Harper, wherever the hell she was, better hope he never found her.

If he did, her life was his, and he intended to make her pay for everything.

Chapter One

Harper smiled against her pillow as kisses trailed down her back. The touch was so delicate and intimate, driving her need higher as she woke.

"Hello, sexy lady," Ethan said.

She rolled over as he gripped her hips and sighed. He skimmed his fingers down her thighs, and seeing him do this reminded her of another time, so long ago.

Sitting up, she pushed him to the bed, changing positions. "I want to be on top." Pushing the memories back, she smiled down at her boyfriend. She met Ethan when he came into the florist shop two years ago. He'd been buying flowers for his mother, and they'd hit it off. She hadn't realized he'd been flirting until it was pointed out to her.

After that, she tried flirting back, giving him back what he gave her, but it didn't feel right. No matter what she did, she always felt … fake.

Anyway, one night after drinks, one too many, she'd ended up back at his apartment, and they'd slept together. Since then, they'd been going steady until six months ago, when he asked her to move in. She didn't have a good enough reason to say no, and so, here she was, still living with him.

It's not that she didn't care about him. She did.

There wasn't a spark between them. She knew he cared about her, maybe even loved her, which was why she tried so hard to forget everything else and to just focus on him, on what he meant to her.

His cock was already hard as rock. He certainly was insatiable when it came to fucking.

Running her hand up and down his length, she smiled at him. Deep in her heart, she wished it was someone else. Another time. The time when she was eighteen years old and willing to take on four men, just to have the one. To be part of their group and have the void filled within her heart that had been left vacant with her mother's death. Only, it had all been torn away from her. Held hostage at Alan's deadly hands. The thought of never having Draven, Axel, Buck, and Jett in her world had nearly destroyed her. They didn't deserve to die because of her.

The threat of death and violence was what kept her away and would always hold her back. She didn't want Draven to die because of her, nor any of the guys. She wasn't worth their lives.

Not for the first time, she wondered if another initiation had begun. If they had a woman between them who bore their names. The thought of another holding their names, of them falling for her, filled her with jealousy. That was supposed to be *her*, not anyone else. Alan had fucked that up, and she hated him for it. She'd hoped Draven would one day figure it out, and come and find her. Only now, after ten years, she hoped he was living a good life.

Ethan had once asked about the ink at the small of her back.

She'd lied. She'd told him it was the names of pets that had passed. He'd thought it was cute and weird.

He didn't need to know it was the name of the guys she once belonged to.

The same guys she'd turned her back on at the threat of one of their fathers. So many times, she wanted to get on a bus and go back to town. To call Draven and tell him what happened. To let him know she was still there, still wanted him. Each time she lifted the phone, the threats would ring around her head and scare the fuck out of her.

So, she never called back.

For a time, she had gone to Europe, traveling around there before finally coming back and getting a job at the florist shop. Alan had demanded her time in Europe. He wanted her out of the country and had paid her to do it. For a few years, he'd even forced her to contact one of his men, who would make her complete a series of tasks. She tried not to think about those tasks she'd been forced to do. Luring young women to these men to be put up for sale. Alan had been sure to hold a great deal of leverage over her head in order for her to do everything he wanted. No matter where she went, there was always someone watching. Someone who reminded her of home. Alan had stopped calling her personally years ago, but his memory always lived on. She hadn't seen or heard from someone in a couple of years, and so, she'd tried to find a life for herself, and not to think about the women she'd hurt in the process. She'd been in Europe for nearly six years—five of those years with Alan calling her, making his demands. There came another year, where she didn't hear from him, but someone was always there, making sure she followed through on the task. Then, after being free for a month, with no one there, then another, followed by another, she finally felt it was time to head back to the States, which was exactly what she'd done. Since then, she'd been trying to work hard to forget all the damage she'd done.

There was no way for her to call Draven. After ten years, she still didn't want to risk killing him by disobeying Alan, and she also didn't want to draw Alan's attention to herself. He had so much dirt and evidence from all the work he'd forced her to do, that there was no one in the country who would believe she was being blackmailed.

She was over ten hours away from Stonewall, the

closest she'd ever been to home. Part of her was tempted to drive on through, but still fear kept her back.

"What's wrong?" Ethan asked.

"Nothing." She kept working her hand up and down his cock, aware of his gaze on her. "You're not liking what I'm doing?"

"I like it, a lot."

She leaned forward, taking his cock into her mouth, staring up at him, distracting him as the taste of his pre-cum flooded her tongue. She swallowed him down, licking and flicking the tip for more. Ethan groaned. His hand gripped the back of her head, pulling her down to take more.

She stopped fighting and let herself go, taking his cock into her mouth, closing her eyes, and thinking about someone else.

Even as she sucked Ethan off, she couldn't stop thinking about Draven.

Ten years was a long time to be without someone, and yet, she found herself thinking about him at the most inappropriate times.

His touch.

His mouth.

His eyes.

She missed them all. Wanted them all. Craved them all.

They're not yours anymore.

"Oh, fuck, baby. I'm going to come."

With her eyes squeezed shut, she swallowed down his cum without making a sound. When he was done, she pulled away, wiping at her eyes that were already watering. This was a weakness he couldn't see.

"Babe, you blow my mind."

"Good morning to you too."

He chuckled, his hand going to her thigh, and she

knew what he wanted to do.

"I've got to get ready for work."

"What about you?" he asked.

She still hadn't turned toward him. "I'm fine. You can make it up to me later." She didn't look back. Going into the bathroom, she closed the door. Staring at her reflection in the mirror, she grabbed her toothbrush and worked the taste of him out of her mouth.

The tears fell down her cheeks, and she hated this, hated feeling so alone.

"You okay?" Ethan asked, calling through the door.

"I'm fine. I'll be out in a minute." She finished her teeth, washed her face, brushed her hair, and when she looked normal, she stepped out of the bathroom.

He caught her hips, trapping her against the door. "Have you been crying?"

"No, of course not." She kissed his lips. "I hate to cut this short, but I've really got to go, babe." She pulled away and quickly worked her pants on, followed by a large shirt. She tucked her raven hair into a bun at the base of her neck, and didn't even bother with makeup. She rarely did.

"I was thinking we could go around to my parents' house this weekend," he said.

His parents were really judgmental and always asking questions. She tried to avoid them as much as possible.

That wasn't true, and Harper hated herself for thinking it. They were kind people, sweet, and they deserved to have a daughter-in-law who cared for their son and loved them. It looked like she wouldn't be getting her wish of avoiding them. There were only so many excuses she could make.

"Of course. I'll stop by the grocery store today on

my way home."

She grabbed her bag and rushed back to the fridge.

"Love you," Ethan said.

"You too."

She rushed out of the apartment, and instead of going to the elevator, she went straight to the stairs, releasing a breath as she broke out onto the busy city street.

Rain was already rushing down, and she pulled the hood of her jacket over her hair and headed in the direction of work.

She stopped off at a coffee stand, grabbing herself a pastry and too-bitter coffee. Still, she didn't have to linger at the apartment, and whenever thoughts of Draven entered her mind mid-cock suck, she always felt the need to get the hell out of dodge, to avoid questions. To avoid everything.

Her life with Draven was nothing more than a memory.

A few short months that changed her life, and yet, she was no better now than she was back then.

It's not like she could go and visit her mother's grave. She'd not been in contact with Ian, her father. All her life had changed because of Alan Barries and his threats. He'd torn her away from what she loved. She could give up her father—she fucking hated him anyway. The others, that was the hardest thing she had ever had to do in her life.

The thought of being in a world that didn't have Draven had killed a part of her. Even though her life was a good one, she knew deep down something was missing. Draven, Axel, Buck, and Jett. They were all missing from her life, and there was no way of getting that back.

She finished her pastry, throwing the wrapper in

the trashcan, followed by the coffee. There was only so much bitterness she could stand before it became too much.

Checking the time, she saw she had ten minutes before getting to work, but decided to be there early. There was nothing wrong with waiting to open up the shop.

Shoving her hands into her jacket, she bowed her head, watching her feet and those around her so she didn't bump into anyone.

The days were getting darker, shorter. It wouldn't be long before winter was upon them. It was already cold.

Ethan liked to snuggle. Most nights she only got a couple of hours' sleep with his constant mauling.

He's your boyfriend. He has a right to snuggle.

She got to the shop and saw the security barrier was already up and Miss Farris already there, setting out the shop.

Entering, she gave her boss a little wave before heading in the back.

She removed her jacket, placing it over the radiator, before putting her bag into the locker she'd been given. In a way, it was exactly like high school, only dirt wouldn't spill out of this one.

Nor would it have shitty, crass names scrawled all over the metal. They never had told her who wrote on her locker. It was going to be one of her tests, and she'd not been around long enough to see it through.

Putting her fingers to the door, she felt the tears sting her eyes and pulled away.

"How are you today?" Miss Farris asked.
"Good. You?"
"Really well. I had a hot date last night."
"Was this with the rich billionaire?"

"Nope. This was with a sweet guy. He's got a couple of scars to his face, but he came in a couple of weeks ago, and you know, we hit it off. He loves the scent of flowers."

"You haven't told me about this guy."

"To be honest, you've looked a little out of it. I didn't think you'd want to talk."

"Oh, I'm fine. You know me. Staring into space. You got a picture of this guy? Is he hot?"

Miss Farris, or Stephanie, was a sweet woman in her early thirties. Harper got her job as she passed the shop one day and it was Mother's Day. Stephanie was completely overrun, and she hadn't walked away. She'd gone into the shop and helped.

Stephanie hired her on the spot.

They were friends in a way. Neither of them hung out or socialized. Stephanie loved going to luncheons and dancing, while Harper preferred her own company and often declined any invitation. It worked for them.

"He doesn't like having his picture taken. I don't know what to say about him. He's fun, sweet, charming. He makes my heart race."

"Sounds like a good guy. What's his name?"

Before Stephanie answered, the door went and Harper cursed. She'd forgotten to lock it.

When she glanced back at her boss, Stephanie shrugged. They weren't due to open for another few minutes, but there was no point kicking out a customer.

Heading to the man, who looked completely lost, she offered a smile.

"Can I help you with anything?"

He lifted his head, and he looked genuinely happy to see her.

"Yes, I need to apologize to my fiancée about missing dinner. Do you recommend groveling of that kind?"

"What did she make?" Harper asked.

"Beef Wellington. She took the day off work for our anniversary."

"Ouch, not only did you miss the anniversary but also dinner." She winced. "I think we've got something for you that will have the right tone of grovel without being too desperate."

"I don't mind desperate," he said.

She laughed.

"You got it." She spent the next twenty minutes helping him to pick the right flowers to make it up to his woman.

Once she made the sale, Stephanie was with another customer and two more were in the shop.

This was what she loved about Stephanie's Flowers—she never had a dull moment. When all the flowers were purchased, all she had to do was fill up all of the empty spots.

By lunchtime she was starving.

Stephanie dealt with a customer, so Harper headed out to get them something to eat. She grabbed two vegetarian kebabs and coffees.

On her way back to the shop, she noticed a really expensive-looking black car. She paused, as it looked vaguely familiar. A man leaned against the car, arms folded, looking all serious. In her mind, it flashed back to Stonewall and to Marseille and Naples and the kind of vehicles she had to lead unsuspecting girls to, but she pushed it aside, and figured she must have been mistaken. Alan had always told her what city to go because of the kind of girls he wanted to get. It always sickened her what he made her do.

There's no way she would see someone from Stonewall here.

She lived far enough away that no one would ever find her. She couldn't believe for a second that she'd tempted fate in some way.

Just as she was about to step back, she saw a man leave the florist shop. She couldn't get a good look at him. His head was bowed over his cell phone, and he looked really deep in thought. Only when she saw them drive off, whoever they were, did she approach the shop.

Stephanie looked so happy as she walked inside.

"Who was that?"

"Oh, you saw him." Stephanie gasped. "He was right here, and he's going to take me out on a date tonight. He wants me to look all pretty, and I think I'm in love."

Harper chuckled. "Go you. You should totally take it."

"My heart is racing. My lips are tingling. I feel like I'm on top of the world. Is this how you feel with Ethan?"

Harper paused and had to keep the smile forced into place. "Yes."

"Women who are in love are so lucky. I can't think right now. I need food."

Harper laughed, only this time it was more on the verge of a little hysterical. Stephanie didn't notice, her attention on the kebab in her hands.

For Harper, she wasn't thinking about Ethan.

No, about an entirely different man.

The one she'd left ten years ago so his own father wouldn't kill him.

She pushed aside the bitterness, the simmering rage that bubbled beneath the surface as she took a bite of her kebab.

There was no point in thinking about all that could have been. At the end of the day, nothing could change what had happened between them. She couldn't wave a magical wand and pretend her life was normal or that her meeting with Alan in his office hadn't occurred.

It had.

Her life had changed forever.

Throughout lunch Stephanie talked nonstop about her new boyfriend, only pausing when a new customer came in. By the end of the day, Harper just wanted to head on home. Hearing about Stephanie's new love interest hadn't exactly filled her with joy. If anything, it only served to remind her of what she'd lost.

With Draven, she'd fallen in love. With Axel, Buck, and Jett her feelings had been different. She cared about them, but with her and Draven, she'd felt a spark. Even when he was pissing her off, she'd been drawn to his green eyes and that smile. It always reminded her of doing bad things.

She stopped off at the grocery store as she said she would, and made her usual trip, picking up the ingredients Ethan always liked to cook with. She cared about him, but was it enough? She knew deep in her heart that staying with him would be a huge mistake. He deserved someone who thought about him all the time, who didn't see his constant love confessions as a pain.

One day she'd have to leave him. She knew that.

There's no way she could be with him for a long time, simply because he should be with someone who loved him back.

Harper wasn't that person. Deep down inside, she loved another and was broken inside, damaged, and Ethan couldn't repair that.

****

The weekend at his parents' house was as perfect as Harper expected. They were loving, and after forty years of marriage, the love still sparkled between them.

She couldn't help but watch them together, remembering her own parents before her mother killed herself, or at least before Ian decided to leave.

"So, Harper, you two look so amazing together," his mother said.

She rested her head against Ethan's chest. "Thank you. That was a really wonderful chicken."

"Oh, I know how to roast a good chicken. Don't you worry, I'll teach you how. I like to make sure our boys are well-fed."

"Yeah, Harper, you're going to have to go through the cooking course that we all did." This came from Fran, who'd married the youngest son.

Harper had no interest at all in being taught how to cook.

"My mom's not that bad," Ethan said, wrapping an arm around her.

"You live in a beautiful area. Would it be okay if I go for a walk? I don't mean to be rude."

"No, no, of course not. You and Ethan go and have some time together. I'll prepare a light snack for when you get back."

His mother was always feeding them.

Grabbing a jacket, she pulled on some gloves, and Ethan wasn't too far behind. Not what she had in mind, but she couldn't exactly complain.

"I'm sorry about my parents," Ethan said.

"Don't worry about it."

"They like you though. I know they want to adopt you. After everything that happened with your parents."

Since Alan had pushed her out of Stonewall with no chance of ever going back there, her parental story had changed. Both of her parents had "died in a car crash." It was a sad event but one she'd moved on from. Yes, there were times she missed them, but she couldn't bring them back. There was no point in going to a town that only held bad memories, or at least that's what she told Ethan.

"It's fine. They don't need to adopt me." She smiled.

Ethan took her hand, and rather than getting the fresh air she felt she needed, instead she felt that crushing weight of expectation. She'd noticed the coy looks his family were giving him. They were all waiting for him to do or say something, and she didn't know why it scared her. Something was going to happen, and the more time she spent with him, the bigger the chance of him asking her or saying something. It would be easier for her to be cruel to him, but again, she didn't have anywhere else to live, and she had moved in with him to make life easier.

"It's getting cold."

"That it certainly is. If you think all that food is a big deal, you should wait for Thanksgiving."

"You dish up a feast?"

"That we do."

She'd gotten out of the last couple of Thanksgivings due to "other commitments." Living together, well, she hadn't thought about how to get out of it this year.

"You have a wonderful family."

It was true. Ethan was wonderful. His family was too. Everyone and everything were great.

She was the problem.

They stopped near a field. The entire ground was covered in amber and fire-red leaves. The scene looked so beautiful. It hadn't been dirtied up yet by the rain.

"Actually, there's something I really want to ask you. I know we're going through a bit of a rough patch right now, and I'm not even going to pretend that I understand it. I don't. I mean, I thought we were in a really great place."

"Ethan, we are. I'm sorry. I'm just. It's around that time. You know, it's hard." Again, the guilt weighed her down. She only hoped it was the same time that she'd said her parents died.

She couldn't go back, and with her constantly looking in the past, she'd stopped herself from going forward.

"I get it. I do. I … I love you, Harper. I love you more than anything I've ever loved in this world. When I look at the future, I see you. I see us together."

"Ethan?"

"Let me finish. I want you to marry me. It's what my parents would love as well. They know I wanted to ask you this weekend. It's why I brought you up here. We're out in the country, and it's beautiful. This scene beats that of the smelly city any day of the week. One day, I want to come back here. Start a family. I want it to be with you. I know I can make you happy, and that's why I'm hoping that you'll consider me. I hope you'll say yes."

Tears filled her eyes, and she looked at him and smiled. This was why she shouldn't be with him. He loved her. He was willing to do whatever it took to make her happy. Ethan was a good guy.

Knowing all of this, she *should* walk away.

She shouldn't give him false hope, and yet, knowing how serious this was for him, she did. She told him yes, and the rest of the weekend was filled with celebration.

His parents were happy. His sister- and brothers-in-law were happy. His siblings were happy. Everyone was so fucking happy.

All the time, Harper played her part well. She kept her smile in place, and no one knew any differently.

They didn't know she was breaking apart or that this wasn't in fact what she wanted. Everyone around her only saw what they wanted to.

So, she celebrated.

She got drunk, and Ethan carried her to bed, and he was sweet. He didn't try to have sex with her.

No, the perfect gentleman.

He was the only guy she had slept with since leaving Stonewall.

She'd never been the kind of woman to enjoy casual sex, and even though there'd been offers, it hadn't been anything she'd taken up. From the moment she'd been forced out of her town, she'd felt dead inside. No one could compare to the men she once knew, not a single person.

By Sunday evening, she wore a ring, her stomach was full, and the apartment looked so dreary compared to the house she'd been in. Ethan was in a particularly chatty mood, so she didn't even have to make the effort there.

Not bad really. Her life was perfect. Only *she* was the one that didn't think it was.

One day soon, she'd see it was better. She'd have faith once again.

That day wasn't today, or even next week.

She only hoped it would happen soon.

Chapter Two

One month later

Harper was grabbing down a box of decorations that Stephanie wanted to use to fill the shop to make it look all pretty.

There was dust on top, and she used a cloth to wipe most of it off. A sneeze broke out. Stephanie had lost her mind the moment she saw the ring, and for Harper, it was getting easier to wear it.

She tended to ignore it, but every once in a while, it caught the light.

With time passing, she had started to come to terms with the new future. She needed to let go of the past, to stop thinking of herself as ever going back to Stonewall.

Opening up the box, she stared inside at all the seasonal decorations that ranged from pumpkins to Christmas fairy lights, and there was even a witch in there somewhere. For some odd reason, she thought about her father.

She'd not given him much thought in so many years.

He was the last person she often thought about, and yet, right now, she wondered how he was doing.

If he'd like to know that she was still alive and safe.

That she was going to get married.

Moving to the desk, she stared at the phone, and before she could chicken out, she dialed the house number she remembered. She was shocked to find that it was ringing.

"Hello," a female voice said after a few seconds.

It had been so long since she heard Hannah speak

that Harper didn't even know if it was the right voice.

"I was wondering if a Mister Ian Miller is there?" she asked.

"Of course. Who should I say is calling?"

This made Harper panic for a split second. "A client."

"Certainly, just a moment."

She heard noise as if someone was walking. Then the muffled voices until finally, he was on the phone.

"This is Ian Miller. Who may I ask is calling?"

Her hand fisted at her side. Even as there was a chill in the air, panic gripped her. She took a deep breath. This wasn't her talking to Draven, so Alan shouldn't hurt him. She was only reaching out to her dad.

"Hey, Dad," she said.

"Harper!"

He sounded shocked, desperate almost. "Fuck, it's Harper. Honey, are you okay? Where are you?"

"I … erm, I'm fine. I've been fine for some time. I just, I needed to call you. I shouldn't really be calling you." What if this did, in fact, break the rules? She didn't want Draven to end up hurting because of her selfishness.

"Are you coming back?"

"No. I don't think so."

"Don't come back, Harper. I mean it. Stonewall isn't what it was. I mean, it's … just don't come back."

Tears filled her eyes, but she didn't argue with him. "So, I'm going to be getting married."

"Married?"

"Yes. I met a great guy. He's wonderful, and I know this is weird, but I felt the need to call you. I really shouldn't have called you. I know that now. I'm going to hang up now."

"Harper, wait. Why did you leave?" Ian asked.

"Why didn't you say anything? Call sooner?"

She thought about it, all the situations going around in her head. "I couldn't call anyone. It was a decision I made."

She'd hated her father back then, but she wasn't willing to have Alan hurt him. No one was going to die because of her.

"I want to be able to call you."

"I'm not going to give you my number. I'll call you when I'm ready." With that, she hung up and took a deep breath.

Lifting up the box of decorations, she headed out of the shop just as someone else was leaving. From the dreamy look on Stephanie's face, it had been the man who was currently rocking her world.

"You keep looking like that and you're going to need one of these soon." She held up her engagement ring.

Stephanie laughed. "I wouldn't mind him wanting to get engaged to me. He's a man that knows what he's doing."

"Sounds fun."

"Yes."

Harper put the box on the floor and frowned. "You know, you've never once told me his name."

"Oh, that's easy. His name's Jett."

This made Harper's heart race. "What?"

"Jett. That's his name. He's a businessman. His company is expanding, which is why he's in the city. He's got to head on home, but he'll be back in a couple of weeks. He wants to have dinner."

It couldn't be *her* Jett?

The Jett from her past.

He didn't own the name. It wasn't like it was copyrighted for only him to use.

"What does he look like?" Harper asked.

"Oh, brown hair, brown eyes. Do not let the suit scare you. He's got some scars on his face that he said were from some accident."

"Do you have a picture?" Jett from her past had black hair, a slightly lighter shade then her own.

"No, he doesn't like to have his picture taken. He told me it reminds him of everything he's lost."

It couldn't be him.

"Oh, well, he sounds like an amazing guy. I've got a question though," Harper asked. "I know it's kind of crazy, but when I was growing up, I knew a Jett."

Stephanie gasped. "Do you think he's one of your friends?"

"No, no, of course not. But, does he carry a knife?" Harper was going crazy.

Her boss laughed. "A knife? No, of course not. He's such a sweetheart. He doesn't carry a knife, or a gun. Just a pen to sign his contracts. I'm starting to wonder about you, Harper. I wonder if that ring is messing with your head. I heard of mom brain, but what about fiancée brain?"

Harper forced a laugh. "Yes, you're totally right. Of course you are." She rolled her eyes. "It's just me. I know I'm going crazy. Let's take a look what we have here."

She dove into the box, more than happy for a distraction. What could she have done if it had been Jett Henry from her past? It wasn't like she could have done anything. Not for the first time, she wondered what Alan had said about her disappearance.

Her dad certainly didn't know. He didn't have a clue. If Ian wasn't told the truth, what did that mean about Alan telling Draven and the others?

Nothing.

He wouldn't have told them anything. For Alan, he needed her out of the picture. She interfered with his plans and was a thorn in his side that got in the way.

Draven would have been made to feel the worst.

Her body tensed up, and it was like a dark cloud fell over her as she thought about what it would mean for her if she ever met Draven again.

Running away, turning her back on them, it was the ultimate betrayal.

Rubbing at her arms, she excused herself to get a sweater. Pulling it over her head, she tried not to think of Draven, what it could mean for her if he ever found out where she was.

For some strange reason, she had a feeling that ten hours' travel away from Stonewall wasn't enough.

****

Draven stood in Ian's home office. It had been a long time since he'd been back at the old man's place.

Ten years.

Ten years since he'd banged on Ian's door and demanded to know what he'd done and what he'd said to Harper. Even though his father had told him the truth, he needed to know if it *was* actually the truth.

Ian didn't have a clue back then. He'd let him inside his home though, and Draven had stood in Harper's untouched room.

She'd left them at the mall. Run away.

Standing in Ian's office, all those feelings came rushing back to him.

Draven ignored them.

They meant nothing to him now. He was a man now, not some boy hoping to have found the girl for himself and his friends.

"It's good to see you, Draven."

"Cut the crap. You know why I'm here. You had

no time for me all those years ago. Nothing has fucking changed. Just tell me what Hannah was so desperate to talk to me about." Even though his father was dead, Hannah's loyalty was still to him. Of course, they still paid her handsomely to do everything they told her to.

Seeing the anger flash across Ian's face, he laughed. "You really think that she loves you?"

"I'm not here to talk about Hannah."

"No, I'm sure you're not. You've still not handed her back though, have you?" Draven shrugged.

"What happened to you, Draven?" he asked.

"What's the matter, Ian? Don't like the man I've turned into?"

"You're a better man than your father ever was, and you know it."

Draven laughed. "If that's what you need to tell yourself to help you sleep at night."

"I got a call from Harper."

This made Draven pause. Hannah had said Ian got a phone call that had spooked him, not who it was.

Now, he was fucking pissed. "And?"

"She … she's getting married," Ian said. "She sounded lost, and I don't know, as if something was bothering her."

"Why didn't you come to me with this?"

"She's my daughter, Draven."

"And she's a woman that is on my ultimate shit list. I think you need to understand here, Ian. You or her."

He pulled out his gun and stared over at Ian. The man went white.

"You think I'm a good guy, but I'm not. I never have been. I'm not a man to mess with, Ian. What else do you know?" he asked.

Ian shook his head. "I don't have anything else. I

don't ... this is the number she called on." He handed him a slip of paper, and Draven laughed.

"Even after all this time, you'll sell out your daughter to make sure you live."

"You don't have to hurt her, Draven."

"You're right. I don't have to. Doesn't mean I'm not going to. So, she's still alive. This is interesting news." Draven laughed.

"Don't, Draven, please, I'm begging you."

"I'll kill you. Would you like that? Life for a life."

"What did Harper do to you?" Ian asked.

Draven stared at Ian, and the temptation to shoot him in the head was strong. He could do it, make Hannah clean up the mess. Maybe he should save it for when Harper was back in town and make her watch as he tortured her father.

He wondered if she'd even care.

Staring down at the number, he smiled.

"She left."

"Women leave, Draven. It's the way of life."

"Your ex-wife killed herself because of a broken heart. It is not, nor will it ever be, the same fucking thing," Draven said. "If you want to save your daughter, then offer your life up on a slab, and I'll kill you instead of her."

He stood, waiting.

Ian did nothing.

He said nothing, and Draven burst out laughing.

"Some men, they think they've got what it takes to make the ultimate sacrifice, but when they're faced with a real challenge, they've got fuck all to offer." Draven lifted up the number. "Thanks for this."

He walked out of the office. Hannah was waiting by the door. She held a smile.

"I did good?"

Draven stared at her.

All of her good looks were long gone. In the war that broke out in Stonewall, she'd put on a considerable amount of weight, and age hadn't been kind to her. He could imagine Ian was regretting his decision to go with Hannah. From what he remembered, his first wife was a stunner even as she aged.

For a fleeting second, he wondered how Harper had aged.

Pushing that aside, he made way for the anger, for the pain that always took its place.

"You're still getting paid, aren't you?" He left the house and climbed into the backseat of the waiting limo.

His driver didn't say a word as they took him to his home. Axel's old place. He wouldn't walk down the street, not to talk to anyone.

They were all afraid of him, which was how he wanted it to be.

Once at his home, he climbed out and headed into his office. Pulling out his cell phone, he dialed Axel's number.

"Oh, yeah, baby, give it to me. Give me that big fat cock. I need it. I want it. Please, Yes, oh yes, oh yes."

There was another feminine scream and Axel's chuckle.

"What can I do for you?"

"Your current girlfriend?"

"You know I love the good girls. This one is so beautiful and sweet."

"What were you doing to her?" Draven asked, mildly amused.

"Me? I was doing nothing to her. I've got my bodyguard pumping away inside her. I have a gift, Draven, you know that. A gift of making a woman do exactly as I want. I use it to my advantage."

"Yeah, well, guess what?"

"You miss me and want me to fuck you," Axel asked.

Draven burst out laughing. "Harper called her father."

Silence from Axel met his reply.

The sex was still going on in the background. The sounds faded to silence, and he heard the door close.

"What do you want to do?" Axel asked.

"What makes you think I want to do anything?"

"I know you, Draven. After all this time, you're going to want revenge for what she did. You want me back home?"

"Actually, I want you to go and pick her up. I think it's only fair. I'll be waiting for you." Draven hung up his cell phone and texted Axel the number that would help them locate her.

He sat back in his chair, and still, he held the number in his fist.

Putting his legs up on the desk, he smiled. When he got her back, Harper was in for a rude awakening. He was going to make her wish she'd never left Stonewall, and when he was finished, he was going to bury her right next to her mother.

Revenge was a dish best served cold.

In ten years, he'd not gotten over her betrayal.

He'd asked her to never run away, to come to him, and she'd ignored what he wanted, and now, he was going to get the payback he deserved.

Chapter Three

"My mom wants us to go to her place this weekend and to eat cake," Ethan said.

Harper frowned. "Why?"

"It's what engaged couples do."

"They eat cake?" She rolled her eyes, pulling out the money the guy needed for her lunch. She was on the phone to Ethan as he was talking about the benefits of heading home, not to the apartment, but to his small town.

"Yes. We've got to pick what flavor we want for our cake, and the frosting. It's a big thing."

"I'm not much of a cake person. You pick it."

"Honey, this is something we do together."

Not when you've got four other men's names printed on your back.

"You want me to help pick out cake. You do know I'm supposed to pretend to be on a diet right now."

Ethan laughed. "Baby, I love you the way you are."

After she left Stonewall, she'd lost weight.

She did skip meals often, and eating, when thinking about all that she lost, it didn't exactly give her an appetite. In the past few years she had put some weight back on, rounding her hips and stomach once again. Whenever she looked at herself in the mirror, she always thought about those girls. The ones that wouldn't get a choice in their life anymore.

"Then we'll go and eat cake. I've got to go. Bye."

She didn't give him a chance to say he loved her.

"A future bride should look a lot happier than you are," the man behind the burger stand said.

"Yeah, well, weddings don't exactly thrill me."

"Tell your boyfriend you don't love him and save yourselves both a lot of money and pain."

She took her change as well as hers and Stephanie's lunches.

There was no witty retort that came to her, and rather than keep the rest of the people in the line waiting, she turned on her heel and walked away.

Tucking her hair behind her ear, she walked back toward the shop.

She noticed the car, once again waiting. Stephanie had looked so happy this morning. She said her boyfriend had made a rare appearance last night, and it would seem he was back.

Entering the shop, she saw the Closed sign had been put into place. The moans coming from the back of the shop, in Stephanie's office, let her know that her boyfriend was very much making up for lost time.

"I've got food," Harper said, shouting as loud as she could to be heard.

Stephanie let out a chuckle, and there was a masculine groan.

"I'll be right out."

Harper sat on the stool, waiting. She opened up her burger and took a large bite. She was staring out of her window, when someone cleared their threat.

She smiled at Stephanie.

"I'm so pleased you came back in time. Harper, I would love for you to meet Jett Henry."

Harper's smile dropped as she looked over Stephanie's shoulder. The man behind her was not the Jett she knew from ten years ago.

No, the man behind her, with a half-scarred face, was Axel Cook.

"You know, Harper knew a Jett from her school. Do you two know each other?" Stephanie asked.

Harper felt a little dizzy. Remembering she had to chew her food, she started to do so, vigorously. This was really bad. She felt sick to her stomach. The food in her mouth no longer appealed.

"I'm sure Jett is a common name."

Axel was in the shop.

Right in front of her.

She'd recognize him anywhere, even with the scars. They stood out, but it also enhanced the side of his face that wasn't scarred. How beautiful he was.

Axel had always been good-looking. To some women, he'd been the best-looking guy of the four of them.

Her heart started to race, and her hands shook.

"I need to use the bathroom," Harper said.

Getting to her feet, she heard the concern in Stephanie's voice. She stood in the bathroom, staring at her reflection in the mirror.

She was white as a ghost.

Her past was back.

With Stephanie's back to him, he'd looked fucking pissed. The ten years apart had clearly made him angry. Axel was angry at her, and she imagined so were the other three.

She couldn't stay locked in the bathroom, and as she turned to leave, Axel was there.

He stepped into the bathroom and closed the door. Before she could do anything, his hands were wrapped around her throat, and he slammed her against the wall, near the mirror.

"So, you've been here, all this time that I've been coming here. How about that, we've been missing each other. I wonder if that was fate interfering, letting you live just a bit longer."

He'd cut off her air, and she grabbed at his arm,

panicking.

"You need me for something now?" he asked. "Oh, you need air?"

He released her neck, and she breathed deeply.

Once.

Twice.

He held her again, cutting off her air.

Tears filled her eyes as she saw nothing in his gaze. The Axel she once knew was gone. All that was there was the cold, blank stare of a killer.

A man who was going to kill her.

Suddenly, he let her go, and she gasped again, stepping away from him, trying to get as far from him as humanly possible, in the small space.

Taking a deep breath, she tried not to panic, but Axel didn't leave her alone. He didn't turn his back on her.

"Where's Draven?" she asked.

Axel smiled. "He's going to be expecting you."

"No. I'm not going back."

"Let's get something straight, Harper. You're coming with me, whether you like it or not."

She shook her head. "Why are you using Jett's name?"

"So much you don't know about. Poor thing. Draven's going to have a lot of fun with you."

Tears filled her eyes.

"You're going to go out there and tell Stephanie how ill you feel. Then you're going to walk a couple of blocks. I'll pick you up, and guess what, we're going home."

"Don't, Axel, please, I'm begging you."

"I always wondered what it would be like to have a woman beg for me." Axel sighed. "It always sounds so … desperate. You'll do it or I will go out there and kill

Stephanie, and it will be all your fault."

"You don't want to kill her," she said, hoping to find the Axel of the past.

"She's been a good fuck up to now, but I don't care. The bitch can die for all I care. Your choice. Dead Stephanie or alive and breathing Stephanie."

She nodded. There was no choice for her. Words failed her. She'd never seen Axel look so mean, so angry. It was all directed at her. Panic filled her, and she tried not to cry.

"Go."

Without argument, she grabbed her bag and jacket. She made excuses to Stephanie, who was filled with concern.

The only thing was, Harper didn't stop at the corner a couple of blocks away, waiting for him. Axel intended to hurt her, and not only that, he gave the merest hint that it was exactly what Draven wanted to do as well. She wasn't about to hand herself over to anyone.

Cutting through the streets, she used all the shortcuts she knew to get to her apartment faster. All she needed to do was grab a few things, leave the engagement ring, and get the hell out of there before Axel hurt her or anyone else she cared about.

Even as tears fell down her face, she didn't stop. With her key in her hand, she charged into the building, taking the stairs. The elevator was the slowest one on the planet, and right now, speed was all she could hope for.

Rushing up the steps, she got to her door.

Her hand was shaking so bad it took her three tries to get the key in the hole.

"Come on, please, come on." She sobbed against the fear that clutched within her chest.

This was not how she imagined meeting Axel or anyone else.

She charged into her apartment, slamming the door as she went to the bedroom. Opening up drawers, she grabbed her passport, some money, and her bag. Throwing in some clothing, she was heading out just as Axel entered the apartment.

Her heart raced as he closed the door slowly, quietly, carefully, his gaze on her.

He'd aged, and the scar across one side of his face let her know that it hadn't been done all that well.

"What did I tell you to do?" he asked.

"Please, Axel, let me leave."

"You mean how you left us once? You just ran away. Didn't even give us a chance to help you, or for you to explain yourself. What it was exactly that forced you away? You betrayed us. You used us for your own gain, and then went into the arms of our enemies."

She had no idea what Alan had told them, but she heard the pain and bitterness within his voice. Her heart broke. Gone was the playful Axel she once knew.

"Please, I don't want to cause any trouble."

"There's no trouble at all. You're going to give me your bags, and we're going downstairs. You're getting in the car, and we're leaving."

"Please, I can't go back there."

He chuckled. "You seem to think this is some kind of polite request. There's no request here, Harper. I'm telling you. You're going back to Stonewall." He grabbed her hand, and she cried out.

"You're hurting me."

"We've not even come close to hurting you."

She cried out, and as her cell phone rang, he wrapped his fingers around her throat once again.

He lifted up her cell phone, and she saw it was Ethan.

"Ethan, who is this? Is this your new little

boyfriend?"

"He has nothing to do with this. He's innocent," she said, gasping for breath.

"Well, let's see if he wants to have something to do with this. I wonder how much Ethan knows about you. Does he know what those names mean on your back?"

She cried out as he let her go but only long enough to turn her and to fist a hand in her shirt, twisting it out of his way.

The tears were coming thick and fast now. Her cell phone stopped ringing. If she knew Ethan, he'd call again.

Axel slammed her back against the wall. His hand was on her neck, but he wasn't squeezing this time.

She knew she'd have bruises from where he touched her. This Axel, she didn't know him, and he was determined to make her hurt. The pain took her by surprise as he kept on holding her.

"Do you love him?"

"Just leave him alone." Her cell phone started to ring again, and she whimpered. This wasn't what she wanted. Why was Axel even here?

"The poor bastard doesn't even know that you don't love him. I'll put him out of his misery."

She cried out as he drew a gun and pressed it against her temple.

The intent was there as he ran it down her face to under her chin.

"I will kill this motherfucker if you don't end things now. If you don't tell him that you're leaving and want nothing more to do with him."

"Please," she said.

"I'm not going anywhere. You'll do as I say or you will hate the consequences. What's it going to be?"

Her cell phone stopped ringing, but she knew it would only be a few seconds before it started again.

Sure enough, it rang again.

"Wow, this guy is persistent. I imagine he thinks your pussy is made of gold."

Taking the cell phone from Axel, she answered it. How she was able to press the tiny button was beyond her. Her hands shook from her fear, and with Axel breathing down her neck, she couldn't focus.

"Hello," she said. Her voice was croaky from Axel's grip.

"Harper, baby, you okay? You sound different?"

"I'm fine. Just ... got a cold I think." She flinched as Axel pressed the gun against her head.

He'd do it as well.

"So, I'm thinking you and I should go to that cute little Italian place I saw around the corner from your shop. What do you think?"

"Actually, Ethan, I ... I can't see you anymore."

Ethan burst out laughing. "What the hell are you talking about?"

"I don't love you. I've never loved you, and I don't see this going anywhere. I'm sorry. But I'm leaving your engagement ring in the apartment. Bye, Ethan. I hope you find someone else who deserves you."

She turned off her cell phone.

Axel took it from her, dropping the device to the floor and stamping on it. She heard the plastic crush beneath his foot.

"Take it off."

"Why don't you leave me alone?"

"What's the matter, Harper? Am I playing too rough for you?"

"This isn't you."

"You don't know who the hell you're even

dealing with."

"I knew you once."

"A lifetime ago."

"Ten years is not that long." She didn't know why she was arguing with him, trying to reach to him, make him remember she wasn't the enemy.

You are.

He slammed his hand against her head, and it took everything in her not to scream. She'd never seen him like this, or at least, his anger was never directed at *her*.

"Do you know how many people can die in that time? What can happen? Look at my face, sweetheart. Do you even remember what I looked like before this?"

"What happened?"

"None of your business. You'll find out all in good time." He grabbed her arm. Just as they got to the door, he glared at her. "Make a sound. Scream. If you draw attention to us, I will make you wish you never made a sound. Anyone who dies from this moment forward, is your fucking fault."

She didn't fight him as he pulled her along, waiting for the elevator.

It was on the tip of her tongue to tell him about the stairs being faster. As she opened her mouth, the doors pinged, and they stepped into the empty metal cage.

She took a deep breath, and Axel smirked.

"You got even hotter," he said.

She glanced down at her body. Torn jeans, Ethan's old faded shirt, and her hair falling around her and messy. She'd not had the time to run a brush through it. She'd gained some weight in the past few months, and her hips and ass had filled out some. She always had large breasts, and that hadn't changed. Most of the time, she hid her curvy body in jeans and a large shirt, but with Axel pressing against her, no doubt he could feel it.

"Thanks."

"I know Draven's going to want to fuck you again."

"Let me go, Axel. I don't want to harm any of you."

He burst out laughing. "Oh, baby, you couldn't harm us if you tried."

"What happened?"

"Life happened." The doors opened up, and she kept with him as he marched out to the waiting car.

Part of her expected him to dump her in the back of the trunk, but instead, he held the door open.

"Your carriage awaits."

She stepped inside and slid to the far door. She tried the handle, only to find it was already locked.

"I love that you're a fighter. It's going to be so much fun watching you break."

"I don't break."

"You're not as strong as you think you are. That's okay. You'll soon learn your place."

"And where is my place?" she asked, snapping out each word.

He smiled.

"With the scum of the earth, Harper. You deserve to rot in fucking hell."

She had nothing to say. His hatred of her shocked her to the core.

All she did was leave Stonewall to protect them. He clearly didn't know the truth. What did she expect though? Alan to tell the truth? That bastard needed to weave a tale that made her look like the enemy.

He'd never tell anyone what he did or what he threatened.

Rubbing at her temples, she felt the first stirrings of a headache. She had a feeling that in ten hours, her life was never going to be the same again.

****

"None of them are any good," Draven said, pointing at the line of women. The stench coming off them irritated him as he stood looking at the merchandise.

"Sir, they are the best on offer."

"I bet half of them are already carrying diseases. You need to learn to keep your hands off the merchandise. I see dried cum on their legs. They are filth." Draven nodded to his man, who raised a gun and shot each woman in turn.

They were all sick, and besides, it would be a more peaceful ending for them than what this piece of shit pimp had planned.

"What the fuck, man? They were good women. They sucked cock."

"I'm growing increasingly bored with your idea of 'good women,' Ralph. Let's get one thing straight, this is not good."

"You're going to pay for them," Ralph asked.

Draven stared at Ralph. He did business with him because he was normally reliable when it came to women who served.

"You dare to speak to me like that?"

"Draven, dude, come on. Times are tight."

"You think I can make that excuse to my clients. The ones that want fresh pussy three times a year. You think I tell them times are tight. Pussy is hard to come by."

Ralph went pale.

"You're one of many kinds of men, Ralph, and I grow increasingly bored."

"Draven."

It was the last word Ralph spoke before his man shot him.

Draven stared down at the bloody mess on the floor. With the stench of sex, death, and decay in the air, he needed a shower.

What a total waste of his time.

"Clean this shit up," he said, leaving the docks. He went straight to his car, climbing in the back, and checking his messages.

Axel: **I've got her. Heading to the house. Be there in ten, maybe sooner.**

Draven kept reading over it.

There was only one person Axel could possibly have.

Harper.

Axel had Harper.

He held his cell phone so tight that the screen cracked. Dropping the device back into his pocket, he'd have to get rid of it safely. He tended to drop his cell phones in buckets of acid so nothing remained.

Rubbing at his temple, he wondered what she looked like. Had the ten years of separation been good for her? It wouldn't matter to him regardless.

Once he got his hands on her, he was going to kill her.

Harper Miller had fooled him once, and he'd vowed he'd never give her that kind of power again.

He watched as the container started to burn. This was the only way to handle the dead bodies.

Rubbing a finger across his lip, his patience grew shorter as he thought about who was coming to his home in a few short hours. He should have known Axel would find her.

His father had been the one to keep close tabs on

her for the entire five years he'd been alive after she left. Every single time Draven had doubts, Alan was always there, showing him how helpful she was being to the enemy. She supplied girls, doing everything she wanted, and with a smile on her face, looking so fucking happy. When he killed the bastard and took over all the reins, the trail had dried up for a long time. Then, he'd been more concerned with his own businesses. Finding Harper hadn't been as important as building up his reputation, and dealing with the men and women who felt he wasn't ready to take over from Alan.

His driver climbed behind the wheel, and Draven gave him the order to take him back home to Stonewall. Sitting back, he thought about Harper. Even now, after ten years, he was so fucking angry.

The last time he saw her, she'd been smiling at him, giving him no hint that she intended to run.

While they'd been trapped in the mall with a lunatic, she'd been running away. He'd been fucking scared. Terrified. Instead of helping Buck, he'd gone to the bathroom to find she'd left.

If he'd not wasted so much time, things may have been different. His father had told him she'd gone to their enemies, men who wanted to know the inner workings of their world, and had sold their secrets. Then, he'd seen the proof. The way she took random girls as she worked for their enemies, looking so fucking happy with her life away from him. Every time he saw her smiling face in the photographs, he'd wanted to destroy her.

Cutting off his thoughts, he stared out of the window. What happened, happened. He wasn't going to change it.

His driver parked on the driveway, and Draven was already out of the car and heading up to his home. Still no sign of Axel.

Taking a seat in his sitting room, he poured himself a large whiskey and waited. The cigars his father used to love were locked away in a safe. Draven never smoked them as he hated the taste.

He drank the entire glass of whiskey and poured himself a second. The time ticked by, and he waited. His patience was wearing a bit thin, but he stayed patient. As with all things in life, patience always paid off.

Axel's car sounded in the driveway.

In a few seconds he'd see Harper for the first time in ten years.

Sitting back in anticipation, he heard the door open.

"Oh, Draven. Come out, come out, wherever you are?" Axel yelled for all to hear.

He didn't say a word.

"Let me go."

Ah, her voice.

The fear echoed down the hall. He heard her release a gasp, and seconds later, she appeared in his office, Axel holding her arm.

She was clearly hurting.

Draven didn't say a word.

He stared. There was no mistaking this was Harper.

Her raven hair was lush and so much longer, it fell to her waist in ringlets. Her blue eyes shot fire and ice just like always. Her curves were still there.

If he was to put her up on the auction block, she'd fetch him a fortune. Shame she wasn't a virgin. He'd have gotten triple for her, but then, he'd taken care of that pesky cherry years ago.

They stared at each other. The clothes she wore did little to hide the woman beneath.

Standing up, he took a sip of his whiskey and

stepped up to her. The scent of citrus still clung to her. She either used a fragrance or soap. Where once it turned him on, it now offended him.

It reminded him of a time long ago, and he hated the stench.

Reaching out, he grabbed her jaw, turning her face to look at him.

"Draven," she said. Her words were almost impossible to decipher as he held her still.

"Hello, Harper. Long time, no see." He turned her face this way and that. "Completely unharmed."

Axel nodded down at her neck.

Releasing her face, Draven pulled the collar of her shirt away to reveal the bruises.

"Was she naughty?" Draven asked.

"She tried to run from me. Thought she could get away." Axel laughed. "You know, she's been working for that florist I've been banging. Fucking tight pussy and dirty to the core."

"She has."

"Yes. I guess it was one of those things where we constantly missed each other. Shame, this could have happened months ago."

Axel stepped away from Harper, and he heard the sound of glass on glass, pouring himself a drink.

Harper stood. He saw how awkward she looked. Unsure. Nervous.

"Look, I can see that you're pissed."

"You think I'm pissed."

"What happened ten years ago, I can explain."

"You want to explain to me why you betrayed me. Betrayed all of us?"

"I didn't betray you."

He stared at her. The urge to hit her was strong, but he wasn't going to. If he started hitting her right now, he wouldn't stop.

He had big plans for her.

"I don't want to deal with you tonight."

Putting his whiskey down on the counter, he grabbed her arm and pulled her along the corridor. He passed men who didn't even look at him.

He forced their loyalty, tested them relentlessly. They all knew not to interfere with his dealings. People who came onto his property were always handled by him.

Draven only employed people who were loyal to him. Those that were loyal, were always handsomely rewarded, and those that weren't, suffered. He made sure every man and woman were given the option. Those that failed didn't live to see another day.

He headed out into the garden, down the steep path, and across the small field.

"Draven, what are you doing? Please, stop. You're scaring me."

He didn't let go even as he heard the fear in her voice.

Ten years ago, he'd have pulled her into his arms, protected her, stopped her from feeling fear or pain, or anything. All fucking four of them would have been there for her. She'd belonged to all of them, but she had to go and throw it in his face, in all of their faces.

Now, he relished her fear, wanted it.

He wanted her to experience everything he'd felt in the past ten years, but also, what he'd had to deal with after she left.

"Will you stop and just talk to me?"

Talking was over.

He got to the building. This was where they kept the disobedient women that were brought here. A couple of days out here in the winter, and well, some women died because of it, men too.

Oh, yes, rather than fight the inevitable, he'd expanded into men but taken kids off the menu. He had some morals still at least.

Harper fought him, trying to pry his fingers from around her wrist. Draven held her tightly and pulled her down into the cells.

Opening one up, he threw her inside and locked the door. Harper cried out as she landed on the hard ground. He held the bars of her cell tightly, staring down at her. She looked so small, so fragile, breakable.

Draven intended to break her. He was going to hurt her. This was just the beginning.

She got up, and the sound of a rat scurrying echoed in the small space. She turned her head, and he saw the tears fall down her cheeks. She looked pretty when she cried.

"What happened to you?" she asked.

He smiled. "What happened to me?"

"You heard me."

"Nothing happened to me, Harper. I grew up. I saw that there was no point in fighting this. Fighting who I am."

She stepped toward the cage, and he saw she limped.

"Who you are?"

He smiled at her.

"You've become the exact monster your father wanted."

"You want to talk about my father?"

"Where is he? Is he laughing right now? Joyous in knowing he got what he wanted."

Draven smiled again. "My father is dead."

"Oh," Harper said.

"Yes, I killed him."

She swallowed and looked away.

"What's the matter, Harper? Can't handle it?"

"You killed your own father and yet you've let mine live?" she asked.

"Oh, yes, you see, my father betrayed me. He didn't like that not only did I take this place, and expand, I moved him from the top. When I decided to help him, to make all of this mine, my end game wasn't the same as his. I'm a fucking king, and there's no way I'd work to put someone else in my place. I don't follow. I lead."

"And now you own Stonewall."

"Yes, I do. People bow as I pass."

"And my dad?"

"He's your dad now?" Draven chuckled. "You called him out of the blue a few days ago. What makes you think he's your dad?"

"He told you about the phone call?"

Draven burst out laughing. "No. Not until I was at his home, asking him. Hannah, his trusty little whore, told me. You know how she works for me. Poor guy though, she's let herself go, and well, I wouldn't want to ride that."

"You're disgusting."

"Be careful, Harper. It's nearly winter. It's getting a lot colder. I leave you in here too long, well, the outcome would be what I want but a little different." He winked at her. "I'm going to go now. It's a little too cold for my taste. I like something warm."

He turned on his heel, and even as she yelled his name, he ignored her.

Stepping back in the direction he came, he walked into the kitchen and found Axel, eating a sandwich.

"She's out in the cells?" Axel asked.

"She's where she belongs."

Axel laughed.

"You knew where she was all this time?"

"No. I didn't. I recognized the number, and I recalled Stephanie going on and on about a chick she employed. To be honest, unless it involves my dick, I didn't pay attention."

"So, what happened?"

"I was fucking the shit out of her, and well, Harper returned with their lunch, and now we're here." Axel took a bite of his sandwich. "Her bag's in the car. I've also dealt with the fiancé."

"How did you manage that?"

"Got her to break up with him over the phone."

"I'm going to need more information," Draven said.

He didn't like that she had a fiancé. That she'd had a chance at a happy future.

"Like what?"

"Does he know where she comes from? Does he know about Stonewall? Will he be coming here to find her?"

"Shit, I didn't find out any of that information. He was a persistent fucker."

Draven clenched his teeth but didn't say a word. He was pissed off. Of course he was.

"I'll deal with her tomorrow. I'll find out what I need," Draven said, heading back to his office. He finished off his whiskey in one gulp. Without another look, he headed upstairs to his room.

He took a quick shower and went to bed naked. As he lay down, he stared up at the ceiling, curious.

Getting to his feet, he moved to his window and opened the curtains. Axel's father had built the cells so that he got a perfect view from his bedroom—the room Draven now had. Everything had been fully refurnished, and it was his space now.

Staring at the building, he knew she had to be freezing.

The cells were not a kind place. The point of them was to break the women who still had a spine, who still hoped to escape and get help.

One night, even two, it helped them to see the error of their ways. If the cold didn't get to them in the height of the summer, the heat did. The sun was always beaming down on the building.

Then if they could handle the extremes of the weather, there were the rats. One or two, just enough to freak them out.

The stench was another thing.

Of course, there was nowhere for them to go to the toilet either.

Draven closed the curtain.

There was a time he'd intended to knock that building down.

Axel never went near the cells. Too many memories and his friend wouldn't talk about them. He stayed completely silent about the entire experience.

Draven hadn't used them in years either. Harper was the first cellmate in a long time. Kind of poetic.

He climbed back into bed and continued to stare at the ceiling. She was back, and he had big plans for her, lots of plans.

He thought about this fiancé. The one who she left behind.

Did she love him? Did she care about him? Was she heartbroken to have left him?

Buck and Jett entered his mind, and along with it, the spark of ice that spread within him, threatening to consume him just by their memories alone.

Whatever Harper had coming to her, she deserved

it.

He was going to have a lot of fun.

Chapter Four

Harper lost track of the time.
There was no blanket.
Nothing.
Just the icy chill of the night.
She sat on the mattress. From the moon shining into the room, she knew it had stains on it.
Blood? Piss? Semen?
She didn't want to think about what went on here.
All she could see was Draven's face, his eyes. He was dead inside. The boy she once knew was long gone.
Resting on the edge of the mattress, she watched the rat that had entered her cage. It scurried along the edge of the walls as if it didn't have a care in the world.
Alan was gone, which meant she was alone now. There was no way of knowing what he'd said to them or made them all believe about her. Draven didn't know she'd been forced out of Stonewall.
Forced to run so that he and the others could have been safe. Her suffering hadn't stopped there. Alan controlled everything, what she did, where she went. There was no freedom. When he told her to look happy, smile, and stare up at a certain guy, she did it. Every single instruction, from each vulnerable innocent girl to each guy he asked her to look at happily, to look proud of what she was doing. Those girls didn't deserve to be taken, to be fooled into thinking they were living better lives, but Alan had made her do it, to keep her guys alive. His threats hadn't stopped there. If she didn't do as she was told, he soon had enough evidence to send her to prison. No matter what, Alan held all the cards, and he relished it.
She didn't see Buck and Jett anywhere. Were

they waiting to take their pound of flesh?

She wiped away the tears and closed her eyes. Sleep didn't come. The cold kept her awake. The time passed though.

She saw it was getting light, and as it did, it lit up the room, and she saw the filth that surrounded her. Staying perfectly still on the mattress, she couldn't stop shaking. She was so cold.

Time still passed.

No sign of Draven. How long would he keep her here? Would he make her freeze to death?

She didn't want to die.

Still, no one came.

Harper got to her feet and moved toward the window against the wall. She saw men milling around. They were smoking cigarettes, talking. None of them were looking toward her.

Stepping away, she went to the cell door. Wrapping her fingers around the bars, she tried to pull, to grip them, to get herself to freedom, to do something, anything, that would help her get free.

"It's pointless."

She released the bars and stepped back as Axel stood in front of her.

He'd changed into a pair of jeans and a shirt. The jacket he wore looked the most inviting of all of his outfit. He placed a finger against the metal. "You think you're the first woman to try these bars?"

"You keep a lot of women here?"

"Surprisingly, no. This is new for Draven. My father loved these cells. They put women in their place. Most of the women serving Draven here are happy. The women we buy, he has places for them that are not in his home."

"You're a pig."

"I'm a pig? Is that all you've got? I've not been here in over five years, maybe even longer, and you think I'm a pig. I've seen what these cells do to a woman." He touched his back. "I got a whipping because of trying to help them."

"What?"

"My dad, he traded in blood, guns, drugs, and pussy. All kinds of pussy in all ranges. You know what I'm saying."

"He traded kids?"

"You got it, princess. He didn't mind at all. You see, Harper, there are a lot of sick people in the world. The kids, a few slaps got in line. Some women had a lot of spine, teenagers too, and he'd send them here. As you know, it's freezing cold in the winter, and in the summer, wow, you are losing water in sweating. One day, I couldn't stand to hear the cries anymore. I was having to train. My dad, he wanted a good, strong son. A fighter. Someone to rival Draven." Axel chuckled. "So I trained. I fought. This one day, their begging got too much. I couldn't stand the noise, so I went inside, grabbed some bottled water and some food, and brought it out."

She knew this wasn't going to be the end of the story.

"Anyway, my trainer was loyal to my father, so, he did no more than alert him to what I was doing. I got caught. I was dragged to the whipping post."

"The whipping post?"

"Oh, yes, my father loved these cells. Then we've got the whipping post, and then he's got an entire dungeon of tricks to train the women to take a cock, a beating, whatever he wanted to give."

She felt her stomach turn as she looked at him.

"I was locked into place, and he gave me ten whips. They cut my back, and because of my insolence and kind heart, he kept me on that post for three days until I was close to death, then he finally let me down. After that, I never came in here again. Until today. There you go, princess, I'm breaking my own rules for you."

"I had no idea you went through that," she said.

"Not a lot of people do. They see the big house and assume that we're privileged, and living the best life imaginable. They don't know what is expected of us. What they want from us. Draven's the same. We're all the same."

"What about Buck and Jett?" she asked.

"Don't you say their fucking names."

"Axel?"

"Don't. You have no right to say them. You speak them, and I'll have you up on the whipping post, praying for death." He slammed his hand against the cage, and she gasped, stepping back.

The violence of it scared her.

"You better hope Draven just lets you freeze to death. It would be a kindness you don't deserve."

He turned on his heel and walked out of the cells. She watched him go.

Gripping the bars that contained her, she wondered if it was at all possible to get out. If after years of women tugging at them, was there any way they were weakened or would she be wasting her time? Her breath? Her everything.

Wrapping her fingers around the bars, she tried to give them a tug and failed.

"Come on."

They didn't give. They were held in place, designed to stay there.

Stepping away from the bars, she sat down on the mattress and drew her feet up to her chin, holding her legs close to her, watching, waiting. Even as she heard men and women laughing, she didn't go and look out the window.

Time passed, and then she heard someone rushing inside the cells. Getting to her feet, she was surprised to see her father on the other side.

"Harper, honey."

She got off the bed and stepped up to the bars. "Hey, Ian."

"No, what the fuck? Why are you doing this?" Ian turned his head, and Harper saw Draven was there, a key in his finger, twirling it around as if he was a madman.

"Be careful there, Ian. You know I don't like any attitude."

"You're going to have her freeze to death."

"I'm teaching her a lesson. If you want, I could have beaten her last night. I wouldn't have stopped at one hit either. I'd have probably sold her to Lucas, and you know what he likes to do to women."

Harper watched her father pale. She stepped away from the bars. "You knew about this place."

Ian couldn't lie.

He didn't say a word, but one look and she knew. He'd known about this place, and still he worked for them, taking money, ignoring that men and women were dying. They were being tortured.

Draven laughed. "You really think your old man made his living by being a good guy? By doing the right thing? He doesn't have a clue how to do that. He's rotten from the inside out. Just like us."

"*I'm* not rotten," Harper said. "I know right from wrong, and what you're doing now, it's fucking wrong."

"Look at you, one night here wasn't enough to break you."

"Is that what you're wanting to do, Draven?

Break me? Is that what Axel hoped to achieve by hurting me?" She held the collar down.

"Harper, don't," Ian said. "You're finally back. Just let this pass. Okay? You can come home and I'll take care of you."

"Stonewall is not my home. It hasn't been my home for a long time." She looked at her father, and she saw how he'd aged. "You want to punish me for leaving, fine. Do it."

She walked back to the mattress and lay down on the surface. There was no point in fighting with them.

"Harper, please, just do as they say."

"I didn't need you ten years ago, and I certainly don't need you now." She shouldn't have called him.

She heard him sigh, and in the next second, his footsteps disappeared. Harper didn't move.

"So, you're still hating dear old daddy?" Draven asked.

She tilted her head down so that she stared at the cell doors. "You're still here?"

"Why not? I own these cells."

"A visit from you and Axel, this must be my lucky night."

"I want to know about your fiancé."

She gritted her teeth. He wasn't going to find anything out about Ethan. He had no right to know anything.

"I want to know about him."

"I've got nothing to tell."

"Come on, you were going to marry the guy."

She rubbed her finger where the ring had been. It was empty now. No ring.

"Are you going to let me go?"

"You want to stay in these cells?" he asked, instead of answering her.

"Why would I want to stay in these cells?" She sat up and looked at him. "What is it you want from me?"

"Me? I don't want anything from you. What I want right now is for you to answer my questions. You do, and you'll get to go to the house to wash." He winked at her. "Come on, Harper. I know how you like to negotiate."

"You don't know a thing about me."

"Do we have a deal?" he asked.

"Fine. What do you want to know?"

"Your fiancé, does he know your history?"

"No."

"You were going to marry someone and he didn't know who you were?"

"It's not like I could tell him, is it? I didn't want anything from Stonewall to come back here. Do you know what your father did?" she asked.

"I'm not here to answer your questions. You're here to answer me."

"Damn it, Draven, I'm not a monster here."

"Don't worry, I am. Does your fiancé know how to get in touch with you?"

"No. Axel broke my phone. Any means he had of getting in touch with me is long gone. He doesn't know where I lived as a child, or what I did. I lied to him about everything so he wouldn't come hunting, or expect me to want to go back home. I lied about absolutely everything. If you're expecting him, don't."

She placed her hands on her knees, waiting, watching.

"You were going to marry a man, and he didn't even know that you'd given yourself to four men?" Draven asked.

She couldn't help it. She touched the base of her

back.

Draven burst out laughing. "You still got the ink?"

Harper kept her lips pressed shut. This wasn't going how she thought it would, if this ever happened. What did she expect? For Draven to welcome her home? She had no home. Draven was doing this because he felt betrayed. He believed Alan, just as she had.

"How did he fuck you seeing other names?"

"I let him believe I was going through a morbid phase and they were my dead pets."

This dropped the smile from his lips. The anger was back.

She got a small glimpse of the old Draven, but now, he was gone, and all that stood in his place was a monster.

"I answered your questions."

"That you did."

He flicked the key around his finger, and finally, he opened the door.

She got off the bed and took a step toward him, and another, and another. Just as she reached out to grip the door, he locked the cuff he had on his own hand around hers.

She stopped and tried to pull away from him.

"Draven, what the hell?"

"Axel has the key. You're stuck with me until he comes back. Let's go."

"No. I don't want this. Send me back to the cells."

"Too late for that."

He pulled her out of the cells. She didn't look at anyone as she passed, or at least, as Draven dragged her past them, into the house.

She wanted a shower. To relieve herself during

the day, she'd pulled her jeans down and squatted in the corner of the cell. It shamed her to know she'd done this, but it was all she could do.

No amount of begging stopped Draven. They entered his home, and as he dragged her upstairs, men and women who were there stopped to watch.

Draven didn't stop.

No one spoke to him. No one stopped him. He was a force to be reckoned with.

She saw the fear in others' eyes as he passed. Everyone was afraid of him. This stopped her from fighting. She was fighting with a man she didn't know, not anymore.

He opened a large door at the end of a long corridor. Once they were inside, he closed and locked it.

"What was that?" she asked.

"Don't worry, that doesn't concern you. You stink."

"Is this your bedroom?"

"You want to fuck me already, Harper? You are a little slut, aren't you?"

He didn't make a move to touch her, and in the next second, they were in the bathroom. He turned on the lights, and seeing the toilet, she felt so much relief flood her.

"Draven, please, I need to use the bathroom."

"You need to go, then go."

"Draven?"

"I'm not going anywhere, and neither are you. You may as well stop fighting and accept what is going to happen."

"You can't be serious."

"Believe me, I am."

"I need to pee."

"Then pee. You think in the past ten years I've

not seen it all? I've seen a woman piss and shit herself. I've also seen them begging. Their pussies so wet as they want cock."

She went to lift her hand to hit him, but he caught her, letting out a tut.

"Let's get one thing straight here, Harper. You hit me, I'll hit you back."

"So you're a big, strong man that hurts women?"

Draven laughed. "Oh, honey, I can hit you back in many ways that don't even involve me touching you."

His warning sent a chill down her spine.

"Come on. I'm bored."

She pulled her hand to her pants, and Draven followed as they were cuffed together. Pushing them down, he followed her movements. Sitting on the toilet, she held her hand up, and just tried not to look at him, trying to give them both as much space as humanly possible.

Once she finished, she wiped herself and was about to pull her jeans up.

"Unless you shower fully clothed, I wouldn't bother with your clothes."

"How am I supposed to get completely naked?"

He reached into his jacket and pulled out a knife. The blade looked incredibly sharp and familiar.

"Isn't that Jett's knife?"

Draven tensed but didn't say a word. They were facing each other now.

"Step out of the jeans."

She wanted to protest. The thought of a shower was far too tempting to give up.

She kicked aside her sneakers, jeans, and panties.

"The rest."

She removed the shirt, but the arm of her cuffed hand pooled at her wrist. She held it for Draven to cut, tensing up whenever the blade got a little too close to her skin.

She didn't want him to cut her in any way. Fear was a great motivator for her doing as she was told.

With the shirt gone, he flicked the blade beneath the strap, and she gasped as the cold metal touched her skin. The bra strap opened and fell to the floor.

She was now naked in front of Draven.

One glance at him, and he was removing his clothes, one by one, but keeping the blade in his hand.

She saw the scars that decorated his chest. Some wounds look like he'd been shot while others appeared to be from a knife.

Biting her lip, she watched him, fascinated, as he moved, as he got naked.

Much to her shame, she felt a stirring of lust deep inside at seeing him like this, at having him close. Her feelings for Draven had never diminished.

Once he was naked, he smirked at her.

"Look at you. I recognize that look. I have to wonder if your fiancé even knew how to take care of you. Did he make you come? Did he make you scream his name as he pounded inside you, over and over again?"

Ethan never had her screaming in pleasure. Sex had been … enjoyable. She was always wet, but it had never blown her mind. Never made her want to do crazy things.

Draven put the blade down, and his hand touched her face.

She didn't flinch away from him. Staring into his green eyes, she could kid herself that they were still eighteen again with so many plans.

He stroked his finger down her neck, running down her back until he grabbed her ass. She cried out as he gripped her. The pain was instant, but she didn't fight him as he pulled her close.

She knew she stank, and yet, she tilted her head back, looking up at him.

"You really are a slut." He traced the ink across the base of her back. "I wonder if he ever did this while he was pumping inside you."

Harper tried to pull away, but he wouldn't let her.

"Let's see how wet you are. I can smell you right here." He slid a finger between her thighs even as she pulled away.

She was no match for his strength as he found the evidence of her arousal.

He plunged two fingers inside her, and she cried out, moaning as his thumb stroked across her clit.

She closed her eyes, ashamed that she was turned on by this. By his brutality. This was wrong. She shouldn't be enjoying this, shouldn't be wanting this, and yet, when he added a third finger, she took it.

"Look at you, Harper. You're so wet you're dripping onto my hand."

"Stop it." Even to her own ears she knew she wasn't putting up much of a fight.

There was no fight to have.

He was the one in control, not her.

Back and forth, around, across, he teased her nub all the time, finger-fucking her hard. She rode his hand, feeling that orgasm begin to build. The only way she'd been able to feel any kind of release was if she was touching herself. Ethan never knew which parts of her to push to get her to come.

He tried. He just never succeeded.

"Please, please, please," she said, hating herself for begging for more. This wasn't fair, but she'd rather beg than him stop.

"You're so desperate, aren't you, babe? You want to come on my fingers."

"Yes."

"You want me to make you come?"

"Yes, yes."

"Scream my name."

He twisted his fingers inside her, and as she came, she yelled his name. Draven held her up, and she rode his fingers, begging for more, wanting more. Hungry for more.

Once she finished, she came to, her head resting on his chest.

Lifting up, she looked into his eyes and saw the smirk staring right back at her. Draven wanted to make her come.

He pulled his fingers from her pussy and held them up for him to see. They were coated with her release.

"You see this. This is what I do for you, and yet, you thought to give your pussy to another man."

"Draven."

He silenced her by putting his cum-slicked fingers against her mouth.

"Lick it off. Taste yourself."

She stared at him and knew he wouldn't stop until she did his bidding.

Flicking her tongue across his finger, she tasted herself, and he smiled even wider.

"That's it, Harper, taste your pussy. Suck it off my fingers. That's what I do for you."

She cleaned him up and waited, defiant. If he intended to break her, she'd fight it. Draven wouldn't win this. She wasn't going to cower in a corner.

He shoved her into the shower and turned it on. The icy cold water sprayed her, making her cry out. Her body had already been cold but was now even more so.

Draven held her beneath the water, and she felt his eyes on her at every turn. He spun her around so that she faced the wall and he was behind her.

"When do I get to see Buck and Jett, or are they planning something else for me to hate?"

"You didn't like the orgasm I gave you?" he asked.

She stayed silent as he chuckled against her neck.

"It's okay. I know how much you wanted it. I wonder how many men have used you. Taken what you offer and tossed you aside."

"Why?" she asked. "How many women have you been with? I doubt you've waited for me."

"You're right. I've not. I don't take women though, Harper. They know the score when they fuck me. They get one night. If they entertain me enough, they get to worship my dick for a second time."

"You're a pig."

He spun her around, and what shocked her was how easy it was for him to use the hand that was cuffed to hers. He wrapped his fingers around her neck, right next to the marks she knew was there from Axel.

"You like to throw insults around."

"You keep calling me a slut and you can't even handle being called a pig? Grow some balls, Draven."

He laughed, and she gasped as he pressed his cock against her.

"I've got some balls, Harper." He held her shoulder and shoved her down to her knees so that she was right in front of his length.

Draven was long, thick, and pre-cum already coated the head of his cock. Nerves chased up her spine.

She'd sucked Ethan's cock but never Draven's.

"Let's see how much you've learned, shall we?"

He wrapped her hair around his fist. No matter how much she tried to tug away and to put him off balance, Draven was by far stronger than she was. She couldn't pull away from him.

He held all the power.

"If you bite me, I'll choke you."

"Stop this, Draven," she said, even as she licked her lips.

"Why should I stop something you want?" He placed the tip at her lips and trailed his pre-cum across them. "Lick it off."

She didn't, glaring up at him.

He tugged on her hair so hard it made her gasp.

When she opened her lips, he slammed his cock deep inside, choking her with his length. He didn't pull out for a few seconds, and when he did, she gasped for breath.

"Let's try this again. Lick it off."

Tears filled her eyes, and she knew it was going to get worse. The Draven she once knew was gone.

The boy she'd loved was gone. She never even got to tell that boy all those years ago that she loved him.

She licked her lips, tasting his pre-cum.

He did it again and again until he put the tip of his cock against her mouth, and she sucked him inside.

The urge to bite him was strong, but she held off, instead, licking and sucking at his cock as he asked her to. When he thrust forward, hitting her throat, she gagged, and he tutted.

"It looks like you're going to be spending a lot of time with a cock in your mouth. Don't want your vomit on my dick, but you're going to learn to take it, Harper. To suck on cock."

She swallowed him down, bobbing her head, pleasuring him as he groaned. She tried to ignore the pulse between her thighs and the heaviness of her breasts as he held her head, and made her take his cock.

This wasn't something she liked doing or enjoyed. She had to remember she was being forced to do this.

Liar.

Even though Draven was forcing her, she enjoyed it.

He held her head still, the grip in her hair tightening even more as he pumped harder, faster.

He was so close. She felt it in the hardness of his cock, the increase in his thrusts. When he came, he went to the back of her throat and erupted his load into her mouth.

"Swallow it all. Don't let a drop go to waste."

She swallowed him down, drinking every single drop of his release.

Once she was done, he pulled out of her mouth, picked her up, turned her toward the water, and washed her body.

He didn't say anything, not a word.

Her cheeks were flaming, and she was aroused.

He cleaned her up, and still, he didn't say anything.

It was like they'd not just done … *that.*

She knew they had. She tasted his cum on her tongue still.

"Draven."

"Shut the fuck up, Harper. I've got nothing I want to say."

"I've got something I want to say."

He slapped her ass hard. It wasn't playful. "You'll learn to do as I say."

"Or what?"

He hit her again, making her cry out. He tugged

on her hair again, pulling her back. The angle hurt her arm, and she screamed. It didn't matter what noise she made, no one would be coming for her. She was all alone with a monster; only, this monster, she craved with every fiber of her being.

"Do you think I've got a problem hurting you? I don't. I don't give a shit about hurting scum, and that is what you are, Harper. Scum."

"Why do you hate me so much?"

"I could have given you the world. Everything your heart desired, and yet, you ran and went straight to our enemies. I don't forgive that. I'll never forgive that. Now shut up."

He let her go, and she was so relieved to no longer be in pain, she didn't say another word. She stayed perfectly silent as he cleaned her body, washed her hair, and when he was done, he climbed out of the shower.

With how strong Draven was, she didn't have an option about stopping, or forcing him to listen to her. All she could was follow his orders. When he tugged her left or right or straight forward, she had to go.

Entering the bedroom, she discovered Axel sat on the edge of the bed, waiting for them. His gaze roamed up and down her body.

"I see you've added to the marks I've already given her." Axel pointed at her neck.

"She wouldn't shut up."

"Does she really think talking to us is going to help?" Axel asked.

Draven shrugged.

"Here you go, at your request." Axel held up the key.

Harper lunged for it, but Draven already had it. She watched as he opened his side of the cuffs, but then she cried out as he dragged her to the bed and locked her into place on the bed. She didn't have much room.

Draven stepped back.

"Now that is a pretty sight."

"Have you already fucked her?" Axel asked.

"Screw the both of you." She tried to pull free, but nothing was working. She cried out as the cuff seemed to dig into the flesh of her wrist, making her gasp.

Axel moved up behind her. Even though he was wearing clothes, there was no mistaking the arousal there. He pressed against her ass, and she paused.

"One day soon, Harper, you're going to be fucking us. You should hope to keep us entertained because you're going to be using that cunt to save your life."

With that, she watched as both men left the room. Draven wore a robe while she was still naked.

"You can't keep me here against my will," she said, hoping to reason with them.

Draven stopped at the door, staring at her. "You shouldn't have run away."

"Draven, didn't your dad tell you anything?" she asked.

"He told me how you tried to blackmail him. How you wanted out of Stonewall. Away from all four of us. He told me about the ten grand you had. The secrets you were willing to spill to get away from us and how you ran into the enemy's arms."

Each accusation was thrown back at her, cutting her like a blade.

No! No! This isn't fair. This isn't fucking fair!

Alan had blackmailed her.

He'd put Draven's life in danger, and she'd seen it with her own two eyes.

"You're wrong. Draven, I swear, he lied."

"Well, it's not like I can ask him if your version of whatever happened is true or not. You were gone, and I told you to come to me when you were going to run."

"Draven, I swear to you I would have—"

"I don't need to hear any more lies."

"Damn it, Draven, listen to me."

He closed the door, and she heard the lock.

"Open the fucking door. You bastard. Cowardly fucks! Where's Jett? Where's Buck? You can't keep me here forever. How dare you?"

Anger hit her hard, and she tried to get the cuffs off, crying out as she tore at the skin. Tears spilled from her eyes, and she screamed. Grabbing the lamp nearest her, she launched it across the room. It hit the wall. She opened the drawer and emptied it out, throwing everything she had in her grasp.

Some items hit the wall, others hit the door, and most of them fell in a path, until she had nothing else to throw.

She collapsed on the bed, ass in the air, exhausted.

She couldn't get comfortable, not with her hand tied above her.

Sobbing into the pillow, she couldn't believe that Draven trusted his father over her. Yes, she'd run, but part of her had hoped he'd find her. He'd asked her to never run, but didn't he at least doubt Alan? She'd been with him for so long, and she belonged to him. He took her virginity, and she gave him everything. She really had hoped he'd come. When he hadn't, she'd lost hope. Alan still made his demands. No matter where she went, he was there, close by. If she didn't do as he told her, Draven, Axel, Buck, and Jett were the pawns he used. She had run from Stonewall, but she'd not been free.

Alan had used her as a puppet. Wherever he wanted her, she had no choice but to go. He'd sent her to Europe to do his bidding, and she tried to run so many times, but Alan always found her. She worked every single day just to afford rent and food to try to get away. Nothing helped until one day, five years ago, he simply stopped calling, and eventually even his men on her disappeared. By then, it had been too long, and she'd tried to move on, always afraid he was watching her, waiting for her to fuck up.

Her life had become nothing more than survival.

Now Draven was intent on killing her, and it wasn't fair. It wasn't fucking fair. None of it.

No matter what they did, she wouldn't break.

She was stronger than this.

She'd fight, and she would win.

Chapter Five

"It has been three days," Axel said.

Draven looked up from his paper to his friend. "And?"

"You're not going to talk to her? Bring her down here?"

"Are you wanting to fuck her, is that it? Go in, use her, you might as well."

"Draven, look at me."

He lifted his head up and stared at the only person in his life who he'd ever let talk to him like that, even as his hand twitched to touch Jett's knife and kill him.

"What, Axel? Do you need my permission now? Okay, I give you my blessing to go and fuck the whore."

"You know for a fact she was more yours than ours."

Draven threw down the paper. "What do you want me to do right now? If I put my hands on her, I'll take her to the fucking whipping post that hasn't been used since your father was in power here. I will make her bleed."

"You don't want to?" Axel asked.

"I want to, Axel. That's the point. I want to hurt her until I hear her beg me to stop. That ink on her back, the one that says our names, I want to take this knife." He pulled out Jett's blade. "And slice the skin right off so she knows just what she did. I've got no problem with you taking your pound of flesh. You knew the moment you brought her here, her days were numbered."

"Then why didn't you kill her last night?"

"I liked having her choke on my cock. I decided I'm looking forward to breaking her. She stares at me like she wants to kill me." He smirked. "It kind of reminds me of high school."

"And why do you find that so amusing?"

"Because I fell in love with her in high school. I fell in love with that spirit, and it was all a lie. I'm going to break her. When she no longer looks at me with that fire in her eyes, I know I'll have done what I need."

"And then what?"

"Then she goes up for auction. She'll be a prize to any man. A submissive hole for them to use at their will or something to beat and hurt." Draven smiled.

"When are you going to tell her Buck and Jett are dead?"

"It bothers you, doesn't it? That she doesn't know."

"She's asked about them."

"I know she has."

"Don't you think it's fucking time she knows what she did? What she caused?"

Draven watched the young woman he hired to cook and wait for him.

"Laurie," he said,

He watched her flinch, but he knew she was loyal.

He'd stopped one of his colleagues from raping her, and since then, she'd been a loyal little servant, always willing to do his bidding, even wait on the ungrateful slut upstairs.

"How is my guest?" he asked.

Laurie's head dropped. "She hasn't eaten anything, sir."

"What?"

"Her meals are always left untouched."

"She goes to the bathroom."

"Yes, Philip is always there. She, erm, she has new bruises on her face."

Draven noticed her hands were clasped together, and she was shaking. "Have you seen Philip strike her?"

She looked up at him, and he saw the fear in her eyes.

"I'll protect you." He didn't like that Philip had scared this young girl. She had no family of her own. He knew that because he'd gone looking for them, hoping to return her. She'd been one of the women from Ralph's last good batch.

He'd gotten the details from her and ran a check. Ralph had killed her entire family. Laurie would have fetched a lot of money, only Ralph had raped her, taking her virginity and in the process, had scarred her. Now, she was used and damaged goods, which was why he allowed her to work for him.

He wasn't entirely cold.

"He ... touches her. He hits her, sir. He knows that you don't go up there."

Draven was out of his seat in a second. Laurie jumped away from him.

"Go into the kitchen. Do not come out until I say so."

"He was heading up to her room, sir."

Axel was already out of the door.

Philip was ... dangerous.

Draven had hired him to keep the girls in line, as he didn't have a problem with hurting them if they needed to be given a warning.

Everything he once hated, he had become. There was a time, he would beat the women to keep them in line. His father demanded it of him, and each strike had been torture to his very soul. Alan had tried to break him, and failed.

Women, drugs, guns, anything that had a price tag, he sold, apart from children.

He drew the line there.

Yeah, it makes a total difference that you have standards.

He stormed into the bedroom, and just in time as well.

Philip had Harper bound. Her other hand was locked into place, and he had her spread. He saw something inside her ass, and Philip's pants were down around his ankles. He was about to pull his cock out.

Draven saw red.

He gave Philip one set of instructions: to help Laurie assist Harper. When he was ready to give her to his men to use as he saw fit, he would do it. His instructions, his very fucking law, had been ignored.

Harper's body was covered in bruises. Some of them, he and Axel had put there.

"I've not touched her," Philip said.

"You were about to."

"I didn't touch her though. Come on, Draven, she's still yours. I was just giving her a taste of what was to come."

With Jett's knife in his hand, Draven slid it into Philip's abdomen. Philip grunted, his grip weak as he tried to stop him.

He liked to keep Jett's knife sharp so all it took was a flick of the wrist and the person who defied him was dead.

"When I give an instruction, I expect it followed to the very letter. You have failed me, Philip. I don't like failures, and you know what I do with them?" He pulled the knife out, only to pierce the fucker's heart. "I dispose of them."

He pulled the knife out. It was covered in blood.

There were two gaping wounds, the one on Philip's stomach leaking blood onto the carpet, where it was soaked, and the other out of his chest.

Sobs echoed around the room, and Draven turned to see Harper.

Philip had pushed a dildo into her ass. He saw the lube, and it looked like she'd been whipped with a belt as well. There were welts over her back and thighs. He watched as Axel pulled the dildo from her ass.

"Let me go. Please." She tugged on the cuffs that bound her.

Axel looked toward him.

"Get her out of here."

Axel released her from the bed and left the room.

Draven stared down at the mess and called his cleaning crew. Giving them the order over the phone, he went into the bathroom and cleaned the blood from his blade. Next, he removed his clothing, and as he left the bathroom, his men were already in the process of removing the body.

"Here, take this." He tossed them his blood-soaked clothing, and went to his closet. After pulling on some clothes, he found Axel on the second floor, outside one of the guest bedrooms. "Why are you out here?"

"I wanted to give her some privacy."

"Why?"

"She won't stop crying." Axel rubbed at his eyes. "Fuck, it reminds me of when we were younger. I know it's fucked up, and she's going to die. Just give me a fucking minute."

Shaking his head, Draven entered the room. Harper was curled up on the floor. She looked a mess. Her hair was wet, and he figured she'd had a shower.

"Is that what your orders were? To have a man come and beat me? Rape me?"

"No. He was to assist you to the bathroom."

"So none of your men listen to you. Good to

know."

"Philip has been dealt with. Get dressed."

"Screw you."

Draven smiled. "Even beaten and nearly raped, you still have a spine."

"Do you know what he put in my ass?" she asked, lifting up from her spot on the carpet.

"It wasn't his cock."

"I can't even believe you're saying that."

"What, you think you're the only woman on the planet that has a cock in her ass? I've seen a woman take two in her ass, and it wasn't even on porn either."

"Huh?"

"You've heard of anal, right?" he asked.

"Yes."

"You've never done it?"

"Of course not. It's gross."

He laughed. "Some women love it when a man fucks their ass."

"I'm not having this conversation with you."

"Get dressed," he said.

"I don't trust you. I'm not going anywhere with you."

"I'm taking you someplace. Get dressed or I'll send a man who will show you exactly how he fucks an ass."

She got to her feet. "I don't have any clothes."

He went to one of the drawers. He kept spare clothes in every single room of the house.

Grabbing out a pair of sweatpants, he threw them at her, followed by a shirt.

"I'll have your sneakers downstairs waiting for you."

"What about underwear?"

"You don't need it. The clothes I've given you

are sufficient." He left the bedroom, and Axel was there. "Bring her to the car when you're done. You're coming with us."

"Where exactly are you taking her?" Axel asked.

"You wanted her to know the truth. I agree. It's time she knew it as well. I'm taking her to Jett and Buck."

"Now? After what she has just gone through?"

"Wow, you know, I wonder about you sometimes."

"Come on, Draven. This isn't about me. It's about you and how you're dealing with her being here. I saw the look on your face when you saw him. You may hate Harper right now, but there's a part of you that still wants her."

"You're fucking clueless, Axel. I don't want her. She's going to be punished for what she did. Harper's strong anyway. We got there in time." He shrugged. "You don't think she's going to experience worse by the time we sell her? Come on, put on your big boy pants, and shut up moaning. It's boring, and tedious, and I don't have time for this."

He turned on his heel, walking away.

"You're sure you're not going to regret this?"

Draven sighed and looked back at Axel. The scars on his face made him an ugly fucker.

"What am I going to regret?"

"Treating her like this? Pushing her aside. Selling her off? Killing her? You had feelings for her once."

"Not anymore!" He yelled, silencing Axel. "This is one of the many reasons why I'm the boss and you just work for me. You're way too emotional. Do you remember why we lost Buck? Jett? Do you remember why your face is scarred?"

Axel nodded his head.

"At every single turn, we were looking for her. Jett died because he was convinced Harper didn't run, and his message is still unclear to me. He called me out of the blue and said he had reason to believe something wasn't right, and he paid with a bullet to the head after being tortured for hours. You heard the autopsy report. Jett was alive while they tore him apart until finally putting a bullet in his head. Buck, he got it easy, didn't he? One bullet, and where was I instead of helping him?"

"You were going to check on Harper."

"That's right. I was going to see that she was okay because of there being an active shooter in the mall. I tried to find her. She was gone. She made a lucky escape. Your face?"

"I'd been following a lead when I didn't realize I'd been tailed and my face was pressed against hot metal," he said.

"Now, you tell me why I should give a fuck about waiting to tell Harper the truth? How we were all nearly killed because she left?"

"Don't you want to hear her side, just in case? I know you, Draven. You're angry now, but what about after?" Axel asked.

"Right now, I don't give a shit what lies she wants to spill. I told her to come to me. You know she hated being called a slut and a whore. Being with us, it wasn't enough. She ran and joined our enemies, working for them, and guess what, she now gets to pay that price. I don't care what she has to say. Stop with worrying about me, Axel. I'm not going to regret a single fucking thing I do to that bitch. Some may think this is petty. I don't. I think it's time she paid for what she did. You got a problem with that, then you get the fuck out of my house until I'm done, or you stick around and see what I've got in store for her."

Draven didn't give him time to answer. He turned away and walked off.

Axel had never had it in him to lead, to take control.

It had been Draven who killed Axel's dad. He'd taken him out to the whipping post, and where he'd tortured women for too many years, Draven had whipped him, over and over again. He'd made that son of a bitch bleed like others had before him. He left him out for dead, letting animals eat whatever they wanted.

Draven went back a week later to just a corpse, which he buried in the woods.

He'd never claimed to be a good man.

Maybe with Harper, he had some redemption, but that had been taken from him. With every person he killed a piece of his soul was taken from him. Any light he had was wiped out, smeared by the darkness that had taken his soul.

When the time came to kill his father five years ago, he'd done so with relish. He made his father think that he was on top. That Alan Barries was the king. He poisoned the whiskey, and as his father got drunk, he killed him. Not before he killed the cook though, and his mother. They were all loyal to Alan.

Anyone who was loyal to his father died. The only people that survived were those that answered to *him*.

He sat in the back of the car, and he didn't have to wait too long for Harper to appear. She looked small, pale, and even vulnerable in the clothes he'd given her. Next to Axel, she looked so weak.

The spark was there in her eyes, so she wasn't broken. It would take a lot more to break Harper. He hadn't forgotten the strength of her, the darkness that swirled in her eyes, calling to him.

He did see the bruise on her cheek from being hit, which he didn't like. Philip wasn't given the order to hit her or in any way lay a hand on her, only to restrain her. It didn't matter now. He shouldn't be dwelling on what happened because it was over with. Philip had done the damage, and now it was time to move on.

Axel opened the door, and Harper paused when she saw him.

She gripped the jacket she wore a little tighter and climbed in. When she noticed Axel moving in behind her, she had no choice but to slide closer to him.

He stared at her, and she looked at him. He chuckled as she looked away.

"Where are we going?" she asked.

"It's a surprise."

"I don't like surprises."

"Everyone likes a surprise," Axel said.

"You mean like that guy who touched me? Who wanted to rape me and stuck a … thing up my ass?"

"I see it's not affecting you."

"Can we just stop this nonsense? I didn't do anything wrong. This is all wrong, just stop." She ran fingers through her hair. The jacket she wore rolled down, exposing her bruised wrist.

"Why didn't you scream?" Draven asked.

"I did. No one came."

They hadn't heard.

"Where are we going?" she asked.

"We're taking you to Buck and Jett."

"You're taking me to them?"

Draven heard the hope in her voice. Looking over her head, he saw Axel was glaring at him, but Draven didn't give a fuck. He didn't have any feelings when it came to Harper. His friend didn't need to worry about him. Any love he had for this bitch had left him ten years ago.

She'd find out sooner rather than later. Sure, he could tell her now, let her down gently, but he didn't want to give her anything. His mission was to make her as miserable as possible.

"You now live in Axel's home," she said, rubbing her hands across her thighs.

"It's my home," Draven said, staring out of the window.

"But I thought that was Axel's dad's place." She pointed behind her.

"It was. It's not anymore."

"Where do you live?" she asked, turning to Axel.

"I live there. I just don't own it."

"And you're okay with that?"

"I don't exactly mourn the place, Harper. It's just a building and bricks. It has no real value."

She sighed and sat back. "I remember when it was easier to talk to you guys."

"You mean before you ran away and left us without a backward glance? Into the arms of the enemy just to get away from us?" Draven asked.

"Why won't you listen to me? It wasn't like that. I don't know why you won't listen to me. I don't even know your enemy. I worked for Alan, no one else."

"Let me guess, you're going to blame Alan for everything?" Axel asked.

Silence met his question. Of course she'd blame Alan. His father had told him that she would. He rubbed at his temple.

"Wow, he really did think ahead, didn't he?" She folded her arms, and he saw her rub at the corner of her eye, clearly wiping away a tear.

"It's wrong to talk ill of the dead."

"You killed your own father. How could you

have any respect for a man you killed?"

"Simple, I did what I had to do. I imagine he's happy that he nurtured such a cold-blooded killer. I won't let anyone take my place."

"Not even Axel?"

"Hey, don't even think of getting me in this place." Axel held his hands up. "I want no part in your two's squabble."

"So you're happy being his slave? Second best."

Draven chuckled.

"First of all, I'm no one's slave. I'm not second best. I work with Draven. We're a fucking team."

"And where do Buck and Jett fit? I haven't seen them around the house or even heard about them. No one talks about them. Have you passed them off? Kicked them out? Were they not as good as you?"

Draven shook his head at the anger he saw in Axel's eyes, anger which was directed at Harper. She didn't have a single fucking clue. It was sad but not unexpected.

"I guess you'll find out soon enough."

Axel stared out the window.

Even now, it still grieved him to have lost their friends. This was not what they envisaged when they planned to become leaders, to take over from their fathers. So much had changed.

For one, they were still in the trade of human flesh, trafficking. Men and women passed through their hands as if they were nothing more than cattle.

Draven had learned not to think about it, to ignore it. Life was a lot easier if he ignored what he did. There was no room in this life for weakness. Men and women died, and that was a fact of life.

Staring out the window, he saw the cemetery coming into view. He rarely came here. He didn't know about Axel.

For him, it was too much.

When it came to Buck and Jett, he'd failed them. As far as he was concerned, he'd been too obsessed with Harper, and because of that, his best friends ended up dead, and the surviving one had scars.

"Who trashed my locker?" Harper asked, looking over at them.

Axel smirked. "That finally bugging you?"

Ten years ago, someone had trashed Harper's locker with vile words written across it. He, Axel, Buck, and Jett had discovered the identity of the person who had done it. They were going to let Harper deal with it when she was ready, not long after the initiation. Harper had left before they got a chance to tell her.

Draven snorted. "You were going to find the answer to that if you stayed. You don't get to know." The girl who trashed Harper's locker had been the cheerleader screwing Ben, the guy who thought he could touch Harper's ass.

The car came to a stop, and Harper looked past him, her hand going to his thigh as she lifted up a little in her seat.

"Why are we at a cemetery?"

"Don't worry, princess. We're not going to make you dig your own grave," Axel said.

"I don't like this."

"I never at any point told you that you'd like what you're about to see." Draven climbed out of the car and waited for her. He held his hand out like he'd done many times before. Harper hesitated. She stared at his hand as if it was infected.

Maybe in a way, it was.

People died at his hands. He was probably haunted by the ghosts of all the people he killed.

She slowly slid across the seat, taking his hand as she climbed on out. He felt the faint tremor as she held him.

Once she was safely out on the sidewalk, he let go of her hand, slammed the car door, and put a hand to her back.

A couple of older women were walking down the street. One look at them had them crossing to avoid him.

Axel smirked.

He liked to have this power over Stonewall, or at least, over wherever he went. Draven didn't care so much, but then, he had power no matter what. Men and women bowed before him because they knew he'd hurt them, even kill them if he didn't get what he wanted.

Entering the cemetery, he felt Harper tense and try to hold herself back, but he wouldn't let her. Pushing her along, he stopped at the two end graves.

"What is this?" she asked.

"Say hello to Buck and Jett!" Axel waved at them. "Hey, guys, we got her. Look, here's our queen. You know the one, that was supposed to stay by our side but in the end decided to go running off because she couldn't deal with us. You know the one."

"No, this is a joke," she said.

"This is no joke, Harper. It's why I have Jett's knife. He died, and so did Buck."

She shook her head.

"You can think we're lying, but this is where they are," Axel said. "Our two best buds. The ones that were supposed to help us rule this world. They're dead and gone. Have been for a while now."

He saw the tears in her eyes, and Draven was shocked as she sank to her knees and simply stared at the graves.

"They're really gone?"

Her voice broke, and Draven watched her. Tears fell down her cheeks, and she looked as if he'd just given her the worst news on the planet.

"Yes," Draven said.

She covered her face with her hands, and he watched as she sobbed.

"This shouldn't have happened. How did this happen?"

"The usual way."

"No, this is not the usual way."

When Axel went to say more, Draven shook his head. She needed to grieve right now. Clearly, she'd thought they were still alive and were just pissed at her. It was so far from the fucking truth.

"I can't believe this is happening," she said, sniffling. "They didn't deserve to die. They were wonderful."

Draven gritted his teeth as he thought about Buck and about Jett. They were the best friends anyone could have had. Sure, Buck was a joker and Jett the more serious of the two, but they were more family to him than anyone else.

He missed them.

If he could go back at any point in his life, he'd change what happened to them. He'd give anything to have them standing by his side right now, with Harper there at their feet.

"Time to go."

****

Harper couldn't believe they were dead. Even now, hours later, staring at her reflection. What had happened to her this morning, it seemed inconsequential against the pain that filled her chest at knowing she'd never see Jett smile or eat a damn apple with his knife. The same knife that only days before had been used to help remove her clothing.

She placed a hand against her shoulder, near the spot where the strap of her bra had been.

The cool metal had terrified her, and yet when Jett held it, she always found it a comfort, seeing as he always used it for comfort.

Running a hand down her face, she tried to clear the fogginess from her mind. She stared at her reflection, and all she saw was a woman's messed-up face from tears, her eyes bloodshot and puffy. There was a bruise from where Draven's man hit her, but it was just a bruise. Compared to what happened to Buck and Jett, a bruise was nothing.

What *did* happen to Buck and Jett?

She didn't have a clue how they died or why they died, only that they had died.

Getting to her feet, she wore a long shirt that Draven had left for her. She tested her bedroom door, and it was open.

For a split second she thought about running, but one glance out the door, and she saw guards were everywhere. They didn't stop her as she moved past them.

One by one, she felt their gazes on her, and wished she'd put on some pants or something. Draven still didn't allow her to wear underwear. She figured for him, it was a power trip.

Clenching her hands into fists at her side, she made her way down the long stairwell. At the bottom, she saw there were two men near the front door, and three men along each side of the wall leading up to the stairwell.

Each of them stood perfectly still. Like soldiers, ready for battle. Ready for anything.

She took a step forward, and the first two men

turned to look at her. The one on the right spoke.

"His office is that way. You may go to him or go back to your room."

He didn't say another word.

She looked toward the door and knew running wouldn't help her. If anything, it would probably end with her being thrown back in the cells. No matter how stubborn she was, she didn't want to go back to those cells, so without another look, she made her way toward Draven's office.

The door was shut, and as she lifted her hand, she paused. Could she go in there?

What would she find? Did she want to know more?

Draven wasn't the guy she once knew. She'd seen the way he handled his man, the one who'd been intent on raping her. He'd killed him without even looking like he cared there was a body at his feet.

When she couldn't handle it anymore, she knocked and instantly winced at the loud sound that echoed around the walls of the empty house. No matter how many people she saw, the house was still empty, old.

She hated it, but then she'd hated it ten years ago as well.

Axel opened the door and smiled at her. "Well, well, well, look who has come to join us."

"You left my door unlocked," she said.

"At my orders. I've got plenty of men, and they all know not to let you go," Draven said.

Axel opened the door wider, and she saw Draven sitting in a chair, drinking some dark amber liquid.

The door closed behind her, and she stared at Draven as he glanced down the entire length of her body, only to look back up again.

An answering heat filled her just from his gaze alone.

They still had that chemistry, and she couldn't deny it, even as he kept her prisoner and she knew he intended to make sure bad things happened to her.

"Want a drink?" Draven held his glass up as he made the offer.

She nodded.

"What do you drink?" Axel asked, going to the stand, ready to pour.

"I'll have whatever he's having."

Draven chuckled. "You can now handle your liquor?"

She didn't say anything.

"Take a seat," Draven said.

When she went to lower herself onto the sofa, Draven told her no.

"Have a seat." He pointed at his feet.

She stared into his face and saw he was serious.

Fine.

He wanted to play this game.

She moved toward him, and as she went to sit just a little out of reach, he snagged her around the waist and pulled her closer, forcing her to sit close at his feet with the chair at her back. His hand stayed on her shoulder, and Axel watched them.

"You always said you wanted her at your feet," he said.

"And she's going to do as I tell her for once in her life."

She felt heat fill her cheeks as they talked about her as if she wasn't there. She wondered if she was even there for them.

Axel handed her the glass, and she took it. Staring at the amber liquid, she swirled it around, watching.

"I wouldn't drink too much in one gulp if I was you. This is a drink for men," Axel said.

Harper took a sip, and sure enough, it burned on the way down. She didn't let them see exactly how much it burned though. Gritting her teeth, she held the glass in her hand and tried not to cough.

"She's a stubborn one, isn't she?"

Draven hummed his agreement. "But then, we knew that in high school with how she was. She'd never talk about her feelings. No, you always had to wait for some catalyst that would make her break. I wonder what is going to make her break now."

"You're not prepared to listen to what happened for me to run all those years ago. Why should I keep trying to tell you the truth?" she asked.

"Should we amuse her? See if her story matches up with your dad's?"

"Another time, I have no interest in hearing her lies tonight. One day, I may, especially when her pussy is soaking my cock."

She took another drink from her glass while her pussy seemed to like that idea of making him wet. She'd missed him. At least, her body had.

The asshole he'd become, she hadn't missed.

"How did they die?" she asked.

Silence met her request. One look at Axel and he was staring at Draven, the anger clearly there as his jaw clenched.

"You really want to know?" Draven asked.

"I wouldn't have asked if I didn't want to know."

"She's still got fire. It's going to take a lot to break her, Draven."

"I know, but that's what we adored about her, remember. Stand up." He tapped her shoulder, and she stood up, using his leg for leverage to stand.

He held his hand out, and she gave him her drink. She watched him place it down on the small table beside his chair, and once again, his gaze was on her, waiting, assessing.

"Buck and Jett would have liked the way you look. These nice big tits, full hips. You're not skin and bones but fucking curvy."

Draven ran a finger across his lip, watching. Not for the first time she wondered what he was thinking. The heat in his gaze gave her a clear indication of what he wanted from her.

"I think for us to tell her what happened, we need to see her naked. What do you think, Axel?"

"I always love to see a woman in her birthday suit, so I'm game."

"Draven?"

"You want to know the story, strip," he said.

"You can't be serious."

"You want to know more, strip. I'm not going to tell you again."

She saw the truth within his gaze. Glancing behind her at Axel, she saw he smirked.

"Don't look at me, beautiful. I'm not going to help you. Not even a little bit."

"What's it going to be, Harper?" Draven asked.

There was the challenge. She could walk away, never knowing what truly happened to Buck and Jett.

Just thinking about them reminded her of the rare occasions she saw them smile. They rarely had anything to smile about if at all. Most of the time, she saw Buck joking around, but his smile never reached his eyes, and with Jett, well, his knife that Draven seemed to favor was his favorite toy.

"What are you thinking right now?" she asked, genuinely curious about what was running through his mind.

"I'm wondering what it's going to be. Strip to find out the truth, or don't strip and go back to your room."

"I'm not a child."

Axel laughed.

She gritted her teeth, hating them both right now. She turned on her heel, about to leave them both to their misery.

But what about Jett and Buck?
You need to know what happened to them.
Why did they die?

She didn't leave.

She stopped at the chair and slowly began to remove the shirt she wore. No underwear as none of hers had been returned to her. Neither had any of her clothes.

She had nothing.

Was that what they wanted? For her to have completely nothing and to rely solely on them? For ten years she hadn't relied on anyone, not even Ethan.

Completely naked, she folded the shirt up and moved to stand in front of her two men. While she still thought of them as hers, she could do this. She could stand naked with her head held high and wait.

"Well, well, well, what do you think, Draven? Has she surprised you?"

"I guess she feels something for Buck and Jett."

She turned her gaze toward him and waited. She felt something for all of them. When it came to Draven though, he was her weakness, and what was more, she was sure he knew it as well.

He got up out of his chair.

"It makes me wonder exactly how far she's willing to go." He circled her, very much a predator circling his prey, waiting to strike.

She stood tall, refusing above all else to back down. He wasn't the only one here who was strong.

He cupped her cheek, and against her will, she pressed hers to him, revealing so much, and hating herself. Draven laughed.

"Buck was the one to die first out of us all."

"He was?"

"Yes, to know more, go and kiss Axel."

"For crying out loud, enough. I get it. You hate me right now, but I'm here. I'm naked."

"I never said I'd tell you the *whole* story just by stripping. You know the order they died in. You want to know more, kiss Axel, or go to your room. How important were Buck and Jett to you?"

Was this some kind of test?

She moved toward Axel, leaned down, and just as she was about to kiss him, Draven's tut interrupted her.

"No, straddle him. Feel his cock, feel how hard he is, and kiss him like you mean it. Not like he's someone you barely know. Remember, Axel's been inside your pussy. He knows how tight you are, or at least how tight you once were."

Axel sat back, and he had this smirk dance across his lips.

Gritting her teeth, she climbed into his lap and waited. His hands went to her hips. She recognized how good they felt on her body. How perfect. How much she'd missed them.

"Damn, Queen, you feel good."

"Don't call me that," she said.

"You were supposed to be our queen."

"I wanted to be your queen."

She gasped as he tugged her hand. Her lips smashed against his, their teeth clattering against each other, and she moaned. She sank her fingers into his hair, holding him close, very much aware of how dressed he was compared to her. Her pussy rubbed against him, wanting him to put his cock inside her, to fill her up, to fuck her.

It was like a drug, and she could do no more than ride his body to her completion.

Only, her orgasm was held from her.

Axel slid his hands down her back, cupping her ass, spreading the cheeks. He broke from the kiss, his lips trailing down her neck.

"How does she look, Draven? Does she look like she needs a nice big cock sliding in that asshole?"

She tensed up, looking back at Draven as he watched her. His gaze was on her ass. The heat in his eyes was so easy to detect.

He wanted her, no doubt about it, he wanted to fuck her, and thinking about him fucking her, taking her asshole, it filled her with need.

He stepped up behind her, and she wondered for a split second if he'd do it. If he'd take her anus, make her his. One touch. He slid a finger down past her puckered hole to circle her entrance. He slid a finger into her pussy, then two, and she cried out.

"She's soaking wet." He pulled his fingers from her pussy, and ran them across her back so she knew he saw how wet she was.

Pressing her face against Axel's chest, she waited.

Axel chuckled. "It seems our girl has gotten dirty since we last saw her."

"It was always there, Axel. You just couldn't see it. I could."

"What happened to Buck?" she asked.

She didn't want them talking about sex or her pussy, or how wet she was. She needed her sanity right now.

Harper couldn't recall a time in her life she'd been this aroused just by touch alone. Climbing off Axel's lap, she gave Draven her full attention.

"Buck died from a gunshot wound the day you decided to run away."

"What?"

"Yes. There was a mass shooter in the mall. I was too busy being worried about you."

She shook her head.

"No, no, that wasn't a mass shooter." She couldn't believe this. "Your dad organized that shooter to be there."

She cried out as she was suddenly pressed against the wall with Jett's blade against her neck.

"Draven, man, focus."

"I'm sick and tired of her blaming him. Take fucking responsibility for what you fucking did."

The blade pressed tight against her skin, not yet cutting, but all it would take was the right motion, and she'd be dead.

Tears fell down her face as she felt fear unlike anything she'd ever felt before. Not in the ring all those years ago, not even facing his father.

With Draven, she really feared because that one look, and she truly believed he'd kill her.

The anger. The rage. It consumed him.

His father had won.

"You won't say another fucking word about my dad, will you?"

"No," she said. She'd been tempted to shake her head, but one wrong move and she was gone, dead.

"Now, do you want to know what happened next?"

"Yes."

"Good."

Draven stepped back, and she saw Axel watching Draven as he breathed a sigh of relief.

Holding herself together, she ignored the temptation to touch her neck and instead looked at Draven.

"What happened to Buck?"

"Suck Axel's cock."

"What?"

"You heard me."

"I'll tell you exactly what happened to Buck and Jett. I want you to suck Axel's cock until he comes in your mouth. I want to see it there, filling your mouth before you swallow it."

"Draven?" Axel asked.

"If she wants to know what happened next, she has to pay the price. It's not that hard a price to pay and you get to have your dick sucked. It's a win-win."

Draven sat down.

"What do you get out of this?"

"I get to see how far you'd go for information about two men you swore your life to. Your body to. Your soul to. The very ones whose names are still inked on your back like you have a fucking right to them."

She reached behind her, touching them. They would always be there. She'd never get rid of their names or what they meant to her.

Sinking to her knees before Axel, she reached for his belt. Her hands were surprisingly steady as she unbuckled him and eased out his already hard cock.

One glance up at him, and she saw how much he wanted this. The tip was already wet with pre-cum. His cock seemed to pulse as if in anticipation. Gripping his cock, she circled the head.

"Fuck," he said.

She kept on circling the head, taking his pre-cum into her mouth before she covered the entire head, sucking down until he hit the back of her throat.

To Harper, this was at times a lot easier than having Ethan's hands all over her. He'd want to lick her pussy, to try to bring her to orgasm, but she couldn't stand it all the time. Sucking his cock, kept him happy and her as well.

Up and down, she licked, sucked, tasted Axel, getting him nice and wet with her saliva, coating him.

She glanced up and saw how much he was enjoying this. The weight of his cock in her mouth told her the same story, but seeing how needy he was, it turned her on even more, made her feel so fucking powerful as he pumped into her mouth.

"How good is she?" Draven asked.

"She's good. So good. Fuck, that feels nice. I'm going to come soon. So close."

Harper had already felt a change within him, and as he got close, she lifted off his cock so just the tip was inside.

He flooded her mouth with wave upon wave of cum. She didn't swallow it, even as she wanted to.

When he'd finished and pulled from her mouth, she tilted her head back, opening her lips so that Draven saw what she'd done. Once he saw, she did no more than swallow Axel's load, wiping her mouth of the remnants on her chin.

Tears in her eyes, she refused to cry again. She wouldn't give him the satisfaction. Within a matter of seconds, she felt dirty.

"What happened?" she asked.

Before he got himself under control, Harper was sure she'd surprised him.

"The mass shooter in the mall killed Buck with a

single bullet. It hit his neck, and he lost too much blood. He was in a coma for a couple of days before dying. He got an infection, and the doctors couldn't control it. The truth was, he died in the mall. With Jett, he met his end brutally. He was searching for you, and seeing as he wasn't paying attention because of the orders I'd given him, he ended up dead as well. Tortured and killed. It wasn't a happy ending for him."

"Oh." Harper got to her feet, and without a second glance, left the room.

Chapter Six

"Are you trying to break her?" Axel asked.

Draven stared at the spot where Harper had been kneeling just a few minutes ago. Where she had a mouth full of Axel's cum.

Yes, he'd been testing her. He'd been curious exactly how much she wanted to know what happened to Buck and Jett.

"She's not here for a celebration, Axel. I'm going to break her, you know that."

"Why use Buck and Jett?"

"She ought to know she's the cause of both of them dying."

"There's no way you could have saved either of them."

"Oh, yes, there is. Jett didn't have to go hunting for any fucking lead he had on Harper. Did he? No. His death is my fault, and let's talk about Buck. That fucker started shooting, and I ran for the bathrooms to check on Harper. All this time she's been in our enemies' arms, helping to steal girls, and fucking her way through an army of men. You think I don't think about Jett and Buck every single fucking day? I picked her, Axel. Me. *I* fucking picked her."

"For fuck's sake, Draven. I don't know how many times I'm going to have to tell you this, but I guess I'll keep on going until you understand it clearly. Buck and Jett were not your fault. You didn't cause their deaths. Not even a little!"

"I could have done something."

"What could you have done?" Axel stood up, putting his dick away. "Buck was bleeding profusely from his wound. What could you have done about that?

There was no stopping it. He was dead already. The only thing you could have done was to stand around, helpless, just like Jett and I did. You think that's easy? You went to search for Harper, who magically disappeared." Axel shook his head. "If you must know I wished I'd gone to check on her."

"You don't mean that," Draven said.

"Yes, I do. You think it's easy for me to go to sleep at night? To know that my best friend died because I couldn't help him? I tried to stop the blood flow, but it kept on coming. I couldn't make him better. I watched Buck die, and all the time, he was begging. 'Tell me it's not bad, Axel. I don't want to die. I don't. I want to have kids. A life.' Fuck." Axel stormed to the drinks cabinet and pulled himself out a bottle of whiskey, taking a large gulp directly from it. "You don't have those memories, and where you fucking hate them, I wish I had yours. I wish I only had that fear of knowing Harper was gone. Not the reality of how fucked Buck was and the fact he knew this was the end of the line for him."

"Axel."

"No. I don't want to fucking talk about it right now. I just had that woman's mouth around my dick and swallow my fucking cum to find out what happened to two of her friends. I think you're forgetting that all within one day she's nearly been raped, found out two of the men she has printed on her back are dead, and she had to strip and suck to find out what happened. It's really clouding my fucking head, because, Draven, think about it. If she really didn't give a fucking shit about them, why would she do that, huh? Why?"

"We know what she's capable of. Don't for a second think we matter to her. She's vulnerable, and using whatever means she can, to make us care," Draven said.

"You know ... fuck it, forget it. Right now, I need a drink and to not talk or remember shit. Her being here, it's bringing back a whole load of memories I don't want."

Axel took his whiskey and left the room.

Draven sat in his own misery while he thought about Harper. When she asked about Buck and Jett, as he knew she would, he'd intended to let her know what her absence caused. He never anticipated this, feeling like he'd gone too far.

You haven't gone too far.

Harper's going to pay.

It had been a long day, and he wasn't about to feel sorry for what he'd done. Harper was no longer his queen, no longer important to him in any way. She was going to pay for what she did.

Besides, the evidence of her arousal, of how much she enjoyed sucking Axel off was on his fingers.

Finishing his glass of whiskey, he got to his feet and made his way to her room. He stood outside her door, hand poised to knock when he stopped.

Why was he knocking? This was his room. Running a hand down his face, he knew she was messing with his head.

The guards had seen her naked. He didn't know why he didn't think of that, but she'd run out of the office without her damn shirt.

Fuck.

Opening the door, he stepped into the room, and saw it was empty. He heard the shower, and he decided against waiting for her.

Removing his clothes, he dropped them to the floor, not caring about the mess he made.

Completely naked, he made his way to the bathroom and found her in the shower, curled up in a ball, sobbing.

The old Draven wouldn't have been able to stand her tears.

He didn't give a shit.

At least he knew she felt something, anything.

"Why are you here?" she asked, lifting her head. "Get out. Just leave. Get out."

He stepped into the shower stall, and she got to her feet.

Fire flashed out of her eyes as she glared at him. "Why won't you listen to me?" She slapped his arm, his hand, and then growled. "Please, just leave. I want you to leave."

He had no intention of leaving.

Grabbing the soap, he covered his hands, and started to work the soap on her body. All the time, she kept on pushing him away until he held her with her back against his chest.

"You're not going anywhere. You need to understand that. You belong to me. You're mine, and if I want to shower with you, I'll fucking shower with you. Do you understand?"

"I hate you."

"Again, I don't give a fuck if you hate me or not. Life is not fair. Deal with it."

He ran the soap down her body, cupping her tits, sliding down to her stomach, stroking through the curls of her pussy before going to her ass.

When he finished, he handed her the soap.

"I'm not washing you."

"You will wash me or I'll make you go out there and suck a guard off. You should be nice to me, I know Axel is clean."

"Fuck you."

"Is that what you want? You want one of my

guard's dicks inside you?"

"Screw you."

He smiled. Her fire was back. She wasn't backing down. Harper was no coward and certainly not one to shy away from a fight.

"Maybe I should bring another woman in here to show you how I like to wash?" he asked.

He saw the jealousy in her eyes, the anger.

"If you'd not like me to find someone to tutor you in washing me."

She grabbed the soap, and he liked that she got jealous, that she didn't like the thought of another woman washing him, touching him.

Harper's hands ran all over his body, soaping him.

She wouldn't look at him, and he was okay with that. The anger emanating off her slowly diminished as she washed his body. He smiled as she got to his cock.

He was human, and when it came to Harper, he'd never been able to think straight with her. She was his one weakness.

She hesitated and finally, after a few seconds, touched him. Her hand was on his cock, running up and down the length, pulling back the foreskin to reveal the bulbous head.

Up and down her hand moved.

Pressing her against the corner of the shower, he tilted her head back with a finger beneath her chin, staring into her eyes.

She'd always had such beautiful eyes, blue. His little fire and ice queen. He slid a finger down her neck, resting against her pulse to see how rapidly it beat. Over and over, against his fingers.

Down he slid to circle one of her nipples, round and round, to move toward her other nipple. He cupped both of her tits, pressing them together, and leaned forward to take them into his mouth.

She cried out as he sucked on one hard bud, biting each nipple before flicking his tongue across the tips to soothe out the pain.

Draven had enough of showering. He didn't need to be clean. Turning off the shower, he picked her up.

"What are you doing?" she asked.

"You'll see."

He carried her to the bed, and as she giggled, he slid her to the edge, spreading her legs open. Stroking his fingers over her slit, he opened the lips of her pussy to see how wet she was.

"How many men have you been with?" he asked.

"How many women?"

He smiled. "How many men?"

Draven stroked her clit before moving down to press inside.

"One," she said.

"Only one."

"Yes."

He lifted her hips and brought her to his mouth. Sliding his tongue across her slit, he watched her as she closed her eyes, releasing a moan as she did.

He loved hearing her sounds, and it killed him to know that he'd missed them. She didn't fucking deserve to have his mouth on her, but he couldn't go another second without tasting her sweet cunt.

She cried his name, thrusting up to meet each stroke of his tongue, and he held her against his mouth, tasting her. He remembered the sweet scent of her pussy as it slid across his tongue, making him hungry for more.

Before she left, he'd not gotten enough of a taste of her, and he intended to rectify that problem. He wanted her in his mouth as often as he could get her before he handed her out to be used.

"Please, Draven, it feels so good."

He knew how good it felt. He was an expert when it came to sucking pussy. Where she'd only had one, he'd had hundreds of women, sating himself in the pleasure of their flesh, trying to rid his mind of what he'd lost.

He didn't want to think about Harper or to ache for her.

Axel and Jett, they had missed her, but neither of them had craved her like he had. It had been a hunger he'd been unable to deny and one he had to wonder if his father knew about. It was the same hunger his father had for the cook, only, Draven knew deep down, if Harper had stuck around, his cock wouldn't have gone near another female.

She'd been his just as he'd belonged to her.

That had all changed, and as he sucked her clit into his mouth, feeling that explosion she was close to, he knew he couldn't fall for her again.

He was Draven fucking Barries. With that came an expectation, and Harper couldn't last long with him. Draven would punish her, and people would know she was nothing more than a body to be used and abused.

Harper had tried too hard to take. He wouldn't let her succeed.

"Draven, I'm so close. So very close."

This once he brought her to orgasm with his tongue, and as she came, she cried out his name, hungry for him, desperate. He loved hearing those sweet calls from her lips.

One day, he'd have his fill and then he'd finish with her.

When she came, he didn't give her the chance to come down from that peak. He flipped her onto her knees, drew her up, and slammed his cock balls deep inside her soaking wet pussy.

Gripping her hips, he held her tightly as he pulled out, seeing the evidence of her arousal coating his dick. In and out, he fucked her hard, taking her.

His hold on her hips would leave bruises as he didn't show any weakness. He fucked her like he'd been wanting to since she arrived back at his home.

"You feel so fucking good, Harper. Just like I knew you would. Just like all those times before."

Only, he wasn't wearing a condom. He should put one on. Draven knew that, but the pleasure of her cunt was too much. He wanted to ruin all memory of the single guy she'd fucked, to fill her up, to mark her as his.

The need was still there even when he didn't want it to be.

Slapping her ass, he didn't slow down his thrusts, making her take as much of him as possible. He felt every single ripple and every pulse, the sheer heat of her driving his arousal higher.

He wanted to come within a matter of seconds, but he held off. Draven wasn't a teenage boy anymore but a full-grown man. When he had control, he wielded it.

This was the most pleasure he'd had in years, and he didn't want to stop, to give it up, but to pound inside her harder, taking her deeper.

Harper took him, begging him for more, and he gave it to her, sliding inside her, watching his slick prick as it took her. Every single inch of him filled her up, driving her arousal higher until she came a second time on his cock.

This time he couldn't take it, and within a few thrusts, he came, plunging deep inside her, and spilling her womb with his cum. Every single jet of it. Not once did he think about pulling away. All he wanted to do was fill her up, to make her drip with him.

****

The following morning Harper sat out in the garden. She wore a long shirt and a pair of sweatpants. Her pussy was sore from last night's sexathon with Draven, but now it made her more confused. The cold of the morning was a welcome reprieve from the ache.

She needed to think, especially now.

Whenever she thought of Buck and Jett, she felt so broken inside, so lost.

Not a second went by when she didn't wish she hadn't gone to the bathroom. If she'd not gone and stayed by their side, or allowed Draven to go with her, Alan wouldn't have been given an opportunity to talk to her. It was that single opportunity that tore her apart. Ten years had been wasted, and now, Draven and Axel hated her. She'd never get to see her four men together.

Running a finger beneath her eyes, she sniffled and hated herself again for being so weak. This wasn't good for her, not even a little bit. It killed her inside.

What also didn't help was her feelings for Draven.

In the past ten years she hadn't forgotten about him, even with Ethan, and that made her feel like the world's biggest bitch. She had a boyfriend, even a fiancé toward the end, and still, she thought about Draven, about what he'd feel at knowing who she was living with.

Her tears fell down her cheeks so fast she couldn't wipe them away, and it irritated her.

This morning she'd woken up with no Draven in her bed. At first, she thought she'd dreamed the entire night. It wasn't until she moved that she knew she hadn't been going crazy. She and Draven did have sex, and it was the best of her life, even better than when she was a teenager.

How her life had gotten so fucked, she didn't know.

She took a sip of her cold coffee and stared out across the gardens. In the distance, she saw a couple of dogs in cages, and seeing that broke her heart. One of the days she'd been given a picture of a girl she had to approach, to lure her out to the car, she'd overheard the men talking. She shouldn't have been listening, but she heard how they kept the women and girls locked up in cells, making them relieve themselves in their tiny cage, treating them like nothing more than dirt. Even knowing what those girls were going to face, and the degradation, she'd done it for Draven, for Axel, Buck, and Jett. To keep them all safe and to keep herself out of prison, with all the incriminating evidence Alan had obtained through blackmailing her. She'd cried herself to sleep at night, hating the very person she became because to keep four of her best friends alive, she had to put so many through hell. She wasn't stupid; she knew they were to be sold. For their bodies, for their pussies, and what men wanted. They were not people anymore, just a commodity, and *she* had been the one to help ruin their lives.

Was this the life Draven knew about? The one Alan told him? What other lies had he manipulated about her? She could only imagine what Alan would say. She doubted Draven knew the truth. She was starting to get a sense of her surroundings, of Draven's new life. A life that his father wanted for his son.

"What are you doing out here all alone?"

Harper turned to see Axel heading her way.

"Just thinking. No one stopped me on the way out."

Axel smirked. "Draven's already given the order

that you can walk around the grounds. You're not allowed to leave."

"And if I do?"

"Pain of death."

"Pain of death?"

"Yes, the guard on duty that doesn't stop you, will die. Simple as that."

"So you guys take lives now without a single care as to who you're ruining in the process? What you're doing?"

"Harper, babe, we've always taken lives. You've just not seen us do it."

She shook her head. "You're not killers."

Axel burst out laughing. "Who are you trying to kid? Yourself? I hate to break this to you, sweetheart, we're killers." He shrugged. "You've got to in this crazy old world, right."

"It's wrong."

"So, the cops are easily bought. In this so-called right world, do you think that is right?"

She gritted her teeth and didn't say a word.

"See, this world is full of hypocrites and bullshit."

"And monsters?"

Axel smiled. "Exactly that. You've just got to see where you fit in the food chain."

"Where did Buck and Jett fit?"

The smile he had disappeared. She wasn't going to apologize. If he wanted to scream about how the world was divided then she wasn't going to pretend that their very friends had succumbed to those monsters.

"They'd been prey, right?" she said.

"Be careful, Harper."

"Just like me."

"Those were good men. I came out here to keep

you company."

"You're keeping me prisoner here, Axel. Let's face it, my end here is not going to exactly be all sunshine and roses, is it? You and Draven have got big plans for me."

"We've got plans, but you don't need to worry about them."

He took a seat beside her, and she stared over at the cages again.

Without asking for permission, she walked across the garden and straight for those cages. One look inside and she saw a dog had given birth to puppies. They looked to be a couple of weeks old, maybe even up to eight.

She knew Axel had followed her, but she ignored him.

Bending down, she touched the cage and smiled as all the pups came close to her, touching their faces near her fingers. They were so sweet, so innocent. In a horrible way, they reminded her of those girls. Their faces flashed before her eyes, making her pause. She shouldn't touch the dogs. She wasn't a good person, but vile. Shaking off the feeling, she smiled as one dog licked at her fingers.

Without another word, she stepped into the cage, being careful not to step in any dog mess.

One by one, the pups yapped at her feet, and she couldn't help the laughter, the joy that flooded her body from seeing them. In the back of her mind, the guilt flared up, threatening to choke her up, but like so many times before, she pushed it down. She ignored the pain and suffering she'd inflicted, and focused on the puppies.

They were all amazingly beautiful white Labradors, so charming, and the mother came up to her, giving her a sniff.

Seeming happy that her pups were safe, she went and collapsed in the corner.

Harper found a clean spot, and the pups moved toward her. One tried to climb into her lap, and she picked it up, pressing her face against the fur, and simply falling in love with the sheer beauty of them.

"They're all so beautiful," she said.

"Draven sells the bad ones."

"Bad ones?"

"The ones that are not going to be cut out for scaring people, Harper."

She held the one in her arms a little tighter, hating that Draven would discard anything he didn't see as having any real value.

They were all magnificent, beautiful, and she loved them all—unlike the women who were sold into a life they didn't want. The same women she'd helped to lead to a life of hell, just so Alan wouldn't kill her friends, only to now know, one had already died, and another wouldn't last much longer and get killed.

Glancing back at the house, she saw several people were arriving, men and women.

"Is there a party tonight?"

"Something like that," Axel said.

She didn't like how vague he was being and knew it would all be revealed soon enough, when they were ready to hurt her some more.

Don't you deserve it?

Buck and Jett are dead because of you.

No, she couldn't think like that. Not now.

They were not dead because of her. They were dead because of Alan. She had to remember that. Her life hadn't caused death, but she tried not to think about the girls, because without her, *they* would still be alive. She thought about her mother and Ian instead.

Cutting off each dead end, she focused instead on the puppies, the ones that were filling her with so much joy and love.

"Axel, you can head inside now," Draven said.

She looked up, and sure enough, Draven was heading in their direction. Part of her wanted to plead with Axel not to go.

For some strange reason, she felt oddly safe with Axel present. Alone though, she couldn't trust herself. One look at Draven and she was already wet and begging for him.

Get a grip, Harper.
He wants to hurt you.
He's not your savior.
This is not high school.
One day he's going to break you.
To tear you apart and spit you back out again as if you're nothing.
Don't let yourself fall for him, not even a little bit.

Kissing the top of the puppy's head, she waited to see what would happen.

"See you around," Axel said.

Harper said nothing, watching Axel leave. He seemed too sure of himself in his movements, but there were odd fleeting glances where it didn't seem to be the case.

"You found the pups," Draven said.

She turned to him, and he was watching her.

She didn't like to be under his scrutiny, so she quickly turned her attention back to the pup in her arms. Nothing could be wrong with giving some loving to the pup.

The other pups kept coming up and nudging her thigh. They were content with a head stroke and then would wander off back to their mother, or play in the cage.

"You get rid of the ones you don't think are good enough?"

"Everyone does that, Harper. It's business."

"You and business. Were you ever like the guy I once knew?"

Draven laughed. "That guy died a long time ago. Probably when one of his best friends didn't make it out of a coma. Then, he died completely having to bury what was left of the other."

She shuddered at his last statement.

What was left.

Her heart broke a little more.

"You were gone this morning."

"This is not a date, Harper. I have no intention of sticking around. We're not together. You're here for my amusement."

Harper didn't say anything more. She stroked the pup in her arms and stared across the cages.

The dogs were at the doors, wanting attention from their master. She knew what that was like.

She missed the kind of attention she got from him that she used to. She'd give anything to go back to that day at her locker when dirt spilled out. It was odd. She truly believed that was one of the biggest turning points of her life. If she could ever make it back to that day, she'd warn him, warn him that Alan would come between them. He'd set a path in motion that would guarantee their destruction.

Still, she said nothing like always, and pretended.

For now, she couldn't tell him what happened that day at the mall. There was no way he'd believe her.

"You're having a party?" she asked.

"Yes, and you're my plus one."

"Do you have a plus one when you're hosting a

party?"

"You do for this one. Come on, Harper. It's time to go and get ready."

He held his hand out, and she didn't want to go with him.

All the times he'd done that ten years ago, she'd gladly taken his hand, trusted him. This, what was about to happen, whatever it was, this didn't make her feel comforted. It scared her, terrified her, and knowing Draven was doing this willingly unsettled her.

She got to her feet, took his hand, and left the cage.

One glance back and the pup she'd been holding was at the door of the cage. She wanted that pup more than anything, and walking away filled her with regret.

She didn't fight though, not as Draven took her through the kitchen where staff she hadn't noticed on her way out were clearly catering to the party he was having.

"Do you ever leave Stonewall?" she asked.

"Only when I have to."

They didn't linger, and he took her straight back to her room. On the edge of the bed was a box.

"That is your dress for this evening. Don't leave this room until I come and get you."

"You're going to lock me up?"

He chuckled. "Harper, get all pretty for me. You never know, I may reward you later."

She watched him close the door.

Going to the box, she lifted the lid and behind it was a beautiful white evening gown. It was sheer, and as she looked in the box, she couldn't find any undergarments.

If she wore this dress, her body would be on display for all to see. At first glance, it looked like a wedding dress, only on the more revealing side.

Running her fingers across the soft fabric, she could at least admire the beauty of it. The softness ran through her fingers.

Sitting on the edge of the bed, she didn't need any kind of warning to know tonight wouldn't end well.

Draven was going to punish her. He was going to make sure that when he came for her, she was under no illusions of who she belonged to.

This was part of breaking her, just a little more.

She didn't put up a fight. Standing up, she made her way into the bathroom to shower. If he wanted to break her, then she'd go with him and let him try, but he wouldn't succeed. She would do whatever he asked because she knew at the end of it, she would win. One way or another, Alan Barries wasn't going to win this one. Not with her.

Chapter Seven

Men and women of all ages were gathered, enjoying drinks and some canapes. Axel looked bored as he always did at these parties. This was one of the occasions Axel couldn't go by Jett's name. Draven was very much aware of Axel using Jett's name, mostly so he could be invisible, but at his house parties it was difficult. Not that this was any party and Draven was already very much aware of how pissed his remaining friend was.

He needed to do this.

After last night, he had to put some perspective on things. On this with Harper. She wasn't here to be his girlfriend or even his mistress. She was a means to an end.

The men and women here, each of them had been present during his father's reign. Draven had not killed them for two reasons, one, their loyalty was to him, and second, they were damn good at what they did. He had no intention of killing people that helped him, and in this room were such people.

They had all hated his father as well. The power Alan wielded had come crashing down the moment Draven killed him, and in doing so, these people had sworn their loyalty to him. In return, he rewarded them handsomely.

Today would be one of the days he rewarded them.

"For a display of power, you've done really well," Ian said, surprising Draven.

Not that he showed it. He turned to his lawyer and smiled. "I don't recall sending you an invite."

"You don't recall a lot of things right now. I want

to see Harper."

"If you mean to take her away from me, be very careful here, Ian. I've got no problem killing you where you stand, or better yet, making you a mockery and sucking all the cock and pussy here. This is a dirty lot, and they love a good show." He winked at him.

"I'm begging you not to do this."

"And I have no interest in hearing you."

"Harper is back now, Draven. She's not leaving you. Can't you just let this vendetta go for the both of you?"

"Her leaving killed two of my friends at different points, Ian. If you don't want to see your daughter naked and punished later, I suggest you leave."

Silence met his request, and he saw Ian was staring at him, really looking at him.

"Your father did finally break you."

"Are you getting sentimental?"

"No, I just know that Harper will wake up and see this side of you. You're going to break the only good thing in your life, and ten years ago, Draven, you cared for her."

"Like you did with her mother?" Draven asked.

He watched as Ian flinched. He had no problem throwing and casting stones where necessary. When it came to Harper's mother, they all knew the reason she killed herself.

"You think I don't know why she ended her life? Why she took a blade to her wrists?"

"And that Harper found her. Don't forget that part. Remember the part where your daughter had to pull her out of the bath."

"Don't you dare even try to pretend to me that you give a shit about my daughter when your sole aim is to hurt her."

"I give more of a shit than you ever would," he said. "Remember I was there for her. I knew how she was hurting. How she was breaking. You just wanted the young pussy my father had fed you. What he'd fed a lot of men over the years."

"And you think throwing that in my face is going to help you?" Ian asked. "After whatever it is you have planned tonight, the hold you have on Harper will disintegrate. She will never look at you the same way, and I will give you this warning, you continue down this path, it'll be you finding her in the red bathtub. I've lived through it. I picked Hannah, but not a day goes by that I don't regret what I did. I made my bed, and I'm lying in it, day in, day out. With Harper, I fucked up. She hates my guts, and I accept that. I've got no choice. Don't make the same mistakes I did."

Before Draven could say anymore, Ian left. He watched the old man go, his grey hair disappearing into the distance.

"You think there's a chance of that?" Axel asked.

Draven finished his whiskey and turned to his friend. "There's always a risk."

"You're willing to take it."

"I think you mistake me for someone who gives a fuck."

"Damn it, Draven. I know you loved her once. I know you loved her all those years ago and that a part of you died having to share us with her. We all saw it. You didn't tell us to stop. You were determined for us to have our shot, but that didn't stop you from loving her. Not even for a second. This, you could lose her. I need to know you're ready for that."

"Axel, keep our guests occupied. This conversation is boring. I'm going to go and get the star of the show."

Draven went to leave, but Axel grabbed his arm. "I know right now you don't care. She betrayed us, and you want to see her hurting, maybe even dead."

"Your fucking point?"

"Are you ready for that? You're my best friend. The only person I've got in this world, and I need to know that you're not going to do something I can't reverse. You lose her, kill her, I can't bring her back from the dead."

He smiled. "Axel, stop being a pussy. Harper's getting everything she deserves. I don't love her. I feel nothing for her."

Axel cursed but took over, mingling with the crowd.

Draven finished his drink and made his way up to Harper's room. He didn't knock and just entered the room. He found her sitting on the bed.

Part of him had expected her to rebel, to not let him see her in the dress he'd specially picked out.

It seemed rather fitting to him for her to be in white. He'd taken her virginity, and now he was going to completely destroy her soul, or at least, what remained of it.

He wondered if Buck and Jett would welcome what he was about to do.

Her hands were clasped together in front of her, her gaze on him.

"You know, I didn't run away," she said.

Draven sighed. He didn't need to hear the lies or the bullshit. He had no wish to hear any of it.

"That day at the mall I was taken from the bathroom."

"Cut the shit, Harper. I don't care. You think I've not been warned about your lies. I saw what you did, what you're capable of. You're not a fucking victim here.

I saw the pictures of you, carrying girls off as if it was a fucking game. You were happy for the men in this life, just so long as it wasn't us, right?"

"What?"

"I know everything about you, Harper. What you did. What you've done. Every little detail of the women that went missing just as you helped guide them to a fucking car. I don't need to hear your lies. I've seen the truth, and it's not pretty."

She paused, not doing anything, but looking ... gutted. It lasted for a few seconds before she suddenly laughed, which sounded forced. "It doesn't matter though, does it? You've already decided that you hate me. That you're going to go through with whatever you're about to."

"Is this where you try to convince me not to?" he asked.

"No." She stood up. "You can try to break me. It's fine. You can punish me whatever way you see fit."

"And what are you going to do about it?"

"Nothing. I'm going to go through with it and know that deep in my heart, I didn't want to run away ten years ago. I ran out of fear, not out of a need. I didn't beg to leave."

"But you took the ten grand."

She laughed. "Yeah, I took the ten grand. Didn't exactly have a choice in the matter. Alan made sure I had no choice. He wouldn't let me leave without it. His poison didn't stop there. I couldn't go anywhere without his say-so. He was the one who held all the cards. The one who made me do all that nasty shit. I had no choice. None whatsoever. I have to live with all I've done, and right now, I really see it wasn't worth it. That's okay though. Think what you want, whatever will help you sleep at night, Draven."

The dress didn't hide anything. It showed her body, the curves that he loved about her. They were as full and round as she'd been when they'd been younger. She still had amazing tits, full, ripe, and beautiful. He loved her hips as well, the way they were designed to he held as he fucked her. Just looking at her, he wanted to do that right now. But so much had changed in ten years.

Pushing those concerns to one side, he took Harper's arm, and for as much as she was showing her strength, he felt the faint tremor of her hand. She wasn't quite as poised and ready for this as she liked him to think.

He walked her downstairs to where the party was in full swing. The moment he appeared, there were a few seconds of silence. If he'd not been holding her, he wouldn't have seen a change within her.

Harper kept her head high, like a queen, even as she shook in his arms.

He saw Axel watching her. His best friend clearly thought Draven was making a mistake and would regret it later.

Moving through the crowd, Draven stopped and made sure men and women looked. She was his prize.

"So, who is this pretty little lady?" Frank asked. He was an older man, late fifties that had a thing for young women and liked to sell pussy for far above its valued price.

Harper tensed up.

Frank went to touch, and Axel stopped him.

"She's to be looked at, not touched."

"Ah, you still have a no-touch policy. You always know how to spoil a party."

"When it comes to the hands of dirty old men, of course," Axel said. "The point is anticipation, and don't forget, he's the one in charge." He pointed toward

Draven.

Draven moved her around the room, making her very much aware she wouldn't find any help tonight.

She was to be on display, ridiculed, humiliated, and to know her place.

When it came time for dinner, Axel grabbed his arm and tried to give him another warning. "Are you really fucking sure about this, Draven? Are you ready for this?"

Draven was done.

Men and women were seated at his large table, the same table that had seen a lot of death. Everyone present tonight had all been witness to a lot of ugly shit.

As Harper went to sit beside him, Draven caught her wrist.

"No, you will sit on the floor."

Silence fell around the room. Harper looked toward Axel, who sat down at the other end of the table. Harper should have been sitting down there, and if she'd not done what she had ten years ago, she would have been. They wouldn't all be waiting for her punishment, to see her hurt.

Axel didn't offer any comfort or protest.

Harper sat down on the floor.

"Kneel up. I don't want to have to work to feed you."

He was treating her like a dog, but she did as he requested.

One glance at her and he saw her cheeks were red. Tears were in her eyes, but she did no more than blink them away.

Dinner started as the waitress brought out the first course. It was soup.

Dropping his spoon into the soup, he tasted it. He didn't have a clue what it was. Drawing another spoonful, he pressed it to her lips, and Harper glared at him as she took from the spoon. She licked her lips.

"She's like a good little dog," one of the women said. "So perfect. I tell you, Draven, if you're ever interested in bringing her for training, I'd like to give her a try." This came from Tillie. She was a known dominatrix and owned a string of BDSM clubs that catered to all tastes.

"You may get a chance at her later."

"Oh, good, I do like a good show." Tillie clapped her hands in glee.

Everyone present here had seen their fair share of darkness. Nothing would surprise them.

"Does she even know what she did wrong? That all the bad girls always get punished?" another asked.

"She knows what she did wrong. She also knows she's going to be punished for it." He saw the anger in her eyes as he finished off the soup.

Draven had only fed her a few spoonsful.

"Would you like to see her in all of her glory?"

The table cheered, and he got her to stand up and to remove the dress that he'd so carefully picked out for her.

Her hands shook as she followed his words.

"Harper, go and serve all the men some wine," he said.

She turned her back to them and went to the wine bottle. The waitress that was standing in the corner held it out for her.

Harper took it, and came to the table, attending them one by one. She started with Axel, who was shaking his head at Draven. It looked like he disapproved of what was happening.

Doing this, there was no way they would ever be able to have her as queen, to have her at their table.

Axel's concerns about his own welfare were completely unfounded. Draven had no feelings for Harper. He just wanted to make her pay.

What Axel failed to realize was he had no intention of keeping Harper. He was going to let his plans play out, and she was going to be broken. The proud woman they saw right now, that would all fall away.

One by one, she filled wineglasses, and as men and women touched her, Draven sat back and watched.

He wasn't immune to what was happening. Sipping at his drink, he waited for her to get to his table, and as she stepped close, pouring him some wine, he slid a hand between her thighs.

She was completely dry. Nothing about this was turning her on.

He watched her, and as he probed her pussy, she winced. Pulling his fingers away, he spat into them, and worked them between her folds once more and she gripped the edge of the table.

He made sure they all saw what he was doing.

"Axel, go and prepare her," he said.

"Draven."

"Now."

His friend didn't argue. He got to his feet and moved toward Harper. It was time to begin her punishment.

****

There was no weapon, nothing.

Harper had no choice but to deal with everyone who touched her as if they had a right to. Her body was her own, but Draven had made sure they could touch.

Axel grabbed her arm and dragged her outside in the cold.

"What is going on?" she asked, crying out.

"You really think it was going to get as bad as last night? You don't think that Draven has other plans for you?" Axel asked.

"I didn't do anything wrong."

"Buck and Jett died because of you."

"I didn't do anything. I tried to make it so you'd all be safe. So you'd all be alive."

"Stop fucking lying."

She pulled on him, forcing him to turn toward her. The cold of the night bit into her flesh.

"I didn't run away. I loved you all, and you know I loved Draven so much. I went to the bathroom and never had any intention of running away."

"The same old story. Cut the bullshit."

"This is not bullshit, Axel. This is the truth. Plain and fucking clear to see. I was taken from the bathroom back to Draven's old house. Alan had arranged it. He arranged the shooter, Axel. I watched what he did." She pulled on him as Axel tried to move her away. "Please, I wouldn't lie to you. I would never lie to you. Please, listen to me. I watched him give the order. I watched the shooter fire into the crowd. I didn't know he'd hit Buck. I called on Alan's bluff. He told me he'd kill Draven. He'd kill all of you."

"Alan would never kill Draven. He was his only living heir."

"I called that bluff, and he gave the order." Harper was sobbing now, recalling those moments she'd seen on the screen. "I watched as he shot into the crowd. I watched you fall, and I had no choice. I begged him to call off the shooter. He told me I had to go. I had to leave. He sent one of his men with me. You can ask him."

"Who went with you?"

"Laser. He was the one that went with me. Please,

Axel, I am telling you the truth. Laser was there."

"Harper, Laser is dead. Alan killed him for betraying him. He's the enemy."

"What?"

"Laser never worked with Alan. He was a double agent, helping the enemy to gain information and to steal his drugs and women. He'd been involved in several of his shipments that didn't make it. He wasn't working for Alan but for one of the enemies that Draven and I later killed. Draven demanded that Alan search for you, to find you, and he did, several times. There were men that went looking for you. Some either turned up dead, or turned sides. We saw the evidence of what you did, the proof of you being the enemy, but we could never get to you in time."

"And that wasn't the least suspicious to you?" She screamed out, desperate for him, for someone, to see the truth.

"He told us that if we ever found you, you'd feed us a story. You'd been tainted by Laser, and he'd been seen visiting your mother the day before she died. You were playing us the entire time."

Harper cried out. "I'm not feeding you a story. That's all fucking bullshit."

She paused when she realized they were heading toward the whipping post.

"Axel, what is going on?"

"I have no desire to do this. I want you to know that. For me, I'd just fucking kill you, but I've got a feeling this is not all what it seems, and I've got to think of Draven."

"Then let me go. Please, let me go. I've not done anything wrong. I swear it. Please."

She fought Axel, but he was too strong. He easily overpowered her and secured her to the whipping post. It was so dark, so cold.

She sobbed as he held her tightly against it, wrapped up, with no way to move. There were cuffs for her hands, keeping her in place. He wrapped a rope around her body, holding her up, leaving no way for her to get away.

Even as she tugged at the bindings, she couldn't get free. She was completely at the mercy of Draven and Axel.

"I wasn't telling a story. I swear it. I wasn't doing anything but trying to make you all live. I didn't want any of you to die." She held onto the post, even though it was so cold. The chill seeped into her bones.

"You're going to kill me tonight?"

"No." Axel stood, looking at her. She didn't know what he was staring at. She'd never been so terrified in her life. "If I try to find this out, if I somehow find anything that your story is true, I'll let Draven see the evidence."

"You'd look for me?"

"Something never made sense all those years ago. Even now thinking about to it, it doesn't all add up. It's too neat, especially with how much Alan hated you."

"It's because it's all lies. I swear it, Axel. I really swear it. Please, I didn't run because I wanted to. I was taken."

"Harper, I'm not promising anything here."

"You're offering to look, and that is more than you gave me a day ago. I swear to you, I'm not lying. I'm innocent. I wasn't … I had no intention of ever leaving."

"If I don't find anything, I will kill you. I won't let Draven break you. That is the deal we make right now, right this second, Harper. If I find something, you walk free. If I don't, if all the evidence I find is of your deceit, I get to kill you before Draven does."

Tears fell down her cheeks, and she nodded.

"Yes, yes, please, I've got nothing to hide. I swear it. I'm innocent. I had nothing to do with Buck or Jett's deaths. It wasn't my fault."

"They're coming," Axel said. "Harper, try and … I don't know. Don't die or kill yourself."

With that Axel stepped away.

He was her one lifeline. Had she made a deal with the devil?

One by one, she saw torches as they approached.

"You know, Axel's father used to love this post," Draven said.

He moved up beside her, but he didn't even look at her.

The men and women of the party had to be standing behind her.

Tears filled her eyes as she knew what was about to happen, what he was going to let happen to her.

It killed her to know he didn't believe her.

Maybe it would be easier to take her own life?

No. She wouldn't think like that. There's no way she'd ever allow them to win. She was the boss here, not them. Draven was wrong, and one day, she'd be here and he'd have to apologize to her.

He touched the post. "Do we even know how many women got whipped here?"

"Plenty," Axel said.

"Draven," she said. There was no need to ask what was about to happen. He was clearly going to whip her. "You don't have to do this."

"My father believed all women were a weakness. To make sure they were good, they had to experience … punishment." Draven stood in front of her, and she glared at him. He stroked a finger down her cheek. "You. You have been a very naughty bitch. It's time you realized your place in this world, and it's not anywhere but fucking beneath me, beneath us all. You are here to be used, and to learn to keep your fucking mouth shut."

"Draven?"

"Shut the fuck up, Axel."

Tears filled her eyes as Draven stared at her. What was he hoping to prove? Why do this?

"They died because of you. For ten years you've been living your life without a care in the world, and now it's time for you to get what is coming to you. Tillie, please, begin. I know you love to teach as you punish," Draven said.

She looked toward Axel, who was now staring at the ground.

"So, you don't want to break her skin too soon. That wouldn't do well at all."

Harper screamed as she felt the first lash of the whip on her skin. She held onto the post, and she couldn't believe this was happening to her. A month ago, she was working at a florist with a boyfriend who cared and she didn't deserve.

Tears leaked down her chest, and she cried out as the next lash cut through her skin. The pain and the cold combined together to make it impossible for her to numb the pain.

Over and over, Tillie showed them how to whip her, and with each lash, the sting burned brighter.

Draven just stood there, watching her. The smirk on his face let her know he was happy this was happening to her.

He wanted this. He wanted this woman to hurt her.

Draven was doing this to prove to her he didn't care. He didn't love her. She was nothing to him. He was nothing more than a monster.

Someone asked a question, and Tillie changed the angle. There was a difference in the sting. It wasn't as sharp, but Tillie didn't stop, and the pain was still there.

Harper burst into tears, but didn't beg the woman to stop. In the back of her mind, she knew she deserved this, and worse. The men and women she lured for Alan, did they go through this? Were any of them experiencing this right now as she was?

There was no way she'd give anyone the satisfaction of knowing the pain she was in.

Tillie whipped her flesh, repeating different strokes and different force, each one creating their own kind of pain, until finally, Draven stepped forward.

Harper was no longer holding herself up anymore, the restraints on the post doing the job. She closed her eyes, not wanting to see, not wanting anything anymore.

This was archaic. It was fucking wrong. One day, she would tear this fucking post out and burn it up, after, she hoped, having Draven in this position.

In fact, she wondered how many of those disgusting assholes had been on a post before in their life? Did they even give a shit what they were inflicting?

She hated them all. This was not going to go unpunished. She'd have her revenge on them, on all of them. Tillie, that fucking bitch would one day know what it felt like, and the others for watching, they would feel it too.

Draven's sting was harder than Tillie's. That first lash she felt cut her skin. Even after the cold and the pain of before, his hurt the most. She didn't know if it was because of how hard he was hitting her, or if it was because he'd been the one to strike her.

"This is for Buck!"

Harper screamed at the impact. Resting her head against the post, she tried to not think, to do anything, but it wasn't helping.

The pain consumed her, and she sobbed for him to stop, to not hurt her anymore.

When it came for Jett, Harper didn't remember anything as she passed out into glorious bliss.

****

Draven held the whip. "Leave!"

The men and women left the spot where Harper was now passed out.

His guards knew what he wanted. They were all to leave, to be gone by the time he got back with Harper.

She was out cold, and as he approached, he saw her back was red, covered in the welts. He'd broken the skin.

He hadn't intended to cut her flesh, but just one look at her and thinking about Buck and Jett, he'd lost control and fucking hurt her.

"Are you satisfied now?" Axel asked. "Have you had your pound of flesh?"

"You want to criticize what I've done? We planned this. You and me. Her punishment. This is what she deserves."

"How did she know about the gunman?" Axel asked.

Draven stopped, staring at his friend. "She's gotten to you."

"What if … she's right? Alan couldn't stand for her to be part of us. It's still pretty fucking suspicious that she'd go to him. You said so yourself, she hated Alan's guts. Why go to him? We were all too brokenhearted to see it."

"She couldn't handle what we dished out. She should have come to us, but she didn't. Buck and Jett are dead because of her."

"She didn't pull the trigger, and she knew about it, Draven. She knew what happened, and if she was gone, how did she know unless what she said is true? Your father had connections, and even to this day you don't know every single one of them. Don't you think it's a little too neat with how this has ended up?"

"For fuck's sake, you're not going to let this go, are you?"

"You want to break her that's fine. Be prepared for what you're causing. Once you break her, there is no going back. There is no Harper. She'll be long gone."

"Your point being?"

"I hope you can handle that. *You're* my concern, Draven."

He rolled his eyes. "Seriously, what are you getting at?" He was done playing these games. It was fucking cold, and he really needed to get Harper out of the cold. He wanted her to hurt but not die.

"You were in love with her all those years ago, and you really think that is just going to disappear? That a love like that fades?"

"I'm not pussy-whipped anymore, Axel. I got over it."

"You did? Then why did you opt for the whipping post? I thought you were going to have your guys use her. Let them wreck her pussy and ass just like the whore she was. You came here and let them hurt her instead."

Draven stormed over to Axel, raising his fist, and his friend laughed.

"I see right through you. I always have. I saw how much you cared for her years ago. It's why I didn't fight you. For you, it has always been Harper. Here she is. She can belong to you. If you're going to ruin her, be ready to lose her forever."

He watched as Axel walked away, and he watched him go without saying a word.

Alone, near the whipping post with Harper, he was lost to his thoughts.

She didn't deserve to be tied up.

Gritting his teeth, he helped her down, taking her weight as he lifted her up. He'd have to take care of her back. A couple of lashes had split her skin.

She deserved this.

He knew deep down into his soul, she had to have this.

But if he truly believed it, why was his gut twisting at what he allowed to happen?

Chapter Eight

Harper gasped as she woke up. Her body ached, and the pain in her back was intense.

"You're awake."

She turned toward the sound, and as she squinted, she groaned. Hannah, her lovely stepmother, sat in a seat beside the bed.

"Have I died?"

"No, not even close. Draven left you too long on the whipping post. The cold, the shock, and you got an infection. It can happen. You've been out cold for a couple of days."

"So why are you here with me?" she asked.

"Because, Draven thought it would be good for us," Hannah said.

Harper watched as she leaned forward and began to pour out some water. There was a straw.

"Here, drink."

She took a sip of the water and groaned, pulling away once she had enough.

"Why would it be good for us?" Harper asked. "I imagine if anyone was going to be worth me talking to, it would be my dad."

"Your father has never been on the whipping post. I was shocked to learn it was still here and that it was also currently in use."

Harper hadn't forgotten what had happened, and it made her shake a little knowing Draven and his cronies had done that to her. She turned her head away in shame. Had she allowed that to happen? What did that make her?

Pain and fear and everything from anger to rage consumed her.

"I know what you're feeling."

"You were on the whipping post?" Harper asked.

She felt the bed dip, and Hannah had moved a little closer to her. Age hadn't done well for her, and she'd lost that chipper, happy look.

"Is being married to my dad what made you so miserable? Sorry, I've got no filter at the moment." Harper saw her flinch.

"Life in Stonewall has never been … a blessing. For the most part it has been hell. Your dad, he makes life … bearable."

"Bearable? Do you love him?" Harper asked.

"I love your father in my own way."

Harper snorted. "My mother died because of you."

She saw shame cross Hannah's face. It was so fleeting that at first she thought she had made it up.

"I never wanted to get between the two of them. I never wanted to get married. Choices are made for women like me."

"What? Women like you? You're not making sense."

"I never had a good life, Harper. I never had a mother or father that cared. I was one more mouth to feed. A body to clothe. Money that wasn't worth it. I know this is not making sense, but if you just hold on and let me speak, it will all make some kind of sense in a way. You'll understand."

Harper stayed silent and waited for Hannah to speak.

"My parents were poor. So poor and greedy that when a man came by on my sixteenth birthday and looked me over as if I was cattle, I was sold. I still remember the last day of school, flirting with the guys. Loving the attention they lavished on me. I was a hottie, and I knew it. They knew it. I loved the control I had. That was all taken away from me. I was stripped of my name, of the poor clothes I had. They gave me a single rag shirt. I wasn't allowed real clothes for a time. It was more of a sack that had been sewn in the right places to make it look like a shirt. In the winter it was so cold, and there were so many kids, younger and some older, and we'd bundle up together to try and get warm. We were like a pack. We all knew what was going to happen. We were all going to be sold. We watched it happen. Men and women would come in, look at us, pick us out, and we'd leave, never to be seen again. I got picked quickly, as much to their shock, I was still a virgin. I was sold to Draven's dad. He took my virginity before I turned seventeen. After he had his fill, I was his property to be owned and dealt with. I was to fuck every single person he demanded in order to earn my keep."

Harper didn't like this story.

"I was a good worker as well. I knew how to keep men and women happy. I hated pain, and so any beating I got, I learned not to do whatever had caused the beating again. It was easy as well. That's all I had to do. Keep on working. Keep my head down. Screw hard, fuck harder, and love the job I did."

"Why are you telling me this?"

"Because one day I had another job. The job to distract a married man. To get him to leave his wife and kid. At first, I refused. I didn't want to get married, and Alan told me that's what I was going to do. I was to become a trophy wife. I didn't get a beating. I was dragged up to that post and whipped until I passed out. I wasn't let down from that post. I was whipped daily, starved, and when I finally relented, that was when the beatings stopped. I was fed, clothed, and given back who I was once was. Hannah."

Tears filled Harper's eyes as she thought about all that Hannah had been through. "You had to make my dad fall in love with you."

"Yes. Alan wanted someone to report back to him on Ian. Your father was important to him with all that he knew. He got what he wanted, but Alan always did. Catherine was gone, and Ian was in his place, doing his job. I know some of the pain you're going through. Being on that post, it kills a part of you inside, and I guess that is why Draven had me come and sit with you."

"To ease his conscience."

"And to also stop the risk of you hurting yourself like your mother."

Harper tried not to think of her mother, Catherine.

"Can you help me leave?" Harper asked. She was done with this, done with all of this. She wanted to leave, to go back to her life.

Not back to Ethan but away from Stonewall.

"I can't help you with that."

"Didn't you ever think of running away?"

"You come to realize that it doesn't matter where you run to. You'll always be looking over your shoulder to see who is following you. It's why I never leave. It's easier to work with them."

"I want to kill them all," Harper said.

Hannah touched her head, tucking some hair behind her ear. "I know."

"Did you ever get payback?"

"No."

"How do you feel about that?" Harper asked. "Aren't you angry?"

"Always. I'm angry that I never fought, but I'm alive today. I've got a loving husband, a daughter, and I'm happy."

"Please go away," Harper said. "I know you

mean well, but it doesn't stop you from being the woman that caused my mother to kill herself. I'm sorry for what happened to you, but we're never going to be friends or have a relationship. Please, leave."

"I'll go and get Draven."

"No!"

She was already going, and Harper couldn't sit up. She couldn't roll over or do anything.

She was trapped, and she fucking hated it. Screaming into the pillow, she moved toward the drawer and looked inside for anything.

"Don't even think about it," Draven said, slamming the drawer closed before she could pull anything out from inside.

Not that she knew what she was looking for.

"Leave me alone."

"I'm not leaving you to do anything. You're going to end up killing yourself," Draven said.

Ignoring the pain, she dropped to the floor. She would try to leave. Getting to her feet, she stared at him. Her legs were like jelly, and she glared at him, aware of how naked she was.

"I want to leave."

"You're not leaving."

She lunged at him. Using her nails, she wanted to claw his eyes out, to make him howl in pain.

He overpowered her. Draven held her hands away from him, and she growled, hating how weak she felt, knowing how easy it was for him to control her.

"I hate you," she said.

"I hate you too."

"Let me go. You're a fucking monster."

He pushed her to the bed, and she screamed. Tears filled her eyes, and he cursed.

"I don't want to hurt you."

"You whipped me!" She yelled the words in his face, finding the strength to fight back. "You got them to whip me. What happened to you?"

He didn't answer.

Draven stood up, and she got to her feet. Glancing behind her, she saw the bed had red streaks.

"They had started to heal. Lie back down. I'll apply more ointment on your back."

"Fuck you." She sniffled.

Walking away from him, she looked in the mirror. Just as she started to look, Draven stood in front of her.

"I want to see the damage you've done."

He did no more than slam his fist against the glass. She didn't get a chance to see as the glass shattered, shards of glass falling to the carpet.

"Real mature."

"Now you can't see."

"There's more than one mirror in the house. You can't hide it from me for much longer."

"Just lie on the bed and let me take care of you."

She wanted to argue, but seeing no point in doing so, she got on the bed and lay down.

Draven moved toward her, and she turned her head away from him.

"How are you feeling?" he asked.

She gritted her teeth, refusing to give him even an inch. She wanted him dead. She wanted to be the one to kill him, to murder him and for him to know what true pain and anger really felt like.

"I'm going away for a few days. I've got business to deal with. Hannah and Ian are going to stop by and keep an eye on you."

"I don't want them here."

"You don't have a choice. I'm not allowing you

out of my sight. The guards know you're not allowed to leave. Your father would like to see you. He's worried."

She finally turned to look at him then. "Are you worried in case I take my own life? You think I'm like my mother?"

Draven's jaw clenched. He didn't say anything, but she saw it. He was concerned, and now he was trying to combat it.

Releasing a breath, she looked away, hating him.

Counting to ten, she refused to even allow herself to like his touch, to like anything he did for her.

One.
Two.
Three.
Four.
Five.
Six.
Seven.
Eight.
Nine.
Ten.

So easy to do. She kept on doing it inside her head as tears leaked out of her eyes.

Once he was done, he sat down beside her.

"Please leave."

"I know you're hurting."

"Have you been strung to a whipping post?" she asked. "Have you been punished with a beating?"

"Yes. As a boy my father liked to mete out his own kind of punishments to make sure he wasn't dealing with pussies. As you can imagine, that wasn't easy to live with."

She turned to look at him, hoping he saw the anger that she felt.

"And now you're dishing it out to a woman you

blame for your friends' deaths. I had nothing to do with Buck or Jett. I tried to stop it."

"When are you going to stop with all the lies?" he asked.

"When are you going to get your head out of your ass and realize your father is the one that lied? Not me. I was the innocent one in all of this. The only reason I left was to make sure you were all safe."

Draven got up, and she growled in frustration.

"Just like a man. You can't handle the truth so what you do is run away. Well, run, Draven. Go ahead, pretend that I'm the one that lies instead of your father, instead of everyone who lied to you. I'm the only one that told you the truth through everything. You know that, and you couldn't handle that."

Draven hadn't left, and she stared at him, hoping just once that he'd see she wasn't lying. That she wasn't running from him. She'd never run from him.

"Hannah and Ian will be here."

He left without another look, and she collapsed against the bed, sobbing. She let out all of her tears.

She didn't know how long he was going to be gone for. All she hoped was that when he was gone, she got stronger so when he got back, she fought him at every single turn.

****

"You should be resting. Not out here, staring off into space at nothing," Axel said.

Harper looked up at Axel.

She'd not seen him since her whipping, and seeing as now her back was healed, it had been some time. Hannah had told her she'd been out of it for seven days, plus another four with Draven gone.

"You've been gone a long time," she said. "You find any evidence you need?"

"No, not yet. I've not had a chance to look."

"How come?" she asked, sipping at her coffee.

"You're not worried that I'm going to hurt you?"

"If you were going to do it, you'd have done it already. I'll worry when you come at me with a gun. Besides, I know I'm not lying." She shrugged.

"Are you missing Draven?"

"No." She spoke a little too fast.

"Are you plotting his demise?"

"Do you have a toolshed?"

"I'm not going to tell you that," Axel said. "I've been out of the country. We've got some Italian contacts, and Draven wanted me to go and check on some … potential family business."

"Are you married?" Harper asked.

"No. You know I'm not." He held up his hand as if that was all the explanation she needed.

"Just because you're not wearing a ring, it doesn't mean anything, not in this day and age."

"I'm not married, Harper. What about you? Missing Ethan?"

Harper stopped. She hadn't thought about Ethan, not really. Not even in the past couple of days after the whipping.

"Did you love him?"

"I didn't love Ethan," she said. "I cared about him."

"If you didn't love him why were you going to marry him?"

She snorted. "Please, as if you care about love."

"I may not believe in it, Harper, but there was a time I was sure I saw it, and knew of its existence. I also know you wouldn't marry anyone unless you loved them, so it makes me wonder, why?"

"I … let it all happen with Ethan. We met, and it

was kind of like moving. You have to keep walking, keep moving because if you stop and allow yourself to think you realize all that you've lost, all that you've missed, and it doesn't help you. It only breaks you apart even more."

"You're broken?"

"A little, yes. I'm broken. I'm damaged. I allowed Alan to hurt me all those years ago, and now I'm paying the price."

"I don't want to talk about that," Axel said.

"You haven't found anything, and you're not here to kill me."

"I'm not going to kill you until I'm sure I've looked everywhere. You know, Draven thought a lot about killing you."

"Wow, you don't want to talk about Alan's lies, but you're more than happy to talk about Draven's desire to kill me. Good talk."

"He was completely in love with you, and I know it broke him thinking you'd left."

She didn't want nor did she need to hear this. She was very much aware of the pain that it caused leaving. Not a day went by that she didn't feel it herself.

Axel got up.

"Is that it?" she asked. "You're not going to impart more wisdom?"

"No. I just think you should realize that he wanted to kill you. Thought about it, talked about how he was going to deal with you, and yet he couldn't go through with it. You're still alive."

"I was chained to a whipping post where he had his little friend hurt me and then did it himself."

"Tillie's not his friend. You were just a plaything. A bad girl needing to be taught a lesson. It's the first one he's ever given on the post, I admit. Usually, they're made an example of somewhere else."

"Forgive me for not giving a shit."

Axel laughed. "It's good it hasn't broken you. I was worried that it would. I'll be seeing you soon, Harper."

She watched him go. For the past couple of days, she'd been watching a lot of people come and go out of her life.

Getting to her feet, she ignored the guard that followed her around, constantly watching her. She hated his eyes on her. She couldn't help but be curious about what he'd do if she made a run for it. He held a gun.

If she couldn't kill herself then maybe using the guards would be her best option.

It was a thought.

One she hated having and yet, it was there.

Moving from her spot near the house, she made her way out toward the whipping post. She would never forget where it was, set back from the house but close enough for one bedroom to see it.

This was Axel's old home, and she had a feeling his old man liked to look out at the women who were chained up to it.

Touching the wood, she couldn't help but flinch away, disgusted by what it represented. Moving away from the post, she figured a garden this size had to have some tools. It had to have something that could make her stop this. Even if she was the only woman to have been whipped on it since Hannah, that was still two women too many as far as she was concerned.

No other woman would ever know the bite of a whip while she drew breath, not when she could stop it. There's no way she could ever let another woman down. So long as she could fight for them, she would, for all the men and women that had come before. She would never lead another to pain and misery.

She kept on walking the grounds, and when she finally found the toolshed, she cried out in victory.

An axe, a saw, and some cutting shears. They were all sharp and kept in pristine condition.

The guard didn't stop her until she got to the post. As she held the axe in her hand, he stepped up.

"You need to go back home, Harper," he said.

"No!"

She drew the blade down, cutting into the wood.

Over and over she kept on cutting, and when he tried to get near her, she lifted it up. "The only way you're stopping me is if you shoot me. If you come any closer, I swear I will hurt you. I have nothing to lose right now. Think about what happened to the last guard who touched me."

The man paled and took a step back.

He didn't leave her alone, but he did grab his cell phone and start talking to someone. She went back to work, attacking the post, wanting it down.

She created a little gap in the wood with the axe, and she started to kick it.

Releasing a scream, she kept on screaming, and finally, after another few kicks and attacks with the axe, the post was down.

She heard clapping, and as she turned toward the sound, she was surprised to see Draven standing there, watching her.

She didn't appreciate his clapping or his round of applause. He was the last person she wanted to see. Dropping the tools to the ground, she stepped up to him.

"I'm the last woman that will ever be whipped on that post. I will fight you. I'm not going to give up easily. One day, you will apologize to me, and when you do, you better hope I'm in a forgiving mood."

She made her way back into the house and saw her father there, staring at her.

"What are you doing here?"

"Hannah told me what you were doing. I came to pick her up."

"Will you stop her from visiting, please? I can't handle all of that," Harper said.

"She likes you."

"Ian, I don't want to get into this."

"You stopped calling me Dad back then as well."

Harper grabbed a bottle of water and rested her head against the door. "Will you help me get away?"

"You know I can't do that."

"Any dad would help their daughter in a situation like this. I don't want to die. Not yet."

"Not yet?"

"I'm not ready to die yet. I have stuff I want to do."

"You sound a little like your mother."

"Cool."

There was a time it would hurt her to hear him say that. Ten years was a long time to get over it.

"When did you get so cold?"

"What do you want from me?" she asked.

"I'm trying here, Harper."

"Trying? I know who you work for. I know what they're capable of. I knew all those years ago, and yet you're still here. You're still working."

"I don't want anything to happen to you."

"Really! Did you not see the evidence of what they did to me on my back?"

"Harper…"

"Why did you work for them all those years ago?" she asked, changing the subject. "You didn't always have a fancy house, or a huge income. I know you and Mom argued at times about money. I heard you. What changed?"

"You really want to know?"

"My life turned. I'm standing in front of you right here right now, and I think I have a right to know."

"I got a job offer. Alan Barries needed me to get one of his guys off the hook. He offered me ten grand. It was what your mother needed for a new kitchen. Easy money. Something I could do as there was no evidence of murder. It was an open and shut case. I did the job, and I got the money and it started. Once I did one job, it was another. I couldn't walk away. When you become part of this, there's no walking away."

"And Mom?"

"She begged me not to do it. She hated what it was doing to me. What it was turning me into."

"She signed her own death sentence, and you went to Hannah," Harper said.

"I was so sick and tired of hearing her moan, hearing her complain. I was earning good money, and she still wasn't happy. Hannah, she never complained. She never made me feel like a piece of shit. I should have known Alan had set it all up for Hannah to be with me." Ian laughed. "I should have known really. Your mother was incredibly beautiful. Like you are. You've got her hair and eyes. I should have known then that Draven would fall for you."

"He hasn't fallen for me."

"Don't be blind to his feelings."

She laughed. "Are you crazy? He had me chained up and whipped not too long ago. He doesn't have feelings for me, so stop trying to make yourself feel better by thinking it's going to be okay. It's not going to be okay, far from it. It's going to be very fucking hard!" She stamped her foot.

"I know you don't think he cares, but he does."

"Is this what the deal is with you guys? You think hurting us is going to make us fall in love with you? Is that what you did to Mom?"

"I loved your mother so very much."

"Not enough to stick around."

She turned her back on him, looking into the sink, wishing for oblivion.

"Do you ever go and visit her grave?" she asked.

Harper didn't know how he did it, considering she killed herself, but her mother had a resting place. Suicide was frowned upon, and yet there was still a place for her mother to lie. Knowing what she did now, she imagined a lot of money and threats helped.

"Sometimes."

"Do you care for it?"

"I have someone who does it."

"Why don't you?"

"Because as always, Harper, it's too painful for me to go and see that. To go and see what I did. That's why I don't do it."

She turned to look at her father and watched him. He looked genuinely remorseful. A face could say one thing and be thinking another. She'd been living her life for far too long with Ethan.

"I've got to go."

Brushing past him, she didn't stop to his calls, to anything. She kept on walking, needing to get away.

She went to Draven's study and to his table of alcohol. The whiskey she picked up looked expensive, but from the house and his lifestyle, she guessed he could handle the expense of losing a costly bottle of alcohol. She went to leave, but a picture of Alan caught her attention.

Moving to the desk, she lifted it up, and sure

enough, his smile was on display for all to see. Draven was there, and Axel, and Alan looked so fucking smug.

"I will win this. You may have ruined all evidence of that day, but I will win."

She put his picture down, slamming his face to the desk, and wishing she'd done that ten years ago.

There was no satisfaction in destroying a picture.

With her bottle and glass, she went to her room, ignoring the guards that lurked everywhere once again.

Chapter Nine

Draven piled the wood high and set fire to the papers he'd placed in between, watching as the chemicals he sprayed all over to help with the flame lit up. Blowing out the match, he tossed it into the fire and stepped back, admiring his handiwork.

The whipping post should have been removed years ago, when he'd taken over. After he killed his father, five years ago, he'd taken control of all elements of the business. The whipping post simply didn't register to him as a problem. He had more important things to deal with. He'd never gotten around to it. Each time he saw it, he thought about taking it down, and something would drag his attention away until it didn't get done.

He spent a great deal of time wanting to get things done and never actually achieving it.

"This is a little too late," Axel said.

Draven looked to his only surviving friend. Axel looked tired and worn out.

"Harper did this."

"Are you going to punish her for it?"

"No, she saved me a job."

Axel laughed. "That's like Harper. Saving jobs for people. I take it she's not a fan of the whipping post."

"I doubt any woman is a fan of this post." He stared at the flames watching them burn. Harper was proving to be a problem to him. She had spirit, no doubt about that.

"Did you conclude your business?" Axel asked.

"Yes. One of the girls in Tillie's club was finally purchased. Her new Master is taking her for a brand-new life."

"Is she going to end at the bottom of the river for

it?"

Draven shook his head. "No. He wants to make a life with her and in turn, get her out of her servitude."

Axel started chuckling, and it quickly turned into a full-on laugh. He listened to his best friend as he got more and more hysterical.

"I didn't consider this much of a laughing matter."

"You're kidding, right? I don't know if it's Harper being here or if I'm finally waking up to what it is we're fucking doing."

"I've told you not to go there."

"Go where? Go to the reality that we're holding men and women's lives in the palm of our hand. What if that chick didn't want to go with her master? What if she wanted to stay in Tillie's brothel, or better yet, what if she wanted to do neither and just go fucking home?"

"We don't have the luxury of walking away or creating that kind of life."

"Why not? I for one didn't sign up for stealing girls and having them earn us money." Axel stepped right up to him. "We were going to be better than this. You remember that, Draven? Remember when we promised each other a better life?"

"Times change. People change, and we can't keep looking at the past, for fuck's sake."

"We're too busy repeating our fathers' mistakes, and one day we're going to look in the mirror and be exactly like them."

"We inherited their legacy, and we can't turn our backs on it, not yet."

"We helped them build this, Draven. Make no mistake about that. We're the reason this is still standing while they've all been dead. You shouldn't have put Harper on that damn post. We shouldn't be doing anything like this."

Draven said nothing.

This was not the first time, nor did he anticipate it would be the last that Axel had struggled with their reality, or at least, this part of their reality. Killing people, drugs, guns, controlling people in positions of power, Axel relished. Human trafficking, the sale of human flesh, Axel always had a problem with, but then, Axel's father had been a cruel bastard and Draven knew when they were growing up, Axel saw a lot of bad shit that turned him against it.

"I've got to go away for a couple of days."

"Why?"

"I've got business to attend of my own. You think you can keep Harper alive until I get back?" Axel asked.

"You know I can."

"I don't know if you'd decided to kill her for fun or something like that."

"Axel, I'm not a monster."

This time Axel did snort. "Keep telling yourself that. Maybe one day you'll either believe it, or not. I've got to go."

Axel walked away, and Draven watched the post burn until it was nothing more than embers. In his mind, he heard Harper's screams, the sounds of her pleas as she begged them all to stop.

He'd ignored her, and they'd used her back for sport.

Stepping away from the embers, he made his way toward one of the guards, giving him the instruction to keep an eye on the fire.

Entering the kitchen, he saw Ian still in his home, nursing a cup.

"It's coffee. You want one?"

"I thought you'd be back home by now."

"It's my turn to stay with Harper. I don't want Hannah to know I've failed again."

"Why would you fail?"

"Hannah stays with her during the whole of her time, regardless of if Harper even wants her here, and I end up leaving."

"You and Harper still not getting along?"

"I doubt we ever will," Ian said.

"She blames you for her mother."

"She blames me for a lot of things I can't control." He sighed and ran a hand over his face. "Are you going to kill my little girl?"

"Are you going to stop me?" Draven asked.

"Don't make me do this. Don't make me choose."

"I'm not going to make you choose, but I guess I already have my answer, and that is why Harper will never trust you. You're too weak. She doesn't deal with weak men. Only the strong."

"I should have kept you away from her all those years ago."

"You were too busy in Hannah's pussy to even give a shit about Harper. You didn't know what she was going through. How she was dealing or should I say, how she wasn't dealing."

"You just like to keep rubbing it in my face how bad of a father I am."

"No, what I like to do is make sure the men near me take responsibility for their actions. You never do that. When it came to Harper, all you wanted her to be was a good girl. To not make waves. You wanted her to leave you alone."

"That's not true."

"It's why it was so easy to draw her in. To nurture that anger that's always simmering beneath the surface. Harper at times looks weak and vulnerable, but that is because she is a tiger in waiting, ready to strike when she needs to."

"And you're the one that draws it out?" Ian asked.

"I'm the one that doesn't try to keep the tiger at bay."

"I've heard the men talking, Draven. You intend to break her. How is that not keeping the tiger at bay if you intend to break her?"

Draven chuckled. "You should leave. Harper doesn't want you here, and I certainly don't. Get the fuck out of my house."

"One day you're going to have to deal with her. When that time comes, I hope you're ready for the consequences."

Draven was already leaving the room in search of Harper.

One of the guards let him know she'd headed upstairs. He went straight to his room and found her on the floor, leaning up against the bed, drinking from his expensive bottle of whiskey.

"Hello, Draven," she said, holding up her glass.

He closed the door. She didn't sound drunk yet, but it wouldn't take much, not with this brand.

"Did you like my handiwork?" she asked.

"Yes." He moved to sit beside her.

She put a hand close to her side and tutted. "This is for very special people. The kind that don't order whips and stuff like that." She laughed. "Whips. They hurt, you know."

"I know."

"Oh, that's right. You were an abused little boy, and now you're an abuser." She forced out a laugh. "I guess you are like your father after all."

He clenched his teeth together. One of the biggest

insults he always faced was being compared to that man. He fucking hated Alan Barries, and he never, ever wanted to be referred to as his son.

She took a drink. "You know this stuff is nasty."

"Why do you keep on drinking it?"

She found that incredibly funny. "It was only the good stuff that I knew would give me the total buzz I needed. I have to say, using an axe really does a number on the arms. I should totally work out using an axe. I'll look like a badass bitch with cool arms." She snorted.

He watched as she poured out another glass of whiskey, put the bottle down, and started to drink.

"It really is disgusting. It tastes like mold."

"I've got better drinks."

"This one is fine." She shrugged. "I can't be choosy in my choice of oblivion. It just has to get the job done."

"And why do you want oblivion?" he asked.

"Why not? I mean, seriously, look around you. I was taken from my old life and forced out of it by your dad. It didn't end there. Your father controlled me. He made me do things to satisfy his own ends. I had to take innocent people away from their lives and force them into servitude. To pose and to act all because of him. Yeah, yeah, I know, you *totally* don't believe me. That's fine. I don't care. Then I went to my new life, and I've been living it the way I have to. Axel being the knight he is, comes and completely takes me from my life and tries to ruin me. I mean, that whipping post was not fun and games, you know. I guess a lot of people love being on the end of a whip, but not me. My back is killing me." She took another drink, and he watched her.

Her words stopped making a lot of sense, and she sighed after taking another long sip.

"Here, you may as well drink, but keep all your

judgments locked in a tiny ball away from me. I want nothing to do with them."

He took the bottle from her and smiled. Draven sipped from the bottle, knowing how gulping the stuff down didn't help to appease the demons running around in his head.

"I was going to have them fuck you, one by one. Even the women. Tillie is known for being a damn good fuck, even if she's wearing a fake cock."

"How gross."

"Yes."

"What made you stop?"

"I didn't want them touching you."

She laughed. "Wow. You don't want me, and you don't want anyone else to want me. Cool." She rested her head back against the bed.

"I never said I didn't want you."

"You don't go around getting other people to fuck your women if you have feelings for them, Draven. That's not the way it works."

"I never said it was."

"You really can't have it your own way." She drank some more. "I'm getting totally buzzed, and you're ruining it by all your talking. Blah, blah, blah, blah."

"You get drunk, and I'll make sure you don't hurt yourself."

"You know I thought about you all the time that I was away."

"You did?"

"Yep. Every single day I was curious as to what you were doing. If you were happy. I mean, how fucking crazy is that? I'd wonder if you had finally been able to bring your father down. Looking around me, I see you have, but he's not gone. The memory and legacy of Alan Barries lives on." She turned her head. "And when you have kids, he'll continue to live on."

"I thought about you as well," Draven said.

"Ah, you thought of all the ways to kill me." She held an imaginary noose around her neck, tilted her head to the side, and stuck her tongue out.

He rolled his eyes. "Not like that."

"Then what did you think about?"

Draven stared into her blue eyes. "I'm only going to tell you this because I know you won't remember it come the morning."

"That's the whole point, right? To not remember it. To completely forget about everything and anything," she said.

"I thought about running with you. I wanted to find you, and at first, I didn't want to bring you back. I wanted to find you, stay with you, and never look back."

"That's nice."

"Yeah, it is."

"But we can't do that, can we? We can't pretend that it didn't happen. You never came looking for me, and in turn, I stayed alone, hoping for you."

"What were you hoping for?"

"That you'd know the truth. I'd hoped your father didn't have the hold on you that he seemed to have on everyone else, including me. He said jump and everyone always turned around and said, how high. They never considered asking why? Or if he'd jump first. I don't know. I never liked your father. He gave me the creeps. Still does and I hope someone in hell has the luxury of pissing and shitting on him and beating the shit out of him. Ha. Yep, I'm getting the buzz."

He smiled. "I really did miss you."

She turned her head. "I fell in love with you, Draven, all those years ago. So long now. I mean, I'm twenty-eight years old. Not a lot by any means but enough to make me ... feel it. Did you look for me all the time?"

"My father was in charge of keeping an eye on you. His men gave us updates on what you were doing and who you were doing it with. You were not my responsibility. Dealing with the war, I was needed here, not chasing after a girl who'd betrayed me. Then I had to deal with taking over. Jett was the last of us to ever go looking for you. I still don't know why he decided to, especially when we all knew you were gone and why."

"I wasn't hiding from you, Draven."

"We're not doing this now."

"But—"

"No buts. I've told you, Alan dealt with you; I had more pressing issues."

"Then why keep me here? Why not let me go? Why have that bitch whip me, and allow those other ... people to see? Don't you care about me at all?"

"You're here for my pleasure only. I don't have to answer to you."

"You don't make any sense at all, Draven. You know that. You're hot and cold, and you drive me crazy." She ran a hand down her face. "I'm going to have a big motherfucking headache in the morning, and I don't care."

He laughed. Sipping at more of the whiskey, he watched her. He'd missed just being able to watch her, to know that she was okay.

Reaching out, he tucked some hair behind her ear, and she sighed, turning toward him. "That's nice."

"I fell in love with you back then as well. More than I probably should have."

She opened her eyes. "Draven, I was with your friends to be with you. I cared about them, but I never loved them. I went through the initiation because I knew it was what you wanted. I sucked Axel's cock to get information. For me, it has always been you."

Her eyes started to droop, but he wasn't ready for her to be done just yet.

"What about Ethan?"

"I didn't deserve him."

"Why not?"

"He was a good man that wanted a lot of somethings I couldn't give him. I couldn't fall in love with him, or change. He wanted me to be the perfect wife with the kids and the life he wanted, but I couldn't do it. I'm not like that. I need something more. I was going to marry him, and I knew I'd make his life miserable. You shouldn't marry a man that even as you have sex with him, you're thinking about another. It's the man you're thinking about that you should be with."

She fell asleep, the glass falling from her hand.

The liquid spilled to the floor.

He had cleaners for the mess. Sipping at the whiskey, he waited for her to rest against him. He moved up a little closer so she didn't get a bad neck from her position.

With her leaning against him, he closed his eyes, and let out a sigh. Even now, he wanted her.

Buck and Jett were dead.

The life he wanted was gone. He was carrying on his father's legacy exactly how he wanted, even though he'd killed the son of a bitch.

Shaking his head, he kept on drinking, hoping that he'd find the oblivion she'd found.

****

There were some things in life Harper knew she never should try to do. Go bungee jumping off a bridge, eat undercooked chicken, and now, drink bottles of whiskey. She didn't even get down half the bottle.

She opened her eyes, and other than the cutting down of the whipping post and the conversation with Ian, she couldn't remember anything else.

Scrap that, she remembered the bottle of whiskey.

Yep, no way she could forget that.

Opening her eyes, she turned her head and froze.

Draven was looking right at her.

"Please tell me you're awake and not one of those creepy people that sleep with their eyes open?" she asked.

He smiled. "I'm awake. I find it interesting that you've woken to me in your bed and yet all you care about is knowing if I'm awake or asleep because open eyes creep you out."

She shrugged. "Well, seeing as I don't have to be freaked out anymore, why are we in the same bed?" She rolled over and was surprised to find she didn't have a hangover, not even a headache. "I'm going to vomit soon, aren't I?"

"Oh, yes. Your entire guts."

"You spent a lot of time in the bottom of a whiskey bottle?"

"Not a lot of time but enough to know it's not fun coming up. It burns."

"Until that happens, want to tell me why you're here?" she asked. "In my bed?"

"It's technically my bed."

"If you want to get technical, it's Axel's."

"It's not. I own this house and the land, and everything that is on it."

"Including your best friend?" she asked.

"I don't own him. He can come and go as he pleases."

"The rest of us need permission."

"To get out of this house, yes."

She wished she remembered what happened last night. Staring at Draven, she knew they had to have talked.

"Do you still hate me?" he asked.

"Yes."

"It didn't go well with your dad."

"Of course not. We're not the same person, and he seems to think that blaming other people for his mistakes is okay. It's really not okay."

Her stomach started to turn, and she placed a hand over her mouth, knowing she didn't have long.

"Go," Draven said.

She pushed the blankets off her, and only just made it in time to the toilet as she started to vomit.

Draven was there, holding her hair back as she threw everything that she'd eaten and drank back up. The vomit kept coming, and throughout it, she felt Draven's hand on her back, one hand in her hair, keeping it out of the way.

"I don't want to do this," she said.

"Just keep on being sick. I'm not cleaning vomit up."

She laughed. "As if I could go anywhere."

"Once you've done this, we'll go and have some breakfast."

The thought of breakfast didn't help her, and she kept on throwing up. Draven stayed with her for the next ten minutes until she finally stopped.

He had a toothbrush ready for her, along with mouthwash. She took them from him gladly, brushing at her teeth.

From her reflection, she saw it had been a bad couple of days. Beneath her eyes were shadows, and she looked exhausted.

With Draven watching her every move she didn't

check out her back.

He turned on the shower, and she stopped as he started to get undressed.

She saw his heavily inked body. It hadn't been so inked the last time she saw him. There had been more words and drawings added to his flesh.

He removed his pants and boxers, and he stood in the shower. "Come on."

Every instinct inside her was screaming at her to run.

In her mind, she saw the Draven from the past, and this new man. The deadly one. The one she knew she should fear and at the same time, screaming at her to take care of him.

You're fucking crazy.
He had people whip you.

She removed her clothes, aware of how naked she was as she stepped into the stall, and ignored it.

Covering her chest, she tilted her head back and looked up at the water. It was warm, and Draven stood behind her.

The space in the shower seemed to get smaller.

She stared at his arms as they reached past her head and grabbed the soap. It wouldn't take a lot to kill her, to squeeze the very breath from her body and to make her scream in pain.

He'd done so before.

The pain of the whip.

Of his hands.

Of his words.

All of it adding up to where they were right now.

In the shower, completely naked.

"Can I have the soap?" she asked.

He held the soap out for her to take and placed it in her hand.

She took it, running her hands over it, lathering them. She put the block back in the dish and started to run her hands all over her body.

She wondered if he saw her, if he liked how she was washing her body.

She changed a glance behind her and saw him watching her, staring at her hands as she moved them down her neck, over her breasts, and then to her stomach.

His cock stood out, long, thick, and proud.

Rubbing her body, an answering heat filled her with shame. This man shouldn't evoke any feeling from her body, and yet, he did.

You can't deny that you want him.

She watched as he wrapped his fingers around his length. Her gaze locked on the action as he moved up and down. Each glide made liquid heat pool between her thighs.

Would it be so wrong to watch him? To see him complete?

"You want this?" he asked.

She turned her back, not wanting to know the answer herself.

When it came to Draven, her reactions scared her. She knew how she *should* react, and yet her body, it did different things. He stepped up close, banding his arms around her, stopping her from touching herself.

His cock pressed against the base of her back, and the warmth of him surrounded her.

"Are you wet for me right now?"

She stayed silent.

He chuckled against her flesh. "That's okay, I don't mind finding out for myself."

She didn't put up a fight as he teased through her folds. His fingers found her clit, touching her. He didn't linger there for long, and she whimpered as he thrust two fingers inside her cunt.

"Now that is what I'm talking about."

She gasped as he added a third finger and made her take it. "Fuck my fingers, Harper. Take them."

Spreading her legs, she took them, doing exactly as he demanded and not complaining as he forced her to fuck them. He plunged inside her, over and over again.

She whimpered his name, begging for more.

As quickly as he built up her need for him, he took it away, pulling his fingers from her pussy. She watched him as he licked them, tasting her.

"What are you doing?" she asked.

"You want to deny what I do to you, that's fine. You're not going to touch yourself all day. You can only touch yourself when you beg me to fuck you."

"That's not going to happen. You can't do that."

"I've got nothing better to do than babysit you all day. I'll be sticking around to watch you." He winked at her.

She couldn't believe it as he climbed out of the shower.

"Where are you going?" she asked.

"To get dressed. I suggest you do as well."

"Nothing can stop me doing this." She put a hand between her thighs and stroked her clit.

He grabbed her wrist, pulling her out of the shower stall. The wet tile caused her to slip, but Draven didn't let her go, dragging her into the room.

She fought him as he pulled her over his knee. His hands held her down, and she screamed as he slapped her ass.

Not once.

Not twice.

Repeatedly until she was weeping and begging him to stop.

He dropped her to the floor, and when she was on her knees facing him, he cupped her face. "I've got no problem playing this game with you. You don't *want* to want me, fine. It doesn't change the fact you *do* want me. You'll always want me, and I know you can't accept that." He slammed his lips down on hers.

The kiss was bruising, brutal, nearly to the point of breaking skin.

"But don't ever fucking think to test my strength like that again. You will lose, and next time, I won't hold back."

Her ass was on fire. "That was you holding back?"

"I don't do anything by half, Harper. You should know that by now. I'm all in or not at all. Now, I suggest you change. We need to get some breakfast inside you."

He let her go, and she watched as he pulled on some clothes.

She wasn't willing to test him for a second time that day. She rushed around getting dressed into the clothes available to her.

"When will I be allowed my bag of clothes?" she asked. Harper missed her bras, her panties, her jeans, all of the clothes she had.

"When I say so."

Draven left the bedroom, and she sat on the edge of the bed, shocked by what had happened. Her ass was still on fire, and she guessed there would be bruising there as well.

He'd not held back, or at least, she didn't think he had. Her ass burned.

She didn't have long for her pity party as one of the guards entered the room. He held a gun against his chest and didn't even look at her.

Draven wasn't joking around.

When he shot out threats, he intended to see them through.

Running fingers through her damp hair, she was tempted to dry it before joining him. Her stomach rumbled, and she changed her mind. Food would be better, even if it did mean sitting opposite a man who had her blood boiling.

She hated him and yet wanted him with what seemed like equal measure.

Did she love him? What had they talked about last night? Why was he in her bed?

So many questions that would remain unanswered because she had no intention of asking for them. Especially not from Draven.

The only way to keep herself together with him was to be around him as little as possible. It wouldn't be easy seeing as she was in effect, his prisoner, but for now, she was going to try.

Of course, it meant sitting at the table with him.

She made her way to the kitchen and found Draven at the counter, reading his paper and drinking coffee.

He didn't even look in her direction. She hated that he didn't even care enough to give her a few seconds of his time.

Fine.

He wanted to play hardball. She could play this game.

Only, she didn't know how to play or what his endgame would be. They were no longer kids in high school, and she didn't know what he wanted from her.

Axel was nowhere in sight, and rather than ask, she stayed silent.

She had to survive.

Whatever this was, it would pass.

Chapter Ten

Harper didn't come back to him that day, or even for the rest of that week. Draven stayed home dealing with work and whatever held his attention. Ian kept turning up, and he saw the older man wanted to make a relationship with Harper, only she wasn't giving an inch. Not that Draven blamed her.

Axel had still yet to arrive back home.

He'd gotten a call three days ago that he was fine and not to worry about him, but worrying was Draven's middle name, or at least in recent weeks it had become that.

Tillie had also been in touch about the new wave of women that were at the club. She also recommended he take Harper with him. She'd enjoyed whipping his woman, but Draven had no intention of letting any of the men or women touch her again.

He wasn't going to think about why he felt that way. There was no room in his life for doubts.

By the end of the second week, he sat in his office, Harper on his sofa, across the room reading the newspaper or a book. She had both beside her, and each one she kept looking at, growling in frustration, and then moving back to the other.

She'd also snapped at several of his guards this week.

On a few occasions he thought a couple of them were going to retaliate and hit her back. He wouldn't blame them, but then he'd kill them for touching her.

What Harper needed to realize was he was the man in charge here.

The one they all feared, and if she ever betrayed him again, he would kill her. He hadn't ruled out killing her yet.

There were still moments when he thought about it, especially when Buck and Jett entered his thoughts.

"What are you reading?" he asked.

"Nothing." She put the book down, and he watched as she ran her hands down her thighs. "You've got nothing interesting here."

"There's an entire library of books."

"And clearly I want to read the book you don't have."

"You think getting smart with me is going to help you."

"I'm not one of your minions, Draven."

"No. You're my prisoner," he said.

She pressed her lips together before looking away.

"You don't like that?" he asked.

"You think I should?"

"Why not? I don't see why you should hate being my prisoner. You get fed. Free rein, the works."

"I can't go out. I can't leave. I get chained to a whipping post and beaten."

He smiled. "You've still got an issue with that."

"You think I'm going to stop having an issue with that?"

"It wasn't so bad. Other women didn't get the luxury of walking away from it."

"Great, so I was held to a post that other women had died at." She stood up and grabbed her books.

"Where are you going?" he asked.

"To go and try and find a book I want to read, you know, seeing as I've got less than thrilling conversation."

He watched her go.

The clothes she wore hid her body, and he didn't

like that. Staring at his computer screen, he had nothing of any importance and so got to his feet and headed toward the library.

He rarely ventured in here as it was a place with a horrid smell. The books had never been read, at least not by him.

Harper stood against one of the walls. Her back was to him, and he saw her hand reaching out. The tips of her fingers touched each spine, and she read the title and moved on.

"What is it you're looking for?"

"I don't know."

"Are you looking for a romance?" he asked.

"Could you blame me if I was? I happen to like them."

"Did you always read them?"

"Yes."

"With Ethan?"

"Ethan mocked them like you did. He had no problems when I used him for sex though. Not that he was ever any good."

"Sex?"

She picked up a book, brow raised as she looked at him. "Some of the books are very sexy. Very kinky."

"They are?"

"You should read one and find out."

"Is that what your problem has been? You're horny."

"I have no idea what you mean."

He laughed. "You've been more cranky than normal. You snap at most of the guys that are only here to make sure you're safe and protected."

"You mean I'm not safe and protected unless I'm here with you or with one of the men assigned to take care of me."

"It's not a safe world, and I've made a lot of enemies," he said.

"You really need to consider the kind of people you meet. It's not all bad."

"You know that from experience."

She shrugged. "I've done some traveling. I've met a lot of different people."

"Yet, you're still here."

"I'm a prisoner."

"Would you have ever left Stonewall?" he asked.

"No."

"You didn't even hesitate there. I think you're lying."

"I seem to recall an initiation." She turned and lifted her shirt. "The names look familiar. I took my vows that night very seriously."

"And yet you still ran because you couldn't handle it."

"I'm not going to get in this with you. Not again. You're not listening."

He held his hands up. "Truce. I'm never going to believe you when it comes to the reason you ran, and you're never going to give up. Let's not talk about it and talk about your current problem instead."

"What do you consider my current problem?" She folded her arms beneath her breasts, pushing them up.

Again, the shirt she wore was too damn big for him to be able to admire them, and it pissed him off that he didn't get to see her.

"Yes, your current problem."

"Why is it taking forever to get an actual response out of you? I don't have time for this."

He smiled. "Your horniness."

"Oh, please, I can handle myself."

"You can't touch your pussy." If the guards were

not around her, he was in the shower with her and at dinner and even in her bed.

There was not a moment when she wasn't attended.

He made sure to keep an eye on her, not giving her a chance to go out of his sight.

She stared down his body, and her hand cupped his dick.

"And you don't have a problem either?"

The evidence of his own need filled her hand.

"You think I can't wait? Believe me, this is nothing."

"You like having blue balls."

"I like having a willing cunt dancing on my cock a lot more."

"I'm not going to be willing."

"Who are you trying to kid? After everything we've done and been through, you still want my dick deep inside you. I bet you'd love for me to blow my load within you. To fill you up. To have you dripping with my cum."

"Do you read these romance books?" she asked.

"I just know what I want and what I like." He stroked a finger down her neck. "So how about we make this interesting?"

"In what way?"

"We play a game."

"We're a little old to be playing games."

He took her hand. "You're never too old to play."

Leading her out of the library, he went to the pool room, closing the door and flicking the lock into place.

"Don't you ever get bored of having to find your own space in your own home?"

"I do what I have to do. The guards are necessary."

"Why?" she asked.

"You really want to know?"

"Clearly Stonewall got interesting when I left."

"Stonewall has always been interesting. You've just not seen what's hidden beneath the surface."

She walked to the pool table, her hand running along the fabric. "I don't know how to play pool."

"That's fine. We're not going to play an actual game. We're going to pot the balls," he said, lining the balls into the triangle.

She grabbed one of the sticks and handed it to him.

"Were you tempted to beat me with it?"

"Not at all. I know to hurt you it's going to take something a lot harder than a piece of wood."

"I'm not indestructible."

"See, there you are with the ego." She shrugged. "Anyway, pot the balls?"

"Yes."

"Anyone who doesn't pot the balls, an item of clothing has to go."

"This is already not fair. I'm not allowed to wear any underwear. I think it's unfair because I've got big tits and they hurt when I don't wrap them up." She folded her arms beneath her breasts and lifted them up.

"It would look even better without your shirt on."

"Is this how you imagined life?" she asked. "Being in this big house. Commanding lots of men. Having the world bow down before you."

"The world is a bit much, but it's exactly how I imagined."

"It is?"

"Yes."

She didn't need to know anything more. "When all the clothes are gone, what do we do?"

"We'll get to that."

"Fine. Fine. I'll let you shoot first."

He leaned forward, lined the stick with the triangle of balls, and shot.

Two balls landed on his first shot. Rather than take another, he stepped back.

Lady's turn.

Much to Draven's surprise, she sank two balls.

He watched her as she bent forward. The shirt was large enough to show off the curves of her tits.

"So, once you let your party rape me, what would you have done?" she asked as he lined up his shot about to take it.

He missed.

She smirked.

"You did that on purpose."

"Actually, I'm curious. You knew I didn't want it. Felt how dry I was and I'm just curious about what you would have done."

Draven removed his jacket. "It didn't happen, so the point is moot."

"It's not to me. You've taken the time to plan a great deal of punishments at my expense."

She leaned forward, and he let her have another shot. The ball went into the hole, and it was his turn again.

Tuning her out, he sank a ball, and it was her turn.

"I would have thrown you into the cells," he said.

She missed the ball. She cursed and pushed down her pants. The shirt was large enough to cover her ass and some thigh for now.

"You like those cells."

"I've never been in them on a personal level, but I know a lot of women have. Men, too."

"Why do you still have them?"

"They have a purpose." He shot another ball.

So did she.

He missed his next ball as she bent over. The shirt she wore rode up, showing off a great expanse of thigh and ass.

His cock hardened, and he wanted inside her.

He removed his shirt, and it was enough of distraction that when it came to her ball, she missed again.

The shirt went, and seeing as she had no more clothes on, she was completely naked, at his mercy. Just how he liked her.

"I like this look on you."

"How do I stop you from taking out more punishments?" she asked, surprising him and causing him to miss a ball.

Once he removed his pants, he turned toward her. "Was that to get me to miss a ball or are you serious?"

"I don't want to be punished. Alan is not around, and even though you don't believe me, I know what he's capable of. I know what he would have done if I didn't run. I didn't want to, and it came with a cost. I'm willing to do whatever it takes to stop this. To stop the punishments and for you to trust me again. I'm not going anywhere, Draven. I mean that."

****

There was no life for her away from Draven or Axel. To Harper, it was really about Draven, but they came as a team, she knew that.

Fighting with him wasn't helping her. She didn't wish to be part of another whipping night or whatever punishments he had in store. From what she'd seen of Alan and what she knew already, they were not short of hurting women.

That alone scared her.

Also, Draven was ... unpredictable.

He'd always been a force to be reckoned with growing up, but now it was more intense.

She wasn't afraid of *him*, more of what he may do if he completely lost it.

There were times she caught him looking at her, and she didn't for a second think he would ever hurt her. Then there were moments, she truly believed he was going to kill her.

Had Alan done that big of a number on him that he fought constantly with what he felt he had to do, or what he wanted to do?

Ten years was a long time, and she already saw the darkness that surrounded him.

"You must vow your loyalty to me and to Axel. Only in time, during situations will I be able to trust you. I can't give you more than that right now."

"So there's nothing I can do to prove it to you."

"You can prove it every single day."

"How?"

"By your actions. I'll see it when I look at you. When I see you. When I know that you can be trusted above all others. Your turn to shoot."

She bent forward, aware of how close he was.

When he touched her ass, the tips of his fingers sliding across her flesh, she moaned and completely forgot about the game.

He chuckled.

"You've lost the ball and have no clothes. What am I going to do with you?"

She turned, and Draven didn't let her get too far. He stood right in front of her, trapping her between the pool table and his body. His hands on the edge of the table kept her locked into place. She had no desire to run, even as he pressed his body against hers. The hard length of his cock brushed her stomach, and arousal flooded her body.

"What do you want to do?"

He cupped her tit, and the roughness of his hands took her by surprise. It showed he didn't always sit behind a desk while other people did his dirty work.

"I want to see your pussy."

She went to move, but he wouldn't budge.

"Where do you want me?"

"Right here."

He gripped her hips and helped her to sit on the edge of the pool table.

She held his shoulders trying to balance herself. He pushed the balls out of the way, and she leaned back, spreading her thighs wide.

"Now show me that pretty cunt."

She lifted her legs up, keeping them open for him to see. With her hands on the lips of her pussy, she opened up for him.

"You're already so wet for me."

She gasped as he stroked a finger through her slit, teasing her.

"You want my cock?"

"Yes."

"Well, you're going to have to earn it. Once you start this game, there's no stopping it."

He stepped away from her and helped her off the table.

"Debt is paid for now."

She grabbed her stick and watched as he sank a ball. She did the other, and he missed the next one.

He was in his boxer briefs now, the hard line of his cock pressing against the front. He made no move to hide it, and she didn't want him to either.

When she failed to sink another ball, Draven smiled.

"Get on your knees."

She sank to her knees, keeping her gaze up on him as he approached.

"Touch my cock."

She lifted her hand, and he shook his head, pushing her hand out of the way.

"I didn't say to use your hand."

With his boxer briefs on, she pressed her mouth to his cock, touching him.

He gripped the edge of his briefs and pushed them down.

"Use your mouth."

She licked the tip and took him between her lips, moaning as he filled her mouth. When he hit the back of her throat, she pulled back up. He didn't force her to choke on his cock this time.

Up and down she slid her lips over the length of him, coating him with her saliva until he let out a curse.

After several minutes he stepped back, tucked his cock away, and went back to the table.

She got to her feet, aware of how wet she was. The tops of her inner thighs were slick from her own arousal. Harper still tasted him on her tongue.

She took her next shot and was shocked by how it went into the hole. Each time a ball went into a hole, she wished she'd missed.

When they had done all the balls and the table was clear, she thought they'd move on and fuck. No, Draven reloaded the tray and started all over again. Not that she had a problem with that.

Especially as the next ball didn't go into the hole.

Draven went to the corner of the room and opened up a drawer.

"Hold onto the pool table, bend over and don't look."

Harper followed his instruction even as she wanted to ask him nonstop questions. Holding the edge, she counted to ten in her mind, hearing him do something.

When he stood right behind her, she didn't look back as he'd told her not to. Gritting her teeth, she waited. He cupped her ass, spreading the cheeks wide.

What made her gasp next was how he stroked over the puckered hole of her anus. "Have you ever been fucked here?"

"No."

"Good. I don't want anyone to fuck you here."

She looked behind her, but Draven didn't allow that, so he slapped her ass hard. Crying out, she quickly turned her head to look forward rather than back. Her ass was on fire from his spank.

"Hold your ass open," he said.

She spread the cheeks of her ass. Her face was flaming.

His fingers returned to her ass, coating her with some lube. She knew it had to be. It was cold and slick. She gasped as he pressed a finger to her anus.

"What are you doing?"

"You'll see. You'll love it, and besides, you're going to have to get used to this."

"Why?"

"You're going to be taking my cock here soon. So very soon."

She groaned as he began to push past her muscles. It burned, but it wasn't too uncomfortable. It was just weird and strange, and everything she didn't think she wanted.

With her face to the fabric, she breathed in and

out, trying not to think about his finger in her ass, or anything else.

"So pretty."

He pulled his finger from her but made no move away.

Next was something hard and a little thicker. It was slick, and she cried out as he filled her ass. This went deeper and spread her ass wider.

"Now that is a pretty sight. Seeing you completely spread open. Soon you're going to be spread over my cock, begging for it." He reached between them and started to stroke her clit.

The pleasure was intense, and as he touched her, she knew she was only a few strokes away from orgasm.

Before she could even reach it, he pulled away, not giving her a taste of what was to come. The thing in her ass was also removed, and she whimpered. That surprised her. She wanted it back.

"Stay there."

He left, and behind the bar that was in the pool room there had to be a sink. She heard water running, and then he was back, wiping her up.

"You can stand now."

She did so on shaking legs, watching him. Seconds passed, maybe even minutes, and he finally came back and grabbed his stick. He didn't miss the next three balls, and neither did she.

When it came to the final one, he missed his shot, and he lost his boxer briefs.

She watched and waited.

His cock stood out, long and thick. The tip was already wet with pre-cum.

He looked toward her, dropped his stick, and pointed for her to come stand right in front of him.

She wasn't about to argue. He was the one in

control.

Her entire body was tense. She wanted an orgasm more than anything else, and as he stared at her, waiting, she would have given anything.

Draven was in no rush though as he stroked a finger across her nipple. The first touch made her gasp.

"So sensitive."

"Please, Draven."

"What is it you want?" he asked.

"You know what I want."

"I've got a good idea of what it is you want, yes," he said. He stroked across her chest, circling her other nipple. "But you see, I didn't ask for me to tell you. I wanted to hear it come from your sweet lips."

"Draven?"

He stepped back, and she caught hold of his arm, stopping him from leaving her. She didn't want him to walk away.

"You know what you have to do."

She hated to beg him, but to get what she wanted, she was going to have to. There was no way she could be stubborn, not with this need building inside her.

"I want you, Draven. I want your cock. I want your mouth on me. I want it all."

She cried out as he lifted her up. He placed her on top of the pool table, and within seconds his lips were on hers. He kissed her so hard that their teeth clashed together. She moaned, holding onto his shoulders for support.

He held her still as he kissed her. He drew her to the edge of the pool table, and his lips were all over her. They trailed down her body, going to her neck and then her tits. He sucked each nipple into his mouth, cupping the mounds and flicking the tip.

She said his name over and over, wanting more,

begging for more, hungry for more.

He gave it to her as well.

When he got to her stomach, he opened her thighs, and then his lips were on her pussy. His tongue stroked over her clit, teasing her, driving her need for him higher. She chanted his name.

When he pushed two fingers inside her, stretching her, she knew she was so close to orgasm. He wouldn't let her go though. He kept her at the precipice, refusing to let her fall over the edge into bliss.

She whimpered, begged, pleaded, and didn't want him to stop.

Draven stopped touching her. He stepped back, and she watched him as he started to touch his cock, his hand running up and down the length.

"You want this?"

"Yes."

"Then spread yourself wide. I want to see how wet you are for me."

She lifted her legs, exposing herself to him. He stepped forward.

"Watch as I fuck you."

He put the tip of his cock at her entrance, and she cried out as he sank inch by inch within her, driving deeper. He pulled out, and she saw the evidence of her pleasure on his dick, how slick it was.

"I'm going to fill you up, and we're going to watch it spill out of your pussy, baby. I want you to see whose cum is inside you. Who owns you."

He pushed back in, holding her knees for leverage as he pounded inside her, making her take all of his cock. He was so long and big that it was at the point of pain. She didn't protest though. She took his cock and begged for more.

Draven didn't let up, and when he finally brought

her to orgasm, it was the most amazing experience of her life.

He didn't stop, and as he fucked her, the pleasure of his cock prolonged her orgasm until she came a second time. He held her still, keeping her in place as he got closer to orgasm.

When he finally found his release, she felt each pulse as he filled her with every single drop. He held himself still within her, and she stared up at him, shaken by how intense that had been.

Draven pulled out of her, and true to his word, they watched as his cum spilled onto the pool table, their combined releases soaking the fabric.

Chapter Eleven

"We're going out," Draven said, entering the library three days later.

Harper looked up from her book, and he saw the question in her blue eyes. After they had fucked all night long, he'd abandoned her to take care of business.

He knew she was upset from being left alone, but he didn't have time to babysit her feelings, and he needed to get some fucking perspective on his own. Not to mention, Axel was still fucking nowhere to be found and wasn't answering any of his calls.

Tillie was demanding his presence at her sex dungeon, and an MC deal had gone in the crapper.

All in all, he wasn't ready to deal with Harper or what she wanted to talk about. He had his own problems, and they didn't include her.

"Where are we going?"

"First, we're going shopping. I looked at your clothes and they're all crap."

"Hey, don't talk about my clothes like that. They have feelings too."

"No, the person that wears them has feelings."

"Exactly, and this person is a little pissed off right now."

"And I don't give a shit. Get ready. We leave in ten minutes."

"Hold on a minute," Harper said. "You're going to come in here after three days, making demands, and I don't even get a 'Hi, Harper'?"

"Hi, Harper. Get your shit together."

"Draven."

"Not fucking now. Do you really think I've got time for all of this girly shit right now? I've got things to do, and it doesn't involve holding your hand. Get ready."

He slammed the door closed and didn't look back.

The guards stayed silent as he stalked past them. He went to his car, climbed behind the wheel, and waited for Harper to arrive. She didn't keep him waiting long.

She didn't change out of the sweatpants and shirt, and her hair looked like it hadn't seen a brush. She slammed the car door closed.

He didn't care. Pulling off the drive, he headed in the direction of the city.

"We're leaving Stonewall?"

"Yes."

"Where's Axel?"

"None of your business."

"You've not seen him? Heard from him?"

"Nope. He's doing whatever he wants to do."

"Do you know he was screwing my boss? Was he supposed to be doing Stephanie? She was a good woman. A nice woman. A little naive when it came to men, but I don't want her hurt."

"Harper, the only reason Axel was there was to get an easy fuck. The fact you were working there was a mere coincidence, nothing more."

"Are you going to tell me why you're in a pissy mood?"

"Nope."

"What are we doing then?"

"We are going shopping. Then afterward, we're going to have some fun."

"All out of Stonewall?"

"I'm not trapped there, Harper. If you want to stay there, be my fucking guest and go back there. I've got other things to do." He brought the car to an abrupt stop.

"I'm good."

"Seriously, I'm not in the fucking mood for whatever bullshit you're playing."

"I'm not playing any bullshit, Draven. I just, it has been three days."

"Is your pussy missing me?" He knew he was being a prick, but right now, he didn't want to be anything else.

"Why are you being a prick?"

"I want to have some fun, babe. You want to make this hard, then you can go back to the cells. I'll gladly put you there, or are you going to prove to me that you're loyal to me?"

"I'm ready to have some fun." She stayed looking at straight ahead but not at him.

He wouldn't allow her to put on music. The drive helped him to unwind.

After a few minutes, Harper leaned back, and she fell asleep. The silence was a welcome reprieve from the darkness swirling inside him. One of the jobs he had to deal with was a girl. She'd been taken off the street and put in one of the brothels he owned. She didn't last a weekend. A couple of clients decided to use her as a punching bag, and Draven had to clean up the mess.

The men were two well-known businessmen, and he was already working on dealing with them.

"Pussy is all around you, son. You got to learn to cut yourself off. They earn a living. They could be on the streets, but they're not. They get tested regularly, and they take cock. Expensive cock. You want to be weak, cry for them. You'll dig your own grave."

Draven ran a hand down his face, trying to clear the disgust from his mind. His hands shook, and he gripped the steering wheel even tighter.

He shouldn't care.

But he did.

For a long time, he'd cut off all feeling, all caring for anything and everything. He didn't give a shit about anyone or anything.

A few weeks of Harper in his life and the rage that bubbled within him threatened to spill out and completely destroy him.

Harper let out a moan and turned over. He glanced over at her, and she looked so peaceful in sleep. So beautiful and innocent.

He thought about what they did on the pool table, seeing his cum spill from inside her.

It turned him on knowing there was nothing between them. She belonged to him just as he belonged to her.

He was falling again. He had to stop that shit.

She didn't want any more punishments, and yet, could he trust her?

According to the guards, she made no attempt to escape. She always stayed within the grounds and didn't even try to tempt them to leave.

She'd asked Ian and of course Hannah to let her go, and she repeatedly asked him to let her go.

He couldn't bring himself to let her though. That wasn't the plan. The plan was to keep her around and to use her before throwing her aside. So far, that hadn't worked.

One look at her, and he knew he couldn't do that, not after being balls deep inside her.

His father always had the evidence of Harper's misdeeds, whenever Draven felt … the need for her. She'd betrayed them all, but Draven had never admitted to anyone how he felt. There were moments in the first five years, where he would miss her, crave her touch. In those moments, it was like his father knew, and he'd get to see how fucking stupid he was. Harper wasn't the girl he thought she once was, but something far deadlier.

He held onto the steering wheel driving them for three hours straight. His first stop was to get her some clothes.

Draven liked to look at her body, and the only way to do that was to dress her appropriately.

They entered the first store, and Harper dragged her feet like a damn child.

"You're not leaving here until you've got clothes, or I'll start making you walk around my house naked."

"You're a sadist."

"Not even close," he said.

His threat seemed to do the trick as she picked up some jeans, shirts, and he got her some dresses to try on.

She wrinkled her nose, but he ignored that. She was going to look amazing by his side, and of course he loved seeing her walk around his home.

When he was in his office and Harper walked the gardens, he often stopped to watch her. He didn't know what it was, but seeing her, knowing she was close by, it offered him a comfort he didn't realize he needed.

Once they had all of her clothes that she'd need, he spared no expense. He could afford it.

Next was that night's evening gown. He had no interest in returning to Stonewall. Draven ordered for his woman to look the part for a date, and the staff accommodated him.

Much to Harper's annoyance, she was cleaned up, hair done into a neat style, and of course, her nails, makeup, and dress were dealt with.

It took them two hours, but as Harper left the room, Draven could only stare.

When they walked into the store, she'd looked like she walked off the streets in comparison. Her hair was glossed and falling around her in ringlets, her skin flawless with a hint of makeup. The dress, which was black, molded to every single curve and seemed to help enhance her beauty.

She looked stunning. There was no other word for it.

Actually, she looked like a queen. His queen.

She ran her hands down her stomach. "How do I look?"

"Beautiful."

"Well, they pulled and pretty much stitched this into place." She shrugged, wrapping an arm across her middle.

"We're heading out to dinner."

He held his hand out, and she took it.

They walked to the payment desk, and he handed over his card. He struggled when it came to not looking at Harper.

To him, she had always been a looker.

Her icy blue eyes, raven hair, and curves. Some boys or men liked a woman with no extra flesh, no weight. For him, he loved to feel her body against him, her softness, even when they were younger.

Having her in his arms was like a fucking dream to him.

Harper hadn't lost her curves, and since he'd been feeding her, she seemed to have this glow about her, this natural beauty that just drew him.

Draven arranged for the rest of her packages to be brought back to Stonewall, and when they were done, he took her hand and led her back to the car.

"Do you still love Italian?"

"Of course."

"Good."

He drove them to one of the best Italian

restaurants the city held. It wasn't one he owned either. His reach was far but not this far. Was that why he picked this? To be far from any of his influences?

He wanted to remind Harper that he was more than what his father had made him.

The valet opened the door for Harper, but Draven rushed around and took over. No one but himself was going to be touching her tonight.

There was no way he'd even be able to share her, not with anyone.

"I'll take it from here."

He held her hand, and he went to the maître d' and gave his name. Within a matter of minutes, they were seated.

The soft candlelight gave a romantic feel to the room. He stared across the table at her, and she looked around her.

"This is a really nice place," she said.

"I heard they have the best pasta in the world."

She laughed. "That's Italy."

"And this is a little slice of it."

"So, are you going to tell me what is wrong with you or are we going to pretend everything is more than fine?"

"I had a trying day at work, Harper. Let's say, it was one of the worst I've had."

"You keep a list of worst days?"

"Yes. Two of them are because of Buck and Jett." He saw her wince. He liked seeing her pain.

In a strange way, it was her punishment for knowing they died because of her.

"You must really hate me. You keep throwing their deaths up in my face, and you always look satisfied when it hurts."

He sat back. She made no move to run. They

were in a different city. There were no guards around to keep them both in check.

He was on his own when it came to her, and yet, if she did try to run, he'd catch her. She'd been gone from his life once, but never again. Her time for running was over.

She flicked a hand back, and he watched her hair fall away.

The waiter came to get their drinks order. He opted for whiskey while she just took some water.

"Not feeling well?" he asked.

"I'm feeling fine. I just don't want to not remember the night before."

"You don't remember the night?" Draven asked.

"No." She shrugged. "That's why I'm going to keep a clear head."

The waiter brought them their drinks. He took a sip of whiskey. It would be his one and only for the night.

Harper looked through the menu, and he was more occupied with her.

"You're staring," she said, looking up.

He smiled. "You look pretty."

"It's amazing what a couple of hours can do, right?"

"So true." He winked at her. "I couldn't see you sitting through all that in high school."

For the first time that day and night, he saw her smile.

"Could you imagine? No way in hell would I allow someone to poke and prod me. It would drive me insane."

"And now you sat through it willingly."

"You look so very proud."

"I am."

Silence fell on their table, but it wasn't awkward or uncomfortable. It was … relaxing.

He signaled the waiter over and gave their order when they were ready, and Harper sat back, sipping at her water the moment they were alone again.

"I could get used to this."

"There's nothing to get used to. This can all be yours," he said.

"You wanted to hurt me, Draven. Are you telling me that is not the case anymore?"

"I'm saying to you that I'm willing to put the past behind me. No more talk of you leaving. Nothing about you running away. Not even my father."

"And in return?"

"I want you by my side. As my wife."

Those words took him completely by surprise. From Harper's open mouth, it had her as well.

"You can't be serious."

"I am deadly serious. This is what I want. You and me. Like it was always supposed to be. Us together."

She ran her fingers through her hair. It was the only sign of nerves he'd seen on her. She sipped at her drink.

"See, this is why I shouldn't be allowed alcohol, ever."

He smiled.

"You're being completely serious right now?" she asked.

"Yes. Totally serious. No more talk of the past. Of my father. Of anyone else but us. You and me. No one else. I don't want to know what you did or why you did it. I want us to start over, a clean slate."

"This is also for you?"

"Yes." He didn't need to bring up the whipping post or anything else. He watched her.

"As your wife?"

"Yes."

"Does that mean I can come and go as I please?" she asked. "No more prisoner status?"

"You'll be free to do what you want, but knowing there will always be a guard on your side. I hope Axel will consider it."

She leaned forward, and he knew without even looking that she was touching the ink on her back.

"What about the initiation?" she asked. "What does that mean?"

"Axel has shown no interest in being with you, with us. He's a man of many mysteries, and he likes to keep his life away from me and away from what we do."

"It's dangerous."

"It's life, and it was the one we were born into." He took a drink of his whiskey, a little shaken he'd offered her marriage. "The offer is open until the end of the night. When morning comes, it's gone."

The waiter brought them their food.

Harper looked a little pale, but she didn't require him to force feed her.

She ate the food, and they made conversation about nothing. The food. The restaurant. The weather.

Anything that wasn't related to the topic of a wedding.

"Harper, is that you?"

Harper looked up from her dessert menu as a man with short blond hair and green eyes approached.

"Ethan," she said.

Draven's hands clenched into fists as he saw the man that had been willing to marry her. He didn't like him on sight.

"I've been trying to call you. To find you."

"I dropped my phone. I didn't want to be found."

He found himself watching her, seeing her reaction.

She held a smile, but it didn't quite reach her eyes. It was forced. For a woman who was going to marry this man, there was no love there.

Draven sat back.

"I wanted to talk to you about what happe—"

"Are you here on a date?" she asked, interrupting him.

"Yes."

"Then I really think you should go back to your date, Ethan."

"You're just going to leave it like that?"

"I left the ring for you. I didn't force you to marry me, and I'm not there to be the perfect little wife you want. Besides, I'm on a date."

She turned her smile toward Draven.

"Pleasure to meet you," Draven said, holding out his hand.

Ethan shook it, and he noticed he didn't even have a firm grip. That wouldn't do, not for Harper. She could probably crush him.

"You were cheating on me?" Ethan asked.

"No."

"I've been in Harper's life since we were kids. We had a … quarrel some years back, but now we're together. She's also agreed to be my wife," Draven said, taking her hand. "We're going to have the most beautiful children."

She was shooting fire at him.

It was a good job that nothing could spill from her eyes as he'd be burnt to a crisp, scalded from her look alone.

Ethan watched them, and it took him a few moments to realize he had to leave.

When he stepped away from the table and back to his date, Harper looked a little sad.

Draven didn't like that, not the jealousy that spilled out or the need to show her who she belonged to.

****

Draven slammed her against the door of their hotel room.

"You did that on purpose," Harper said, glaring at him.

He grabbed her hands, pressing them above her head. "I didn't know your fuck was going to be there."

She drew her knee up, intending to hurt him, but he stopped her. His body pressed against hers, stopping her from going anywhere else, and it irritated her.

Seeing Ethan, she was pleased to see him move on, but hearing Draven, what he said, she hated feeling that hope.

His proposal had been a shock, but his words to Ethan had been like he was looking within her, and that she couldn't accept.

She was under no illusion about just how dangerous he was. She had to keep her distance in order to survive.

"Why did you have to say that?"

"Are you missing your lover boy? Does me make you as hot and horny as I do? Is your pussy wet for him like it is for me?" He held both of her hands above her head while he cupped between her thighs. "You drip for me. Remember that." He pressed the dress between her thighs, and she moaned. She couldn't do anything else.

He rubbed back and forth, his actions not smooth or gentle.

They were hard and rough, just the way she liked it.

She slid her legs open, and he chuckled. "You

see? This is how much you want it. You want me to have it all from you."

He lifted the dress up, and sure enough, he found her panties soaked.

She knew as she felt them herself. Draven had this power over her. He made her want him so completely that she couldn't think of anyone or anything else. Why would she want to?

He slid a finger beneath the band of her panties and touched her. That single digit slid between her slit, playing with her clit, then down to her entrance.

"I remember that first time. Taking your cherry. You were my first virgin, Harper. I wanted to make it good for you. To have you screaming for me." He slid two fingers inside her, and she gasped as he started to open them, stretching her. "You're still so wet for me, so tight. I need to get you used to my cock."

"So you can sell me?"

"Become my wife and the only dick you'll be riding will be mine."

"You want to keep me?"

"Yes," he said. "You'll belong to me. Everything I want, you'll give me. You'll want for nothing."

"And what do you get in return?"

"I get what I always wanted: you."

He pulled his hand away, and she watched as he sucked his fingers, licking the scent of her off him.

He gripped her shoulders and spun her.

Putting her hands on the door, she closed her eyes, loving the forceful way he took her. His control drove her need for him higher. He released the zipper of the dress and slid it down. His fingers trailed behind his touch on her back.

"No one will ever mark you like this."

Some of the whips on her back would scar.

She wished she could hate him, and a part of her would always hate what he did, but she couldn't bring herself to hate him.

Was it Stockholm Syndrome?

Was it because of their past?

She didn't know.

He banded an arm across her stomach and pulled her back. The dress fell down to her hips. She met his chest, and he slid his hands up to cup her tits.

He held them up like an offering, teasing the nipples. They were so sensitive that with a few strokes, she nearly came.

"Do you have any idea what it is you do to me?" he said, biting her neck, sucking on the pulse that beat rapidly.

"I've got an idea."

He laughed. "Babe, you don't have a clue."

His cock pressed against her back, getting harder and thicker with every passing second.

"I want to fucking own you. To take you and make you mine, over and over again."

He licked her pulse and then released her tits, pushing the dress down past her hips to pool at her feet. Draven didn't waste time as he grabbed her panties and tore them from her body, throwing them to the floor like scraps.

One of his hands slid between her thighs, cupping her pussy, and his fingers teased through her slit. Each stroke against her clit had her moaning, spreading her thighs for him.

Draven let her go once again, and she growled her frustration.

"Please, Draven," she said.

"I love it when you beg."

He grabbed her hand and moved her toward the

bed. Only, it wasn't to go to the bed. He stood in front of a mirror.

Draven pulled her in front of him.

"Look at you. Look at how beautiful you are. You can belong to me, all of me. You only need to say the words." He kissed her neck.

His hands stroked her body, and he sat them down on the edge of the bed. The mirror was in the corner, large and imposing, but easy to move as well if they wanted. She couldn't help but wonder if that was the hotel's intention. For couples who wanted to watch themselves, they could look in the mirror and see.

Draven sat her on his lap and spread her thighs wide, putting her legs on the outside of his so he had control in opening them.

"Look at that pretty pussy." His hand lay on her stomach, and she did as he said, looking at the evidence of her arousal.

While she was completely naked, he was still fully dressed. Draven touched her pussy again, and this time, she watched as he teased her clit. He'd stroke her nub before moving down to fill her pussy. She whimpered, wanting him to get her to orgasm, not to keep on teasing her.

Actually, she wanted him naked like her.

There was so much she wanted, and yet, she couldn't move, not until he touched her some more.

Draven chuckled against her ear.

"Do you even have any idea what you do to me?" he asked. He pushed three fingers inside her, and he thrust against her ass.

"I've got an idea," she said.

His cock was so hard. She lifted herself up off his lap and turned toward him. She pushed his hand away from her pussy and attacked his shirt.

She tore the fabric open, and the buttons spilled onto the floor, popping off in her need for him.

He let out a chuckle but didn't make any move to stop her.

She was the one in charge here. Her, not him. Running her hands over his body, she loved the look of him. The power of him. The ink that decorated his chest.

She saw her name painted on his flesh. The name that pointed to the other three that bound her to him.

When it came to Draven, she was lost. She wanted him and hated him.

Part of her also wanted to run and another wanted to stay, to prove to him she was a fighter, that she'd had no desire to leave all those years ago.

She never wanted to go.

It was his father who caused it.

Just thinking about Alan filled her with so much rage. He'd won on every single battle so far. The war, it was still raging, and she wouldn't let him win that.

When it came to Draven, *she* would be the one to win.

Tugging down his pants after releasing his belt, he let out a chuckle. "If you wanted to get me naked all you had to do was say."

"I want to get you naked."

He helped her, pushing down his pants and boxers until he was completely naked. His cock stood out. The tip was wet, and she couldn't go another second without tasting him, without taking him.

She moaned as she did, sucking and licking at his cock.

"Fuck, Harper, that feels so good." He drove into her mouth, pumping his hips, making her take all of it.

She swallowed him down, gagging a little on the length until she got used to tasting him. He held the back of her neck as he pumped within her.

As she stared up the length of his body, his gaze was locked on her. They both had the power over each other. Neither of them gave up the fight.

"You're so fucking good," he said. "That's it, babe. Take my cock. Suck it."

She swallowed him down, tasting his pre-cum and moaning as he kept thrusting into her mouth.

He suddenly pulled out of her and lifted her up. Draven spun her around, and she watched and felt as he filled her. The hard head of his cock moved between her folds, pushing inside her.

She seated herself on his cock and leaned back, putting her legs back to where they were so she could see.

His cock was so long as it drove inside her. He split her pussy open. Her lips wrapped around his length and the evidence of how wet she was gleamed on his cock as he slid in and out. She watched as he stroked her clit, and she was mesmerized by the sight of them together. His cock drove inside her as he brought her to orgasm.

With only a few strokes to her clit, she came and did so hard, screaming his name. The sound echoed off the walls, and Draven followed her seconds later, his cock pumping inside her.

She didn't need to see their combined release, and Draven moved them both to the bed. His dick was still within her as he held her close, her ass nestled against his pelvis.

Even though he was flaccid, it felt good to have him inside her.

He kissed her neck, and she felt this peace, this calm wash over her.

"Yes," she said. "I'll marry you."

Chapter Twelve

"You agreed to marry her?" Axel asked, suddenly appearing in his office ten days later.

Draven finished the email he was writing before finally looking up at his remaining best friend.

"Yes. I asked her, in fact. If I knew my current nuptials would bring you back, I'd have told you sooner."

"Did you always intend to marry her?"

"Ten years ago, yes. When you brought her back from the florist, no. I was going to make her pay."

Axel laughed. "You think you haven't? How do you know this is not a trap? One she's setting up?"

"I was the one who asked her."

"Oh," Axel said, taking a seat. "Where is she now?"

Draven stayed silent.

"Oh, come on, Draven, you and I both know you're very much aware of where she is at all times."

"She's at the pool, taking a swim." He ran his fingers through his hair. "Care to tell me what you've been doing?"

"Not a lot and it's not any of your business. So, is this an arrangement between you and Harper? Does she know the truth of everything you do?"

"No, and you're not going to tell her."

"You're going to bind her to you in a marriage she can't get out of without her even seeing the true extent of the hell we create together."

"She doesn't need to know. It won't touch her."

"You're going to keep her locked up in Stonewall?" Axel asked.

"You're paying a lot of attention to my soon-to-be wife," Draven said.

"Don't forget, she was also supposed to be mine."

Draven wanted to shoot him. "You've not been around to stake your claim."

Axel rolled his eyes. "You know what, Harper was always yours. She will always be yours. I don't want her. Not like you think, so you can keep your alpha man bullshit away from me, okay. Just remember, you intended to share her with me, with all of us. That was the initiation."

"The initiation was a mistake," Draven said.

"Now the truth comes out. Is it a mistake now or back then? Come on, Draven, what is it? Or is it only a mistake because there's only me left? You want to be rid of me."

"You're like a brother to me, Axel. I will never want to kill you."

"So I should count myself lucky?"

Draven growled. "What is it with you? Are you happy for me or not? Do you want Harper or not?"

"I guess I want some fucking clarity on what happens next?" Axel asked. "You're the one with the power. You're the big man in charge. Tell me what I should do next."

"Do what makes you happy, how about that?"

"What if killing Harper will make me happy? Taking her up to the spot where Buck and Jett lie and running his blade across her throat. Seeing her blood seep into the earth."

Draven slammed his hands against the desk, glaring at him. "Don't even fucking think of it."

Axel smirked. "You know, she and I, we've got a deal."

"What?"

"That's right. If I can find evidence of what your

father did, she gets to walk free. If I don't, then I get to kill her."

Draven shook his head. "No. She wouldn't make that kind of deal."

"I did," Harper said. She stood in the doorway.

From how pale she looked, she'd heard a lot of their conversation. She had a towel wrapped around her. Her hair was wet.

"I thought I heard you, Axel."

"I've not stopped looking. I've got a few places yet, so your neck is more than safe."

"Okay then," Harper said.

"He's not killing you." Draven shook his head. There's no way he'd ever allow anything to happen to her.

"A deal's a deal, Draven. You know that."

"You're not killing her."

"I guess we'll have to see." Axel got to his feet, and Draven tensed, his hand on Jett's knife that he always kept with him. "I hear congratulations are in order."

Before he could do anything, Axel caught Harper's face and kissed her hard. She held the towel against her and made no move to embrace Axel.

She did, however, kiss him back.

"I always knew it was you," Axel said.

"What?"

"Draven wanted you. Always. It's kind of … sweet. Adios, kids," Axel said.

Draven watched Axel leave, ready to strike if even for a second it looked like he was going to attack.

"How much did you hear?" Draven asked.

"Not a whole lot. Enough to know that you're aware of our deal."

"Yes, what the fuck were you thinking?"

"I was chained to a whipping post, Draven. I was desperate."

"You think your lies are going to save you."

Her hands clenched into fists. "My 'lies' are the only thing that will save me. If Axel doesn't find it, I will let him kill me."

"I won't let him."

"It doesn't matter. He'll find a way. He's part of the Stonewall foursome. You know he'll do what is necessary." She went to turn away, but he caught her wrist, stopping her from leaving.

"Did you enjoy your swim?" he asked.

"You shoot hot and cold so fast you're giving me whiplash."

"Good. It's what I want." He pulled her around to his side of the desk, seating her in front of him.

He sat down, took hold of the towel, and spread it open, staring at her. The swimsuit she wore did little to hide her body.

Pulling out Jett's knife, he watched her tense.

"I'm not going to kill you. I've now got to figure out a way to stop Axel from killing you."

"I find your lack of faith in me insulting."

"I told you, the past is put to bed. There is no room for it in our future." He cut the straps of her swimsuit and pulled the chest away from her, slicing it down the center. Another two cuts and it opened away from her body, giving him an uninterrupted view of what belonged to him.

"You can't change the deal I made."

"I'm not going to have anything happen to you."

She smiled. "Are you worried that I'm going to be able to prove what happened ten years ago?"

"There's no chance of that," he said.

He turned her around so that she was flat against

the desk. Anything in her way or that could cause her pain, he pushed to the floor and ran his hand up her back to cup her neck. He stroked back down to her ass and spread her cheeks.

Draven stared at the puckered hole of her anus and her wet, creamy cunt. Both were begging to be fucked.

He opened the drawer of his desk and pulled out a tube of lubrication. Opening the cap, he pressed some above her anus and watched the clear liquid drip down.

When he had enough on her, he dropped the lube back in the drawer. She gasped as he slid his fingers between her crack, stroking over her asshole.

"What are you doing?"

"I'm playing."

"Shouldn't you be working?"

"Probably, but right now, I want to watch you."

With his other hand, he cupped her pussy, sliding two fingers inside her, watching her open up for him, taking his fingers. Soon, he'd fill her with his cock, and when he did, she'd scream for more.

As he pushed a finger inside her asshole, she let out a pained grunt, and he gave her time to get accustomed to that one finger.

His patience was wearing thin, and he wanted to own every single part of her. With Axel's presence, he felt this overriding need to take her, to claim her, to know that every single part of her belonged to him and him alone.

He pumped his finger inside her ass until she started to wriggle back against him. Her pussy was already soaking wet, and he finger-fucked her with his other hand, working up a pace for her to love it. He added a second finger into her ass and started to spread his fingers so it would stretch her asshole wider.

"I'm taking this today."

She moaned.

"I'm going to fuck you and fill you, baby. You're going to be my own personal fuck toy. No more sharing. No one else is going to see what belongs to me."

He worked her ass at the same time as her pussy, driving her toward an orgasm but refusing to let her find release. Whenever she was close, he'd stop teasing her, and that would drive her crazy.

She'd whimper and moan his name, begging for more of what he could give her.

Only him.

Seeing Ethan, he knew he couldn't allow another man near her. Even Axel was off limits to her.

With her ass prepared, he his cock out of his pants and worked more lube into his length. He let go of her pussy to put the tip of his cock at her asshole. She tensed up, and he gave her ass a slap. "Relax."

"Kind of hard to do."

He chuckled. "You're going to love it."

Slowly, inch by inch, he stretched her asshole, making her take all of him. She let out a little whimper, but it didn't stop him.

When she'd taken most of his cock, he stroked her clit, and brought her even more pleasure as he worked her body.

She rocked back against him, sinking the last few inches of his dick within her. He was balls deep in her tight ass.

Staring down at her body, he continued to finger her clit, and as he brought her to orgasm, he gritted his teeth. The pleasure was so intense it nearly set off his own release, only his control keeping him in check.

He started to pull out of her, and she cried out. Cupping her hips, he rocked back and forth, slowly, taking his time, letting her get accustomed to the feel of him inside her. "I'm going to be the one to take your cherry here as well."

"Fuck you," she said.

He slammed inside her, relishing her moans. "No, babe, fuck you. I can feel how much you love this. You're so wet your cum is dripping down your thighs."

He pressed against her back, kissing her neck, biting her pulse and sucking on the skin hard. He kept on sucking so she'd have his marks. Digging his fingers against the flesh of her hips, he wanted her to wear his prints.

Pulling out of her ass, he slid on inside, the lube making it easier for him.

Over and over, as she got more accustomed to the feel of him within her ass, she began to take more, pushing back against him. Her moans turned to whimpers and pleas, wanting him.

Draven gave her everything she craved and begged for, driving her toward a second and even a third orgasm before he found his own release. He didn't pull out. He slammed to the hilt and unleashed within her ass.

He kissed her neck and pulled her with him as he collapsed in her chair. As he wrapped his arms around her, they were both panting for breath.

"I think I'm just going to die for a few moments," she said.

He chuckled, biting the flesh of her breast. "So, tell me, Harper, was that your first time being fucked in the ass?"

"You know it was."

"I like that."

"You're weird."

"When it comes to you, Harper, I like being a lot of your firsts."

"Am I any of your firsts though?" she asked. She tilted her head to look at him. Her blue eyes took his breath away.

"You're a lot of firsts," he said.

"I wasn't your first lover."

"No. With the father I had, I didn't have time to pick my own first. He did that for me." He tried not to think about the past. Nothing good could come from dragging up the past. That was all over, finished.

"Do you miss your father?"

"No." He gripped her hips and started to move her up off his cock. "It's time for me to get you cleaned up."

"You don't want to talk about it."

"I'm sticking with our agreement, Harper. We don't talk about my father, or about the past. It's finished, over and done with."

"He really did a number on you, didn't he?"

He cupped her face, staring into her eyes. "Let's get you washed up."

****

Draven had an important meeting, and he'd granted her permission to do what she liked for the day but not to go to his office.

Harper stormed out of the house, ignoring the bite of cold as it burned her skin.

She didn't want to stay in the damn house and would gladly move anywhere else. It was Axel's old place, and she found as she explored the actual building, there was nothing of Draven's there. Not a lot of work had been done to it. She'd seen Axel's home ten years ago. He'd taken her on a tour during one of the days she stayed with them.

Why live in a home that wasn't actually his? He'd not made many changes, apart from his bedroom. It was

so ... bland. Black furniture and white walls.
Black and white.
His life was all about the grey.
Good and bad.
She walked past the guards, ignoring their presence. One of them would follow her. They always did. She hated their invasion into her life, and so far, she couldn't get a single thing out of them, not when it came to Draven. She wanted to know more about the man she was going to marry.
Marriage.
It seemed so strange to her; it still was.
She'd never considered getting married before, not even to Ethan. With Draven though, it was different, which was why she accepted. She'd truly thought Draven's proposal was a joke. It wasn't. He had people on hand that she could call to give direction on how she wanted her perfect wedding to be.
He'd even given her an engagement ring. She twisted it around on her finger as she tried to think about anything but the man she was walking away from.
When she made to pass the cells that she'd been locked in, the scent of cigarette smoke made her pause.
Every instinct within her was screaming to leave this place. The cells held a lifetime of memories she didn't want to venture into. Not just for herself, but for the women who were there before.
She stepped inside, and Axel sat on one of the disgusting beds. His back rested against the wall, a cigarette between his lips.
"What are you doing here?" he asked.
"I could ask you the same question."
"This is where I come to think, or at least in the past couple of weeks. It had been years before that."
She looked behind her and then entered the cells.

"Well, well, well, getting engaged has given you a backbone."

"Why are you here?"

"Why are you not at home with your precious fiancé?"

"He's got a meeting. Shouldn't you be part of it?"

"Nope. I have no interest in that meeting." He pulled the cigarette from his lips and billowed out a puff of smoke.

"I didn't know you smoked."

"There's a lot of things you don't know about me, Harper. A lot you don't know about your soon-to-be husband either."

"Then why don't you tell me something?" she asked, stepping into the cell and staring at him.

Axel smirked. "It would be too easy to tell you everything. Some things you need to work out for yourself."

"You're being really cryptic right now."

"I know. It's the story of my life."

She sighed. Glancing out the window, she stared up at the house. "You don't like it here?"

"I've never liked it here. Growing up with Draven and the guys, I'd hoped we'd demolish all of this shit. Put it all behind us and never look back."

"That didn't happen?"

"Nope. It has never happened. You see, Harper, when you left, it set off an entire shitstorm of events. What we wanted, never came to pass." He took another long drag on his cigarette.

"Did you find anything about that day?" she asked.

"Not a damn thing. Don't worry though. I've got a couple of other places I can look. You're still alive and kicking for now. Ready to fight another day and to see what that lovely husband of yours is up to."

"You and Draven are not on speaking terms?"

"Draven and I have our own terms of conversation."

"Have you been to see Stephanie?" she asked.

He laughed. "You're all over the place in conversation. You're terrified."

"I don't know what you mean."

Axel smirked. "Oh, yes, you do. I bet you've got an idea of what goes on in our lives. You're not completely sure, but you're marrying into it, and you know that if you were to know all of it, you may run again."

"Why don't you make it clear to me?" she asked.

"I can't do that."

"Why not?" He was going around in circles.

"I have my reasons, and I'm not afraid to use you to get what I want. You need to see the truth to wake him up."

"What kind of reasons?" she asked.

He sighed. "You know this life isn't normal. Having armed guards around the house. The party you were part of. The whipping post, these cells. It all tells you of a life that happened before Draven became in charge."

"Your parents."

"And they inherited it." Axel ran fingers through his hair and sniffed his body. "I need a fucking shower, I stink."

"Why can't you just tell me?"

"Draven's in love with you."

This made her pause.

"That took you by surprise, didn't it, sweetheart?"

"You don't know that."

"Oh, I know. He's been in love with you for

fucking years. It's because he loves you so fucking completely, which is why I can't tell you what you need to hear. He's still my best friend. My brother, and for Jett and Buck, if I don't do ... this, then I know we're stuck where we are until we die. Fuck, I'm doing this to help him, to help the both of us."

"What are you talking about?" she asked.

"I'll do something for you, and you've got to promise me, you'll never breathe a word I told you."

"Go on, Axel."

"When you go to Tillie's club—and you will. You're going to have to—he's going to get busy. Make sure you go to the basement."

"The basement?"

"Yes. There you will find a great deal of ... insight into part of what goes on here," Axel said.

He got to his feet, dropped the cigarette to the floor and stood on it, rubbing his boot along the floor to rub it out.

"Why did you tell me that?" she asked.

"The clock's ticking, Harper. The wedding is fast approaching, and you can't enter a marriage with someone you don't have a fucking clue about. That's all I'm going to tell you."

He brushed past her, and she looked toward him, watching him go. Axel was so different from who she remembered. Staring at the cells, she rubbed her arms, feeling a chill seep into her bones. Women had been killed here; she just knew it.

The question was, how far did Draven take his father's life?

Stepping out of the cells, she made her way back to the house, to Draven.

She didn't go to his office but went to the library, pulling out the first romance book she could find. She

DAMAGED QUEEN

took a seat, curled up, and read.

Chapter Thirteen

It took Draven three weeks before he mentioned going to visit Tillie at her club. He wanted her to go with him. Harper was torn as he stared across the dinner table at her. She was very much aware of Axel staring at her. He had yet to make a decision if he wanted to kill her or not.

Whenever she asked him what he'd found, he kept saying he was looking.

She didn't know what was taking him so long, but for now, she was just happy to still be alive.

"What?"

"I've got to head out tonight on business, but I'd like you to see something. I'm going to take you to Tillie's."

"The woman who used the whip on me?"

"Yes. You will play nice tonight, Harper."

"Do I have much of a choice?" she asked.

"None. You don't have a single choice with anything. You're going to do as you're told."

"I am," she said.

"Please, Harper. I want to show you something, that's all."

"But you've got business."

"It's another side of that whip," he said.

"Fine." If it hadn't been for Axel's warning, she wouldn't have even questioned him.

Draven's cell phone rang, and she watched him step away to take the call. Since her conversation with Axel, she found herself more and more curious about him, about what he did. The full extent of what Alan had done to him, to them.

"Remember to go to the basement," Axel said.

"Will you stop already? I don't think I can handle this."

"Harper, do you love him?" he asked.

She stared at him without saying a single word. "I don't want to talk about this."

"He's in love with you, Harper. It's why he never stopped wanting to hate you."

"He doesn't even believe me." She got up. "I don't want to have this conversation with you."

"Harper, you need to be ready. What you're going to find out, you're not going to like. That's the only warning I'm going to give you. Draven won't kill you, he can't. You two are both too fucking stubborn to see the truth? Well now, I'm giving it to you, plain and clear, for you both to see."

With that, she left, going straight to her bedroom.

Did she love Draven?

She didn't like the answer that entered her head the moment she thought of the question. He'd been in her thoughts for years, but that didn't actually have to mean anything, did it?

Running a hand down her face, she tried to clear the fog that was there. Everything was moving so fast. Draven, the wedding, life, everything.

She'd been dragged out of her life and thrown into this one, and it scared her. Especially as she knew without a doubt she wasn't going to like the truth. Alan had always been a bad person, but had Draven taken over? Was he just as bad? She put the whipping party aside, as she truly believed it was because he'd been pissed at her, angry. She even felt like she deserved it, after all that she'd done, and she never truly believed Draven was a bad guy.

There was no way she could stay at home, lingering on her thoughts. She took a long shower and prepared herself for the night ahead. She was terrified.

When he knocked on her door, she wanted to run.

She didn't run though.

Harper got up and met him at the door. Straightening her spine, she was ready for whatever she was about to find out.

"You look beautiful," he said.

"You clean up really well yourself. I didn't mean to cause a fight at the table."

He cupped her cheek, tilting her head back, and kissing her. "Already forgiven. You don't need to worry about another thing. I promise."

"You always know what to say. Don't leave me alone with Tillie."

"She's not too bad. Mostly with her, it's all about business."

"Have you slept with her?" she asked.

"No. I've never slept with her. Jealous?"

"Maybe a little."

"Don't be."

He took her hand, and there was no turning back. Not as they left the house, or she climbed into his car. Even when he fastened her seatbelt, she stayed perfectly silent. In her mind, she kept imagining the basement door. Wherever they were going, she'd need to find it.

Would Axel put her life in danger?

Absolutely.

"I don't want you walking off tonight."

"I won't."

"I've also got to give you something. It means no one else will approach you, and you'll be safe there."

She glanced over at him. "What aren't you telling me?"

"I will have to leave you alone, but you'll be in good company."

She'd noticed the tension within him, and it was freaking her out, scaring her.

"I'll do whatever it is you need me to."

"I got a call from the wedding planner. You're avoiding her calls?" Draven asked.

She'd been avoiding the calls since Axel's conversation. "I haven't been in the mood to plan a wedding. It's fine. I'll call her as soon as I know more."

They were silent for the rest of the ride. Arriving at what looked like a club, Draven got out of the car, and she noticed no one made a move to open her door. He handed his keys to one of the men waiting outside, and opened her door. He'd pulled something out of his jacket, and as she got out, he turned her and place something against her neck.

She touched her fingers to the collar, recognizing words.

"It marks you as mine. No one else will touch you."

She turned to look at him. "You don't think it's strange you're about to enter a club where a woman needs to be branded to be kept safe."

He took her hand. "Sometimes questions spoil it."

"Did you really need to bring me here today?" she asked.

"I wanted to share this with you. I feel it's important." He kissed her knuckles, and then they entered ... another world.

At least to Harper it was another world.

Lights were turned down low, but there were stages and different rooms. The music was down low, but it seemed to fill the room. The energy hit her straight away.

Draven put his arm around her, tucking her close to his side, and she looked around, having her fill of every single room.

It wasn't long before Harper recognized the woman from the party. She stayed by Draven's side, but stood in a long black dress, tall and serene as if she was above everyone else. Harper wanted to knock her off that little pedestal.

"Draven, darling, I'm so pleased you could come. And you brought your pet. Would you like me to mark that pale skin again?" Tillie went to touch her, and she stepped back, glaring at the woman, who laughed.

He didn't let her go far. "I wanted Harper to see part of what you did here."

"I have our guest here. Will she be here for that?" Tillie asked.

"No. I want her protected. She's mine."

"Yes, I remember. She'll be safe here. No one will touch her. She's got your mark. That is all that needs to be seen."

Draven turned to her.

"You've brought me to a sex club, and now you're leaving?"

"I've got some business to attend to. Look around. Have some fun. Don't talk to anyone, and I'll be back." He pressed a kiss to her lips.

She watched him go with Tillie by his side.

One day soon, she was going to hurt that woman.

She didn't have time to admire the views. Passing the rooms, she thought about what Axel said—the basement—and went in that direction. When she passed a room that showed a woman being bound and whipped, she had to stop and watch.

Men and women were gazing at the stage with such rapt attention.

Harper saw the whip and flashed back to that night.

Unlike her, the woman on stage relished every sting and bite.

For Harper, just seeing it made her feel sick to her stomach.

She stepped away from the room and kept on with her search. She passed rooms, and didn't go for the stairs. Walking to the back of the house, she saw there wasn't as much activity, and whenever someone passed, she hid in an alcove or a closet.

Harper looked down a short passage, and she saw a guy holding a gun, standing guard near one of the doors. He stood out like a sore thumb.

Why did he guard this one door?

She flicked her hair back, lowered her shirt so that more of her cleavage showed, and made her way toward him. She pretended to be a little high, and certainly very easy.

"Honey, you're not allowed to be here," he said.

"Oh, shoot, did I make a wrong turn? I have no idea where I'm going. It's all so exciting." She stopped in front of him, and she saw him relax. His gaze was on her chest. Pushing some hair off her face, she let out a giggle. "Why are you not part of the party upstairs? You would be so much fun to play with."

He chuckled. "Well, I get off in half an hour. Save me some play time and you can make it up to me."

Harper stepped up close.

All of the training she remembered from years ago rushed toward her, and she caught him by surprise. The man was more interested in getting his dick wet than protecting what was behind that door. Drawing her knee up, she hit him square in the nuts, and slammed her fist against his face. With him distracted, she grabbed the gun and used it to knock him out cold. She held the gun in her hands, and without wasting any time, she stepped over him and opened the door to the basement.

There was a light on, a single light, and she heard sniffling. Tears.

Harper tensed up and held the gun in her hand, not that she knew how to use it.

Walking down the steps, she stopped, and as she took in the cages, Harper just knew.

Women.

A quick head count told her there were at least twenty women spread out on the cells. None of them spoke, even as some of them cried.

She stared at them and felt ill.

"Are you guys here because you want to be?" she asked.

"We can't talk. We're not allowed to talk," one of the women said.

She looked at each of them. Harper walked toward the cages. They were all locked up. She gripped the bars and tried to pull it open.

Did Draven know about them? This?

"You shouldn't be down here," Tillie said.

Harper turned to see Tillie on the stairs, wearing a smile.

"You know, I've got security around every single room of this place. I like to take care of all of my assets."

"They're people," she said. "Real people."

"They're a commodity, Harper. Men and women pay for the pleasure of using them. They're expendable." Tillie folded her arms. "When one of them dies, another will take their place. It's a natural circle of all things. They get fed and are well-kept."

"You've got them in the dark in a cage."

"I feed them. They're allowed to use the bathroom, get washed. I've got ten women upstairs working the men who paid for them." Tillie laughed.

"Draven hasn't told you a thing, has he?" Tillie stepped up toward her. "I thought he was ready to move up in the world when he had me whip your back. Such a pretty back. I offered to take you off his hands. To show him how to treat a bad girl like you. I'd mark you up real good and have all my customers that like to make my women bleed, have their fill of you."

Harper drew her fist back and slammed it against the woman's face. She'd taken her by surprise, and as she held the barrel of the gun, she swung it around, and hit her again.

"You want to try and tame me, bitch? Let's see how you can handle a beating. You like to dish it out. Let's see you take one."

She stepped over Tillie. The other woman tried to fight her, but Harper had years of anger. She was done with being pushed around. By Draven, by Axel, by fucking Alan. It was done. This bitch was going down.

She drew her fist back and hit her again.

Harper got three more hits in before she was pulled off, and she screamed at the unfairness of it.

Draven had her locked against the wall, his hands holding hers above her head.

"Enough!"

"No! Never enough. You knew. Didn't you? This is what this all is. You didn't go your own path. Your father made sure you followed in his footsteps. The women, they've been taken, trafficked out. The sex trade?"

"I'm not talking with you about this."

"You wanted to change. You hated your father, and yet, you've become him."

"Nothing could change, Harper."

"It could change. You could make it so. This is not you. You were supposed to be better than this. You shouldn't be doing this. They're real people, Draven. Real women, just like me. You need to let them go. To let them live. This is so fucking wrong, you don't even know how much. None of them deserve this, none of them." She stopped, feeling a sob work its way up her throat. All of these women deserved a chance. There's no way she could let them down, not again.

"Get her out of here before I deal with her," Tillie said, getting to her feet.

"Come on, bitch, I'd like to see you fucking try. I'll kill you. I swear I'll fucking kill you."

Draven lifted her up, and she was pulled from the room. The guy she'd been teasing was nowhere in sight, and she was so fucking pissed.

Draven carried her out of the car, and she kept on fighting him.

Draven didn't put her in the passenger seat or even in the back. He dumped her in the trunk.

Tears filled her eyes as he closed the trunk, and she kept on hitting it and screaming. All the while her heart pounded with what she knew to be the truth. This was what Axel wanted her to know, what he needed her to know before she committed to this. He didn't like selling people, and it must be why he had an aversion to the cells.

It explained so much. Draven hadn't changed. He was still a little minion for his father.

Tears fell down her cheeks, and the only satisfaction she had was knowing she'd hurt that bitch. All those women. They had to be let go. She had to help them, to do something that would save them.

Time passed, and she wiped the tears from her eyes. Her throat was sore from her screaming. She didn't know what else to do.

When the car came to a stop, she wondered if he

was going to push it into a river or something. She sniffled, hating how broken she felt.

The trunk opened up, and she stared up at Draven. They were back home in Stonewall, where it all began.

He reached for her, and she kicked out, hard. She made sure he felt it as well, sitting up. Draven let out a curse, but he didn't stop there.

When he made to touch her, she slapped him away. She was very much aware of the guards, watching.

"Get off me. I don't want you near me. Get the fuck away from me."

She didn't stop, and he held her, controlling her. He carried her over his shoulder even as she hit him, until they were inside his home.

"Leave us," he said.

One by one the guards disappeared.

Harper pulled off her heels and threw them at him. "You evil son of a bitch!"

When she threw them off, she grabbed a vase and threw it. He dodged that.

"You shouldn't have gone looking."

"They are nothing more than slaves. You are in the human trafficking business."

"You really didn't know."

"I knew you weren't exactly legal. I didn't know the extent of what you did. The fucking cells. The whipping post. I thought all of that was in the past. Something Axel's father did."

"He did do it. "

"And you don't? Those girls are there of their own free will?" she asked.

"Harper."

"No! You will tell me now. Alan wanted to get me out of the way because he knew you would change his ways. He knew his time for power was coming to an end while I was there. You … became him. You became the exact monster he was." The tears fell thick and fast.

"I do what I have to do."

She shook her head. "No. You do what you're told to do. You do what is expected of you." She sniffled. "You're not going to let those women go, are you?"

"They are not mine," he said. "I was there to deal with one that caused a problem."

She burst out laughing. Once she started, it was impossible to stop. Holding her stomach, she kept on laughing, let it out, and snorting as she did.

Someone cleared their throat, and she saw Axel had joined them.

"Well, I guess the joke is on me, right? All those years ago, this was the life you wanted. The life you all envisioned. Pimps, criminals, bullies, rapists, murderers."

"I've never taken a woman against her will," Draven said.

"You help rapists. Every man that touches them, every woman that does the same, you help them because you keep them captured. You paid for them. If not those women in those cages like fucking dogs, then it was others. Other women at other times." She couldn't stop crying thinking about it. She saw Draven from the past. "I ran to keep you guys safe. I don't care anymore if you believe it or not. It doesn't matter. No matter what, I didn't cause this. I didn't make *you* buy those girls. I didn't make you do anything." She stepped back. "I won't be part of this. I can't be, not anymore. Not after all I've done before this."

"Harper," Draven said.

"You can kill me, Draven. I'd gladly die rather than be by your side, knowing that … you take them. They have a life, too. Not working for you. They have worth, so much of it, and I can't do this. Not this." She turned on her heel and was about to walk away to her room. She stopped and walked right up to him. "What is it you do?"

"Go to your room, Harper. Now."

"You can't even say it, can you? You can't even acknowledge what you are? *I'm* a human trafficker! It's what I did. I helped sell girls. There is proof out there about what I did, and it kills me. I can't look at myself in the mirror because of all that I've done. I have to live with that, but I don't pretend I'm something I'm not."

She glared at him, and Draven glared back. He took a step toward her, but she stayed right where she was.

"I'm a murderer, killer, I buy and sell women to be used for whatever purpose their owners want. I run drugs and guns, and I have control of over half a city, maybe even more within a couple of days. I took my father's legacy, and I made it grow. Women earn a lot of money on their backs, Harper. I'm just one of many who use it."

"I was a … member of a group. I was initiated to be with four men. Then to keep them safe, I was blackmailed and forced to … hurt other people. To bring them into a life they had no control over. I knew their lives would be total shit, but I did it for you, for Axel, for Buck, and for Jett. When I stopped being told what I was going to do, I vowed I would never hurt another living innocent soul." She stared up at him, and she clapped her hands. "Congratulations, Draven. You're exactly everything your father ever wanted, too. Just like I became."

Then, she turned away and went to her room. Her heart shattered.

Draven was nowhere near the man she thought he

was. That man had died and who stood in his place was someone she didn't recognize.

****

The moment Harper turned the corner and left, Draven pounded Axel's face. "You piece of fucking shit. Why did you tell her, huh? Why did you tell her?"

Axel didn't hit him back but took the beating he was dishing out.

Each blow cut Draven to the core. He wanted Axel to fight back.

To hurt him.

To deliver whatever blow would numb the pain.

"She had a right to know," Axel said.

This made Draven stop, but Axel still didn't put his fists up. He still didn't fight.

"Why? She doesn't need to know that shit."

"Look at you, Draven. Look at us. We were never supposed to be like this. What would Buck say? Jett? We said everything was going to be different, and you can't keep blaming Harper for what we've become. Take a long look in the mirror. I do so every single day, and I don't like what I've become. Having her here reminds me of what we once were before she fucking left." Axel pointed at his face. "I don't give a shit about the scars or anything else. We were never supposed to do this. You told me I was never going to see another woman on that fucking whipping post or locked up in those cells, and yet, Harper, the woman you fell in love with years ago, was the one I saw again, in both of those places. The fact she hasn't killed you, I'd count myself lucky. You could blame her for a lot of things, I don't care. She fucking walked away when we all asked her not to. She betrayed us and worked for our enemies as a human trafficker, helping them get girls of all ages. The war that broke out, the men that died. Buck and Jett, but we can't blame her for everything. That's why I told her to go to the basement. You want to lock her away in this town and throw away the key. You think you can protect her, but you can't. One day, sooner or later, there are going to be men like us. Men who are determined to make a difference, and that's us gone. I welcome it, Draven. I welcome when they take our fucking legacy from us and destroy it. *We* were supposed to be better than this."

Axel got to his feet, spat at the floor, and walked away.

Draven picked up the picture hanging on the wall and threw it across the room. The shards of glass smashed to smithereens around their feet.

He was so fucking angry. Pissed off. Infuriated.

He didn't want Harper to find out the truth of all that he'd become. No, he couldn't look in the mirror.

So he simply ignored the image staring right back at him. His father had set up deals that Draven had no choice but to see through. They'd been strong, but the men his father dealt with had been stronger.

It was one of the many reasons Draven finally killed him.

He walked into his office and went straight for the good whiskey. No glass needed as he drank straight from the bottle. The burn was a welcome relief from the pain.

He kept on drinking, wanting that blissful peace that would come over him. Staring across his office, he saw the picture of his father. He kept it hanging on the wall so he'd feel the rage the man never failed to inspire within him.

It's what kept him going when deals went sour and he had no choice but to help. Tillie would become a problem. She owned clubs up and down the country. She was a wealthy mob man's mistress, and he liked for her to put on a show. Since taking trafficked women, her clubs had become sought after. Men and women alike enjoyed having no rules, enjoyed inflicting pain.

The girls often didn't survive. Most of the boys lasted longer.

It was a deal his father had struck.

The mob would tear through Stonewall and leave nothing standing. He still had the town to consider. It was what Alan had relished when he told him the deal that would take them to the next level.

It had been the final deal that had brought Alan down. Draven had taken over in the hope of ending it. He'd only become more embroiled within it.

Running his hand across his face, he went to his father's image and set about destroying it, smashing the glass, not caring where the shards fell, and making sure there was nothing left.

With the image in pieces, he threw them onto the fire, and went back to his drink.

Blood coated his hands, and he wiped them down his shirt. The blood stained the pristine white fabric.

He kept on drinking until he started to feel numb, and after finishing one bottle, he moved onto the second.

Halfway down the second, he knew he needed to go and see Harper.

To tell her that he loved her.

He walked up to his bedroom, and when she wasn't there, he went straight to her room. Not the one where he'd killed a man, but the one where he'd fucked her into oblivion.

Draven wasn't quiet as he opened the door. It slammed against the wall, and Harper sat up. She had been lying down in sleep, and he saw her eyes were all puffy, even with his double vision.

"Hello, my queen," he said.

"Draven, what do you want?" she asked.

"You're right. I can't look in the mirror. Not unless I've got you standing in front of me or your pussy is on display."

"Are you drunk?"

"Maybe. I'm a little drunk, but I need to say this to you. It's really, really important, so, shh."

"Draven?"

"Shh." He pressed a finger to his lips. "We don't have time to talk. Not now. I don't look in the mirror. I don't like what I see. I've never liked what I see." He touched his chest. "I've got a darkness inside, and it's spreading. I can't control it, and I want to. I want to make it stop, but I can't. It's always there. Always lurking and waiting to come out. I saw it in you, Harper. You feel pain just like me. When you left, I was torn apart. I didn't want to feel anymore, so I did his bidding. I did whatever he asked for because it was easy. I didn't have to think of all that I lost, and I lost you. I did everything to get you. Got Axel, Jett, and Buck on board. I knew that four of us against our fathers, we'd win. I didn't win. I lost, big time."

"What are you saying?"

"You can run. You can run a thousand miles, and even a hundred million miles, but I will find you."

"You're drunk, Draven."

"I know I'm drunk, and I know that this is going to be the only time I say this. I can't let you go. I don't want to let you go. I know you hate me right now, and you're justified in that. I love you. It's why I can't let you go. Even after everything I've done and we've been through together, I love you. I think you're the best person in my fucking world, and I can't let you go. It makes me selfish. I don't want to lock you in my tower and throw away the key. I want to keep you protected. To love you. To make sure I never break your heart like your dad did to your mom. There's a lot I want to do with you and for you. I can't lose you, Harper. I can handle everything else but losing you."

With that, he fell to the floor in sleep.

Chapter Fourteen

Harper blew across her coffee to try and cool it down. She wanted to be out of the house before Draven finally woke up.

She tried to pull him onto the bed, but he was far too big and heavy. She ended up putting a pillow beneath his head, and some blankets over him.

He'd also snored.

In all the time they were together, she couldn't remember him ever snoring, and the sound had kept her awake all night long.

She looked up as Ian entered the kitchen. It had been a few weeks since she last saw him. He smiled at her, and she simply watched him.

"Is Draven around?" he asked.

"Do you know everything that goes on in Draven's life?"

"Harper?"

"You know all the business deals he's part of. Do you know the complete truth about Hannah?" she asked.

"I know a great deal of it."

She chuckled. "I knew that their parents were into it, but I figured Draven would move on from it." She looked toward her father. "He's not. He's in it deeper than his father, and now he wants me to marry him."

Harper hadn't put on the ring. She'd seen it on the floor on her way downstairs, and had gone and put it in his office so he knew she didn't steal it.

"I know it looks bad right now."

"It doesn't just look bad. It *is* bad. I can't marry him. Not like this. Not knowing that … he's this person. I don't want to do this. There's a lot I can take, but … *people* not being allowed to have a choice. I can't. That's too far."

"I know it's hard."

She burst out laughing. "Hard. You think this is just hard? It's fucking painful." Tears sprang to her eyes as she looked at him. "I do love him, and it kills me. I can't do this. I won't."

"I thought this when I first joined the team."

"I really don't want this talk."

"I had your mother and you to take care of. Bills mounting up, and this job. I was in heaven, but I knew it was a bad choice, and still, I took it. I learned to look the other way."

"You ended up divorcing Mom and being with a woman half your age."

"You know I didn't want to fall for Hannah. She wasn't your mother."

"You're right, she wasn't," Harper said.

"But Hannah didn't judge me when I came here. She didn't point a finger and tell me I was a bad man or that I'd sold myself. She didn't constantly remind me that I fucked up."

"So she became the better option. No offense, you sound pathetic." Harper stood up and dumped her coffee out.

"I know this is hard."

"You don't have a fucking clue how hard this is. I'm such an idiot. You think this is easy for me? I love Draven. Love him more than I've ever loved anyone else in my life, and yet, here I am, considering leaving. I've got to go. I can't stay here knowing when he goes and does his deals, someone will die."

"It gets easier," Ian said.

"For you, for others. Not for me. Not with this." In her mind, she thought about one of the girls, wanting a better life. Harper had convinced her to follow her, that an entire world was waiting for her and she just needed to have faith, to grasp it. Alan wouldn't let a single girl slip through his fingers. Whenever he called, there was always someone he wanted.

Harper needed some fresh air, and she left through the kitchen door, finding little peace in the fresh air as it brushed across her face.

Guards were out in force, and she walked right on past them, going to the cells.

She didn't go inside, not today. Harper paused and said a little prayer for all the women who'd come before her and had died here.

She moved on through the gardens, trying to find some peace, anything that would help her deal with the pain exploding inside her chest.

"I thought I'd find you out here."

She turned to see Axel walking toward her. The first thing she noticed was the bruise on one part of his face.

"What happened?" she asked.

"Draven likes to make sure I know who is boss."

"He did this."

"I didn't exactly defend myself, and I probably deserved it."

"You didn't deserve this."

"You're sweet, you know that, right?"

"I'm not sweet." She reached out about to touch his face, but he caught her wrist, holding it tightly.

"He had a right to hurt me. I told you where to find them, and I set this chain of events off. I'm willing to pay the price."

"According to you and Draven, I did."

Axel waved his hand through the air. "Come on, there's something I want to show you."

He held her hand and started to lead her down

one set of gardens she hadn't explored.

"Where are we going? You know I can get shot from leaving the grounds."

"You'll be safe with me, I promise."

He kept on walking, and they had to have crossed some kind of border.

"Talk to me, Axel. You're scaring me."

"Well, in my search for everything to do with Alan, I went through many of his well-known hiding places. You see, as kids, we had a tendency to spy. When we were about five, we all wanted to become spies. We thought we were so clever. We'd sneak into areas of the house where private conversations were happening."

"I bet you guys saw and heard a lot of stuff you wished you hadn't."

"Bingo. That we did. Anyway, we'd been seeing a lot of shit for a lot of years, and so one day, imagine my surprise when I found that Alan liked to hide certain things. Be it murder weapons, or blackmail tapes."

"He actually had blackmail tapes on everyone?"

"You don't get high in this world without a bit of blackmail. You ever wonder why Draven, me, Buck, and Jett could get away with so much crap?"

"I didn't really think about it."

He shrugged. "It's not a lot to think about. Our fathers had dirt on all the town's people. The politicians, the cops, and they used it to keep them in check and all of us in line."

"I still don't understand why you're telling me this."

"Well, I had forgotten about Alan's hiding place because many years ago, I believed it was haunted."

"This is getting weird now, Axel."

"Oh, I know, believe me, I know. Anyway, just at the peak of the cliff, there's a path that leads into a cave.

Do you know any of the town history?"

"No."

"Oh, good, I can tell you a story then as we walk."

"This is crazy," she said.

"Not completely crazy as an old man filming everything in his office and hiding it, but Alan was never normal. So, story time about our town. Many, many years ago, Stonewall was nothing more than a little, quaint town. They didn't have supermarkets and banks and stuff. They had fields upon fields of cattle and food. Farming. It's how they as a town survived. So, anyway, one year the town suffered a huge famine. Most of the cattle died, and the crops, they didn't grow. Back then, they didn't think it was down to the fact it was too hot or too dry. Anyway, the elders in the town knew they had in some way upset the weather gods, I'm going to call it."

"Is this actually true?"

"I have no idea if it's true. I wasn't born back then. This is the story I was told."

"By who?"

"My dad. Let me finish."

"Fine. Fine."

They kept on walking. Axel didn't let go of her hand.

"Like dirty old men do, they decided the only way to appease their weather god was a virgin sacrifice. You know, the good old reliable woman's blood. I still don't get it, but I digress. The elders convinced the town that the gods would pick a willing sacrifice. The sun beamed down and ta-da, that woman was their virgin sacrifice. Now, any good town story has to have a lot of dirt, so they brought the woman up to this cave. She walked willingly as well, thinking she was doing this for her town's people. So very noble and fucking shit if you ask me. They laid her on the platform within this cave, and according to the rules, they sacrificed her. However, the story I was told, the men couldn't resist her virgin flesh and took her for themselves, each raping her. The six elders took their turn, spilling her virgin blood before slicing open her wrists and draining her. Of course, her neck got sliced in the end."

Harper didn't like this story one bit.

"The next year, a wonderful harvest. Well done, old chaps. You did it. So Stonewall had a couple of really good seasons until, like the weather predicts, it didn't. Another sacrifice. Then they decided to guarantee a good harvest every year, they had to pick a girl every single year. They'd take her up to the cave, rape her, kill her, drain her, burn her, and move on to the next girl. Until, the girls started to realize what was happening. Personally, I think the elders got a little cocky and talked openly about it, and one of the girls told the others. There were no virgins in the village."

"You're kidding me, right?"

"I'm not. It is kind of cool. They spited the village, and the women banded together to kill the elders, on the exact table they had slaughtered so many innocent girls. So that is the end of my tale. Only, the reason I never came here and Draven, Buck, and Jett never did, we were told it was haunted by the ghosts of those dead girls, and if you had hurt a woman or female in any way, they would know. Not only would they know, you'd be dead. Needless to say, to a couple of young boys, we didn't exactly want to plunge to our deaths."

"You never went to the cave."

"Exactly. As kids, we didn't go because we were fucking scared. By the time we were teenagers, I was told the cave had collapsed, and was fucking dangerous. I wasn't going to go and risk my life like that. Then, three days ago, I figured why the fuck not. I'd tried everywhere else. And I discovered the cave hadn't fallen in on itself in any way." They paused outside of the cave, and Harper didn't even want to look over the ledge. Axel pulled a flashlight from his pocket and shined it into the room. "This was the only place I didn't look. The last place I even thought about."

With the flashlight shining into the cave, Harper didn't like being here. However, right at the end of the cave, she saw the files.

"You're really serious right now, Alan hid his files here?"

"This cave is reached from my house. No one can have access to it unless they enter my land. I mean, Draven's land. You get the gist of it. My dad was many things in life, but he trusted Alan. They were a team, and they hid a great deal of stuff here, together. I doubt my father even realized Alan wanted it all to himself. His ... complacency killed him. So, I started looking. The tapes are labeled by date, and seeing as I remember the day you left so clearly, I was able to locate it." He went to a box, opened it up, and pulled out a tape. "Here you go," he said.

"Have you watched it?"

"No. I've not watched anything," he said. "I figured we'll take it home and have a little movie show with Draven. Unless you want me to do the deal today." Axel held a gun up. "What's it going to be?"

"I want to go and watch the tape." She didn't even hesitate, holding her salvation in her hands.

"Come on, let's go."

Harper followed Axel out of the cave with one glance back. She didn't know if the story was true, but her heart went out to the girls if it was.

Axel didn't speak as they made their way back to

the house.

Once inside, Harper went to Draven's office to the wall where she'd seen the old-fashioned VCR. Axel had offered to go and get Draven, to fill him in on the details.

Just as she was about to put the tape in, they entered the office. Draven looked a mess. His hair was all over the place, and he looked a little green from last night's drinking.

She turned back to the television, grabbed the remote, and moved toward them.

"So, when we're ready, I think Harper you should get on your knees and face the television," Axel said, holding out his gun again.

"You're not going to kill her," Draven said.

"A deal's a deal. For Buck and for Jett."

"No."

Harper sank to her knees. "I've got nothing to hide." She clasped her hands in front of her and waited.

Draven took the remote from her hand, and she watched as the screen came to life.

She stared at the screen. Alan sat at his desk. The date was in the corner. He was on the phone or on the computer.

Finally, when it was time, Harper closed her eyes. She didn't need to see this to remember.

The volume was turned up loud, so they could all hear it.

"Hear me properly, I can kill you. I can make the next few years of your life unbearable, but I have a feeling I've got a way of getting what I want, by removing you from the picture and you keeping your life."

"What?" This was her scream as he let go of her throat. She touched her neck, recalling how easily he

could have killed her.

"*I want you gone.*"

"*Not going to happen.*"

His smile. Always that same wicked smile that played inside her nightmares every single night. "*I want you gone. Your bags packed, no trace of you ever. As far as my son and his boys are concerned you skipped town because you couldn't handle being known as his whore.*"

"*He'll know differently,*" She'd been such a fool.

"*You've run away. Gone. You've run at the first opportunity.*"

"*And if I don't do this? What then? You're going to kill me? Draven wouldn't allow that. He'd be your problem.*"

"*If you don't go in the next twenty minutes and be out of Stonewall, I'm going to kill Draven and his boys. First though, I'll make sure that Draven knows you did this. You caused this, and I will make them all beg for mercy before I do it.*"

Even now, she felt that same fear. The thought of losing Draven, of losing any of them had filled her with such fear. She'd never been so scared, not even when she got her mother out of the bathtub. "*You're bluffing.*"

"*I figured you'd say that.*"

Then Alan finally took it to the next level. He made the man show her that Alan was always one or maybe even two steps ahead.

"*So my little guest here knows it's you, turn in a circle.*"

The guy had done just that, had shown her exactly how much control Alan had. How he was willing to kill his son, his friends.

"*Good, I want you to kill all of them,*" Alan said.

This was where her life changed forever. She watched as that gun rose, and with it, she'd seen the bullets, the death, everything that would take the men in her life away from her forever.

Harper opened her eyes and stared at her own reactions. The horror. The fear.

The man raised his gun, and she watched as it went off, the bullets lightning quick as it fired into the crowd.

Harper watched her reactions, and this time she saw how Alan watched her. She hadn't seen that back then. Right then, all she could see was Draven ducking and her hope that the others did as well. Did any bullets touch them? What the hell happened?

She saw the fear again. The pain.

"No! Stop!" She screamed. Again, it didn't show the screen going blank, just the panic and her tears. So many tears.

"Wait," Alan said.

"I'll do it. I'll go. I'll do anything just please don't hurt them."

Alan smiled. "Keep them in your sight. Don't let them leave."

He hung up his cell phone, and Harper watched as he once again grabbed an envelope from across the desk. So many actions she recalled back then that were happening now.

"My guy here, Laser, will take you to the bus stop. He'll make sure you leave."

"Why are you doing this?" she asked, tears in her eyes. Harper had tears in her eyes now. *"I love your son."* The confession he was never supposed to hear.

"Aw, that is sweet. The thing is, I've got plans, lots of good plans, for Draven, and you are standing in my way of accomplishing them. I'm being nice, Harper. Not only am I letting you live, I'm not going to keep you." He reached out, stroking a finger down her breast.

She pulled away. He laughed. He repulsed her then, and still to this day, he did. *"Well, I'd be careful who you go showing your pussy to. You come back here and your life is mine."*

"There's nothing else you can do to me."

"Oh, yes, I can. I can use you day and night. I've got a huge appetite, and seeing as you're fresh pussy and ass, I could work you until you bleed. I'm not squeamish. I'd love to fuck you raw."

She stumbled back, and Alan laughed.

"I'll be keeping this." He held up her cell phone as if it was some kind of trophy. "Harper, if you think for a single fucking second this is over, think again. I'm going to need some ... leverage. If you don't do exactly as I say, I'll make sure Draven says his goodbyes."

"What the hell does that mean?"

Alan smirked as he stepped up to her. "Let's just say I've got evidence of you running off with my enemy. With Draven's enemy. He's never going to want to see you again, and if you want him to live, whenever I need you to do little jobs for me, no matter where you go or what you do, you will do them. If not, I'll make sure to torture every single one of them. Contact Draven, and I will find out. Anything you do, everything you do, is mine and mine alone. Get out of my fucking house. Go."

This was the end of the line for her in that office. She'd never been back, not even when Axel came for her, ten years later.

Draven had moved up in the world, and in doing so, she was no longer in his office.

She watched as Alan whistled, laughed, and clapped his hands. Just then, the cook came into the office.

"Our boy is going to be eating out of my hand," Alan said.

"*Did you really have to get rid of the girl? She makes him happy.*"

The smile disappeared from Alan's face. "*Are you questioning me?*"

"*No, it's just that Draven…*"

She didn't finish her words as Alan backhanded her.

"*My son will do exactly as he's told. The little shit thinks he's better than me. Thinks he can change what he's got to do. He'll stay in line, and now that little slut is gone, he'll be easy to deal with.*"

"I think we've seen enough," Axel said, turning the video to pause on the screen.

Harper stayed on her knees, fresh waves of tears falling down her cheeks.

This was not a victory, not to her. Getting to her feet, she wiped the tears from her eyes. They would know she was crying.

She turned toward them.

Axel's emotions were turned off. He looked bored with everything. Harper looked toward Draven, and he seemed devastated.

"I just … I'm going to go to my room now." She left the office and didn't look back. There was no need to.

What had been done couldn't be changed.

****

Draven stared at the screen. His father looked so fucking happy with himself. His heart raced, and anger unlike anything he'd ever felt filled him up.

"You okay?" Axel asked.

"I…" He moved toward the desk, put his hands flat to the surface, and tried to breathe in. "Why didn't he just kill her?"

"He couldn't just kill her. Think about the mess

and the fact he'd have to come up with a reason for her disappearance. We knew he didn't want her around. This way, Alan got rid of her and made it look like she betrayed us. We fell for his lies, believing the worst of her."

"He figured out I wouldn't be able to forgive her betrayal. Running to the enemy," Draven said.

"But he also had the *evidence* she was still alive. Laser didn't look like the fucking enemy there, Draven. He was working for Alan. Every single time you came close to go to her, he'd randomly find information about her helping our enemies. Another way for you to hate her and to become more and more like him," Axel said. "It was kind of clever, really. I didn't think Alan had that kind of patience."

"He also had the fact that Buck had just died."

"There is also that."

Draven threw his arms across the desk and yelled. "That fucking bastard. I believed him. I believed Harper couldn't handle it, and all that time, all the time he was laughing at me. This was all part of his plan. To take from me. To make me do this … shit!"

The computer, the paperwork, the pens, all of it was thrown across the room.

"Draven?"

"Don't, Axel. Do not come near me. He killed everyone who could tell me the truth. Who could look me in the eyes and tell me that he took my woman from me. He's the reason Buck is not here. He's the reason Jett is not here. It had to be him that set that man on him. We were the only ones that knew what he was fucking doing!"

Draven dropped to his knees.

"I … I had her tied up. I had her whipped and put on display." Tears fell down Draven's face, and he wiped them off.

"You got to get a grip, man. All of that shit happened, but Harper's still here," Axel said.

"Do you want her?" Draven asked, looking up at his friend.

"What?"

"Do you want to fuck her? To take her as yours. Is that why you did what you did?" he asked.

"No. I don't want Harper. I never really did. Sure, it was fun with the whole initiation and what we thought would happen. It might have worked too. I know Buck and Jett adored her. She's not my type."

"What's your type?"

"I like my women who don't attack me. I saw the way she was in the ring. It was fucking fierce, but I guess I like a lady."

"You like a lady?" Draven asked.

"Come on, Draven, you were never going to share her long-term. We all knew that."

He said nothing. What could he say to make anyone else think differently when he didn't even know anything more himself?

"You believed her?" Draven asked.

"I had a ... feeling. I don't know. I just didn't think it was as clear cut as your father told us. I'd seen Harper grow in that short time, and to be honest, I never entirely believed him." Axel shrugged. "Now we've got our proof. It was the last place I looked."

"Where did you look?"

"The cave."

"The one from the story?" Draven frowned.

"Yes. I didn't think to look there." He shrugged. "Why would I? At least the truth finally came out. I'm out of here."

Draven didn't stop him. He stared at the office

that had been his for so long now. This wasn't his place.

Stonewall didn't belong to him. It had been his father's.

Turning to the television, he stared at the man who'd taken everything from him.

Harper.

Buck and Jett.

His plans.

It was all wiped out in a single day.

Alan had known it, had known with Harper around, he would have never gotten what he wanted. Draven wouldn't have unleashed a hell that had changed the course of his life forever.

He knew what to do.

First though, he was going to have one night. One night where he wasn't this man. Where he wasn't accusing Harper and threatening to kill her.

He left his office and went to his room. He took a long shower, cleaning the cuts from his hands until they stopped bleeding, and when he was clean and fresh, he changed into a robe and made his way down to Harper's room.

Draven found her sitting on the edge of the bed, crying. Tears fell down her cheeks, and his heart broke for her, for what he'd done.

He moved toward her side, and she stood up.

"Why are you here?" she asked.

"I've not come to start a fight or to do anything." He held his hands up in surrender. "I just want to spend some time with you. I know you're not going to marry me. I'm not going to ask you to. Just come here."

"What?"

"Please, come here."

She looked around the room, clearly looking for a reason not to even approach him. He waited, and finally she relented, getting to her feet and moving closer to him.

When she stood right in front of him, he stared into her eyes and smiled. "Fire." He'd not broken her.

They were both a little damaged, but he'd not broken her. The fire in her eyes told him that.

He held her chin, turning her face this way and that, staring into her beautiful bright eyes. She looked so beautiful, so fresh, so warm, so amazing.

Harper hadn't changed, not really.

"You know, seeing you again after all these years, I knew I couldn't let you go."

"Draven?"

"I don't care who was there before me. I love you with all my heart. I have done for some time." He took her hands and kissed each of the knuckles. Ones he'd seen bleed from fighting. "I'll always be sorry for what happened here. What happened between us." He cupped her cheek, wiping away the tears. "I'll never ask for forgiveness. I don't deserve it."

He ran his thumb across her lips, staring at them.

Damn, he wanted to kiss her so much, to taste her. He wanted to wipe the memory of all that he had done to her and let her know he was so very fucking sorry.

"Kiss me, Draven. Please, kiss me," she said.

"Harper, I don't think I'll be able to stop. Not if I start."

"I don't care. I need you to kiss me." She held his shoulders, pressing her body against his and moving in close to him.

She was so soft compared to him. Her curves drove his need for her even higher. Beneath the robe, he was naked, and he wanted her.

Just this once, before he took care of business,

one last time.

Gripping the back of her head, he slammed his lips down. She moaned. The sound filled the air, making him ache for more.

With her body pressed against his, he was in complete and total bliss. She was like a drug to his system, and he couldn't get enough of her. She'd been part of his soul, and it had been a slice his father had never been able to rid him of.

Whenever she was near, he had no intention of hurting her, or killing her. He loved her so much, so completely.

Her hands moved down his body, going to the belt of his robe. She opened it up, pushing the fabric from his body to spill to the floor. Her nails scored the flesh, and this time he moaned.

"You drive me crazy," he said.

"Good. You've always been able to do that."

She ran her hands down his body to his cock. She sank to her knees, and he saw the smile in her eyes. Even with them red and a little puffy, she still looked like the most beautiful woman in the world to him.

He loved her more than anything.

Yet, he didn't deserve her. To some they may have been perfect for each other, but he knew it wasn't true.

She licked the tip of his cock, sliding down the length, going to his balls, then back up. Her tongue left a trail of her saliva. When she finally took the whole tip of him into her mouth, he was in heaven.

He hit the back of her throat, and he gripped her head, pushing his cock against her. She didn't fight him, swallowing him before pulling off with a moan.

Over and over, she bobbed her head onto his length, and he loved watching her, seeing her take as much of his cock as she could and then gagging on the length. He gripped her head, using her to thrust within her.

After a few minutes of using her mouth, he pulled out of her and brought her to her feet. Taking possession of her lips, he heard her moan and he stripped her out of her clothes. Pushing her to the bed, he spread her legs open.

"Now it's my turn, and you're not allowed to come until I say so."

"That's so not fair."

"Life's not fair, baby. It is what it is."

She laughed, which turned into a groan as he licked at her pussy. Sucking on her clit, he slid his tongue down to her entrance, pressing within her, fucking her with his tongue.

He held her still, keeping her beneath him as he worked her pussy, wanting to feel her orgasm, begging for it.

"You feel so good," Harper said, gasping. "Please, more. I need to come. Please. Don't be cruel. Please."

"Come for me, baby," he said, finally giving her permission, even though he'd not waited too long.

He didn't know how much longer *he* could wait to be inside her.

When she came, he used his fingers on her pussy, watching her come apart. He loved seeing her orgasm. She always let herself go, and he marveled at the pleasure on her face. He brought her close to a second orgasm by teasing her pussy.

This time, he didn't allow her to come. When she was so close, he moved between her thighs, finding her entrance and sliding deep within.

They both gasped.

Taking hold of her hands, he locked them above her head, keeping them in place. Staring into her blue eyes, Draven lost himself to the pleasure they could experience together. This woman, who didn't even realize it, owned his very fucking soul.

Over and over, he worked his cock inside her, making love to her. He felt every pulse and ripple as she fell apart.

Driving in deep, he pressed against her clit with his thrust, and as she came to her second orgasm, he joined her, filling her cunt with his cum.

He didn't pull away, nor did he let her go.

He wrapped his arms around her, holding her close, knowing in his heart, there would never be anyone quite like Harper. Never again for him.

Chapter Fifteen

Harper woke up alone. She looked across the bed, and the space where Draven had been last night, was gone. Empty.

She touched his pillow and even that didn't have his indent.

She sat up, holding the blanket to her chest, and sure enough, he sat in the chair in the corner. He was fully dressed and ... cold.

Draven stared at her. He held a gun in his hands, and it was pointed at his head, resting against his temple.

"Draven, what are you doing?" she asked.

"I've got shit I need to do. You're free to go."

"What?"

"I want you out of my house and out of Stonewall. If you don't, I will kill you." The gun was now pointed at her.

"I don't understand."

"What? You think because we fucked last night that something has changed? That I've changed? I want you gone, Harper. Out of this house and out of Stonewall. You've got 'til six o'clock this afternoon. I've already called Ian. He's coming to collect you. I suggest you get your shit and leave."

"You have all my shit," she said.

Her heart was breaking, but she couldn't let him see. Not now.

He was pushing her away, and she got it. Boy, did she get it, but why now? He wouldn't let her go every other time, but now he wanted to—and the irony was she didn't want to go.

Draven pointed the gun to the corner, and she turned to see that her bag was waiting for her. It hadn't been touched, or at least to her it didn't look like it.

"I suggest you leave quietly and without causing a scene."

"Draven, didn't last night mean anything to you?" she asked.

"I got laid. That's what it meant."

He left. Harper stared at the door and felt so alone. When she first arrived, she wanted to run, but now, she didn't want to.

Climbing out of the bed, she rushed to the bathroom, and threw up everything she ate last night. After they had made love a second time, they'd gone downstairs, raiding the fridge, and all of that came back up now.

She knew she wasn't pregnant as she'd gotten a birth control implant in her upper arm. She didn't have to worry about the pill or taking shots. For three years she was safe from pregnancy.

Leaving the bathroom, she dressed quickly.

Without looking back, with her bag on her shoulder, she ran out of Draven's house, down toward the edge of the driveway. Part of her expected a bullet in the head. When that didn't come and she saw Ian walking toward the house, she rushed to him.

She didn't throw her arms around him, or say anything.

"Please, get me out of here," she said.

Ian took her hand, leading her to the car. Hannah and his kid were nowhere in sight. She was thankful for that.

Without looking back, she climbed into the car, and Ian took off. She stared at the town she'd not been to visit during her stay, and couldn't believe that this small place held a lifetime of memories both good and bad.

"Do you think you'll be coming back?" Ian

asked.

"No."

"Honey."

"There's nothing for me here. I know you're trying, but we're never going to have that kind of relationship. Never again," she said, sniffling.

"You love Draven, and he's here."

"I loved a lot of things. My mom included, and I didn't get to keep her. Just take me to the city. I'll figure it out from there."

"You can stay with us. I know Hannah and I would love to have you."

"It's not going to happen. I'm not even trying to be a bitch with this. I just need to cut this off. To finally leave Draven and Stonewall behind." They were passing the cemetery, and Harper gasped. "Wait. Stop. Please. I just need to do something."

Ian stopped the car without saying a word.

She climbed out and rushed into the cemetery. On the way to Buck and Jett's graves, she stopped at her mother's. It wasn't as well-kept as some of them.

She kissed her two fingers and placed them on the stone. "I love you, Mom. I will miss you every single day, but I can't stay here. I've got to go. To get out while I can."

Her tears started to fall as she moved to Buck and Jett.

"Hey, guys, I really wish you were here right now. I think you'd have been able to talk some real sense into them. You were gone too soon, and if I knew what would happen, I'd never have run. Never left you guys. If you are watching, please, keep an eye on both of them."

She turned back to the car, climbing inside.

"You okay?"

"No. I'm not okay. I'll never be okay again, but I

had to do this. It was important for me to. I'm ready to go."

Ian nodded and started the car.

He pulled out of Stonewall, and Harper allowed herself to look back, to watch the town she had grown up in and now left for a second time, get smaller and smaller.

A piece of her was missing.

That piece was Draven.

The love of her life.

The boy who'd been a man, and that man who was now a monster. He needed her, but she couldn't stay where he didn't want her. As hard as it was to admit to even herself, she would have taken him, regardless of what he did. Even though it would kill her inside to know he was responsible for taking men and women, for Draven, she would do anything. Ten years ago, she left him to keep him safe, and throughout the years, she'd worked for Alan, to keep him alive. She loved him, always had, always would. He was the other half of her soul. Even as it killed her, she didn't ask for Ian to turn the car around. He kept on driving.

When she couldn't see the town any longer, she turned back in her seat and stared out of the window. She didn't see anything though. She kept wiping the tears as they fell down her cheeks.

"You know, you could go back."

"No, I can't."

"You're a strong woman, Harper. You can handle anything."

"I can handle a lot of stuff, but not this. You didn't see him. He wants me gone, and I'm not going to force him to make me stay." She wiped her eyes a final time. "Please, just, can we just be quiet?"

"Yes, sweetie. Yes."

****

Draven watched Harper leave. He stared out of his office window and saw Ian. She didn't run into her father's arms. She'd never run into Ian's arms for as long as Draven had known her. Not since he broke her trust, and yet last night, she'd been in *his* arms, allowed him to make love to her, even after what he'd done.

He kept on watching until the car drove away.

After that, he got all the guards out of the house. Every single one of them. He told them to leave, to go to their families and if needed, they would be contacted.

Right there, in the office, he poured gasoline over every single piece of furniture and book within the office. Once it was soaked and the fumes filled the air, he stared at the office that he'd once been so fucking proud of, lit a match, and threw it in.

The fire started immediately. He walked out of the house and went to the front. Minutes passed, and he stared as the house, room by room, caught aflame.

An inheritance of evil finally burned to the ground, just like the whipping post.

Turning his back, he walked away from the house, going through the streets as he saw people rushing past him, going to the burning, to the town spectacle of what he'd created. The only good thing that house had done was to burn.

He pulled his cell phone from his pocket and dialed Axel's number.

"What?" Axel asked as way of a response.

"I've got a plan, but I need help."

"Meet me at Buck and Jett."

He didn't wait for an answer.

Draven walked through the town toward the cemetery. He passed Ian's house, knowing Harper wouldn't go there. She wouldn't go anywhere in town.

He made sure of that. He'd never forget the look in her eyes for as long as he lived.

She's been so sad, so unhappy, and it was all because of him. Because of what he'd done to her.

He couldn't back down. Not now. Not after everything he'd already lost.

Entering the cemetery, he went to Harper's mother's grave first.

"Hello, Mrs. Miller. I love your daughter more than anything else in the world. I've been blind to a lot of things, and that has made me hurt her in ways I never should have. One day, I do hope she can forgive me, but I'm never going to ask for it because I don't deserve it. I am sorry for all the pain I've caused her."

He nodded at her side and moved onto his friends.

He stared at their names, and again that old pain filled his chest.

"Well, you're a morbid one in the morning," Axel said, arriving five minutes later. "I saw what you did to the house. I hope you did it. If not, we had one hell of a gas leak. I hope you got Harper out of there as well."

"Harper's gone."

"Gone?"

"Yes. She's gone and not coming back." Draven turned to Axel. "Over ten years ago, we said when our fathers passed, be it by our hand or natural causes, we'd take over and change everything."

"That we did. It never happened."

"I want to do it now."

"Draven?"

"It pretty much means certain death. I know that. We'll have to do a lot of killing. A lot of people are going to be unhappy with us, but we've got a team of men and women who are loyal to us."

"Are you asking me to help you start a war?" Axel asked.

"I'm asking you to help me end one. Once and for all. I don't want to carry on in my father's footsteps. All of this, it dies with him."

"And at the end of it?"

"If we're still standing, we walk. We go our separate ways. This is to the death, if we can do it."

"You mean walking away for good."

"I've already burned down a house. We can go back and burn my father's house. All of it, gone. No more Stonewall. No more us. We move on."

"And you go and find Harper. Live happily ever after with her, is that it?"

"I don't see us living past this, Axel."

"What will happen with her?"

"I've made arrangements for her. She'll always be taken care of. You know I would."

"Of course I do." Axel sighed. "This is a big deal."

"I remember when we were younger, before the initiation, you came to my place, snuck into my bedroom. You were a fucking mess. You told me that you couldn't handle it. What they did to the women. It sickened you. You begged me that if we ever took over, we'd make changes. We'd be monsters with morals. I fucked everything up. I can change that now. We can't go on like this."

Axel was silent for several moments. "I'm with you. I've been wanting out for a while, but you've always been so fucking in it, I didn't want to abandon you. I know these guys would kick my ass if I even thought of it." He rubbed his chin. "Then I guess we're going to start a war."

"You're ready?"

"No, not a chance. I'm not ready, but I'm going to do it anyway, because that is what I do. No one messes with us, and they've been doing it long enough. It's time for us to take charge." Axel held out his hand. "Even if we die, it has been one hell of a life."

Draven shook his hand.

"You got a plan?" Axel asked.

"Yep, and it starts with Tillie. I'm thinking it's time to have another get-together. You know, a new meal."

"A bloodbath? I like it. I'll make sure to take care of the appetizer."

Draven stared at Buck's and Jett's graves. He owed it to them to make this right.

He *would* make it right, and then, if he was still standing, he'd go and deal with Harper. One way or the other, he wasn't going to do another deal or kill another innocent person again. That life was done, it was over.

Alan Barries had gotten his way for too long. It was his time now, and he wasn't going to allow that son of a bitch to have his way. Not now, not ever.

Chapter Sixteen

Two months later

Harper closed her eyes as she inhaled the sweet fragrance of the flowers before her. Some were roses and a few daffodils that had started to appear. All of them were so bright and shiny, and making her feel full of warmth.

"I've never known you to appreciate flowers so much," Stephanie said, coming out of the back.

Harper tucked some hair behind her ear and shrugged. "I guess I discovered a new love right here."

After Ian had taken her to a hotel, she'd asked him for one request and that was to take care of her mother's grave, to treat her with care even though he had fallen out of love with her.

Once he agreed, she hugged him tightly.

"I'm never going to see you again, am I?"

"No. I'm not coming back to Stonewall. I'm moving on, and that means I can't look back. Goodbye, Dad."

She hadn't gone back nor had she talked to him.

Like ten years ago, she had cut all contact off from Stonewall, and she didn't go looking for any news either. She didn't need to see what was going in that world. Not anymore.

Draven had seen to that.

"I've always loved flowers. They're so beautiful, and they give so much to the earth. I know we cut them up, but I feel in some way I bring a little beauty to the world."

"You never told me if you hear from Jett."

"Oh, him, he broke up with me not long after you took off. It was a bad time. He told me that I wasn't what he was looking for. I wasn't his type." Stephanie shrugged. "It was fun while it lasted."

"Men are idiots."

"You don't like men anymore?"

"Nope."

"What happened to Ethan? I know you broke up with him. He came here wanting to talk to you."

"It's all a little fuzzy, to be honest. I didn't want to see him again. It had all moved too fast. The engagement. The wedding. I didn't want any of it, you know? I just wanted some time. The most important thing, I didn't love him."

"And now you know you can't marry him?"

"I can't marry someone I don't love, and I don't love him." She never did. Stephanie liked to talk constantly about feelings. For Harper, she enjoyed the peace and quiet when Stephanie wasn't around, but she wasn't about to tell her very nice boss to shut up.

"I'm starting to think love is overrated, Harper. You need to get back out there. Meet some new guys. You know, have a blast, fall in love. Meet new people."

"One day, when I'm ready. For now, I am content to work, shop, and eat."

They got busy, and Harper used the time to excuse herself to go and get lunch. Stephanie already had something, so Harper decided to eat out. She went to a burger stand, ordered something tall and greasy, took a seat, and watched the passersby as she ate her sandwich.

With most times when she was alone, she allowed herself a few moments to think about Draven. She wondered what he was doing. How many women were being hurt? If he was happy.

She wanted to go to the cops, but she couldn't bring herself to do it. There was not enough evidence. She had nothing, and the cops, they were probably paid to look the other way. Not only that, she knew Alan had evidence of her leading those girls to their dark fate. There was no way she could do turn them in without incriminating herself.

Alan had taught her a lot, and so had life. He knew her hands were tied, and he loved to play his game with her.

Everyone had a price, something they were willing to fight for or at least turn a blind eye to. Hers had been her guys and her freedom.

It didn't exactly fill her with comfort knowing, but she couldn't do anything about it. Finishing off her burger, she threw the napkin in the trash and made her way back to the shop.

Stephanie was still busy with customers, and Harper was more than happy for the distraction. She took care of customers, or told Stephanie when she was out of her depth.

Just as they were closing up for the day, a man entered the store carrying a huge bouquet of red roses.

Harper glanced at them and let Stephanie deal with them.

"I'm looking for a Harper Miller," he said.

"I'm her." Harper wiped her hands on the apron and signed for them. "Did you order roses like this?" She turned to Stephanie.

"I didn't. They're beautiful though. They're for you, so you must have a secret admirer."

"I don't have anything."

"Here's the card," Stephanie said. Harper didn't make a move to take it. She sat and listened as Stephanie read it out. "No amount of roses will make up for what I did. I'm coming for you soon, babe. You better believe it, Draven."

Harper took the card from her and read it. She

frowned. "Does it have a number?"

"Who is Draven?"

"He's an old ... friend."

"Sounds more like an old lover."

"He's complicated."

"The complicated ones are always the best. This is the point I'm making, Harper. We need to get you back out there. Get you on the market, dancing and having fun. This Friday, I want you ready, and we're going out on the town. We're going to hit a couple of bars. Dance, flirt, and maybe make out with a couple of guys."

"What happened to you?" She wondered what Axel had done to her. Stephanie was more open, free, happy.

"Nothing. I just feel different. We have one life. One short life, and I want to live it to its fullest. The only way to do that is to live. I'm not hiding, and I do think making out with a lot of guys is incredibly fun."

"Okay, fine." Harper chuckled. "Friday night, I'll be ready. I want it to be fun though."

By the time Friday night finally arrived, Harper wasn't interested in getting pretty, or even doing anything remotely close to going out and having fun. She wanted to be alone. The roses were a problem for her. She couldn't stop thinking about what they meant.

Draven was back.

Why had he forced her to leave in the first place?

It made absolutely no sense to her why he would contact her like this.

Was it even him?

Get a damn grip, Harper.

She pushed those thoughts to one side and instead finished getting ready. By the time Stephanie picked her up, she was ready for a drink. Lots of them.

"You look ready to party," Stephanie said.

"I am. Come on, honey, show me how to have a good time."

Stephanie let out a whoop, and Harper followed her boss and friend as they entered the first nightclub.

The music was too loud.

Harper went straight to the bar while Stephanie headed for the dance floor.

She ordered herself a shot of whiskey, and knocked it back. In order to get away from the questions rushing in her head, she needed to have a lot of shots and a lot of dancing.

Stephanie dragged her onto the dance floor after her sixth shot.

The whiskey was cheap and not doing what she wanted. She threw herself into dancing. The men who joined them tried to get touchy with her, but she ignored them. If they touched her, she pushed their hands off.

Some of them muttered that she was a lesbian. Again, she ignored them. They could all go and suck on their own cocks. She was here to have fun, not to entertain them.

Stephanie got bored with a lot of clubs quickly, and for Harper, she was more than happy to keep on moving.

From one club to another, the drinks kept flowing. The only problem was during their walks to each hot club, Harper was sure she actually got sober.

She needed to numb her body, to stop thinking.

By the sixth club, Harper downed two shots, one after the other. When Stephanie tried to pull her away, she refused. "I just want to drink. That's all I want. To drink."

"You're sure?"

"I've no interest in kissing guys or having them touch me. I just want to drink."

"Okay, I'll leave you to it." Stephanie left her side and headed onto the dance floor.

Knocking back another shot, Harper, pointed to the bartender and waited, tapping her fingers across the counter.

"You know, it's dangerous to drink so much alcohol."

Harper stared straight ahead of her. She didn't need to turn to recognize that voice.

Licking her dry lips, she finally did turn, and sure enough, Draven was sitting beside her. He looked ... different.

She noticed instantly he had a scar down the side of his face that looked fresh.

He wore an expensive-looking suit, and he nodded to the bartender, who actually came to him to serve.

"Seriously, right here," she said. "I ordered my drink first."

"I'll get it," the bartender said.

"You're going to ignore me?"

"No. I'm going to sit here, wait for my drink and the buzz I'm hoping to get from it."

"You're still very beautiful," he said.

"Don't, Draven. Please, don't." She tucked her hair behind her ears and glanced behind her at Stephanie. Her boss had two men around her and was having the time of her life.

"What is it, Harper? I didn't think you were the partying sort. You know, having girl time and all that."

"I'm not. I'm here, so I don't have to think about you!" Harper got up and was about to leave, but Draven stopped her. He held her arm and wouldn't let her go.

"Where are you going?"

"To dance. To do anything but sit here and listen

to you."

He didn't let her go and instead, followed her over to the dance floor. She didn't go anywhere near Stephanie.

Draven wrapped his arms around her, holding her close even as she tried to keep some distance.

Just her luck, the dance number changed to that of a slow one, and she cursed every single DJ in the land for their inappropriate music changes.

"You look good," Draven said.

Harper tried to ignore him, but she couldn't do it. He wasn't going anywhere, and neither was she.

"You don't," she said. "I'm afraid to ask. I mean, what happened? Why are you here? Is it safe? You kicked me out of your house, and now you're here, talking to me. Do you see what I mean about this whole personal space thing?"

Draven smiled. "Let's have this dance, and then I want to take you somewhere private."

"You're going to hurt me?"

"No."

"Kill me?"

"No and to kill you would also hurt you, and I've covered that."

"Smart ass."

He chuckled. She liked the sound a little too much. Harper had missed him, no doubt about it.

She enjoyed his company, had missed him, and wanted him back. Still, she could do nothing about that. He'd kicked her out of her bedroom after stealing her away.

Now she had no choice but to rebuild her life. It wasn't easy. Not even a little bit.

Her thoughts would always escape back to Draven and what he was doing. Axel as well, but she wasn't kidding anyone about her feelings. The person she loved more than anything in the world was the one holding her. The one she had always wanted since she was eighteen years old. The one who could handle the good and the bad and would keep coming back for more.

"Come with me, Harper," he said.

She stared into his green eyes, and she trusted him. She couldn't explain it as she didn't even understand it herself.

"Okay. I've just got to go and see Stephanie first."

They finished their dance, and afterward she found Stephanie in the bathroom. Her friend wasn't interested in coming out of the stall so she called through telling her she had met someone and would see her the next day at the shop. With that, she left. Draven was waiting.

He held his jacket open for her to slide on, which she found incredibly sweet.

A car was waiting for them, and even as her heart raced, she climbed right on inside beside him. They drove for a short while. She didn't know how long before they reached an apartment building.

"This is mine."

"I figured you'd take me to a diner or something."

"No diner. I wanted complete privacy."

"But not to kill me?"

"Not to kill you."

The car was parked, and Harper climbed out, rounding the vehicle to join Draven. He held his hand out for her to take, and she accepted it as they climbed onto the elevator.

Draven gave an instruction to the driver, and in the next second, the elevator doors closed, and it was time for them to head to his floor.

She watched the light as they climbed each floor, going up and up until they finally reached his floor.

There were only a couple of doors along the corridor, and Draven went to the last one, putting in his key card and entering his apartment.

Harper followed close as he still hadn't let go of her hand.

She wasn't going to complain about that. She liked his touch and had missed it. Even though it was only holding hands, to Harper, it felt really important.

"Would you like something to drink?" he asked.

"A whiskey."

"I want you to remember this. We're going to have something a little lighter."

"You intend to control what I drink now?"

"Yes. I don't care if you like that or not."

She rolled her eyes.

"You know that just makes you look sexy as fuck."

She smiled. "I'll take that as a compliment."

"Do."

She chuckled.

"I'll get wine."

He let go of her hand, and she watched him walk away.

Staring around the apartment, it didn't give anything away about the man. Draven had always been a private person, and he never trusted anyone. Even when they were kids, she never saw anything that screamed it was his room or his space.

He returned with two glasses of wine, and she took a long drink.

"You're nervous?" he asked.

"Wouldn't you be?"

"I guess I would. Especially if I didn't know the truth."

"You've got a couple of scars you hadn't before."

He rubbed his face and smiled. "Yeah, I do."

They sat in silence for a few moments. Harper drank her wine, and the nerves hit her hard.

"I'm out," he said.

"What?"

"I'm out of the trafficking, the drug trade, the guns, all of it. It's gone. I'm done. A clean slate. After everything, I'm all out."

"I didn't think it was possible for you to do that." She frowned.

"It's always possible. There just have to be certain sacrifices. You've just got to learn to sever ties where necessary, cause a shitstorm of problems, and all the while, know what you're planning to do."

"I don't understand."

"I had Axel by my side. He never wanted any part of this and had hoped we'd be out of the trade forever."

"It never happened?"

"No. When you left, I didn't even question my father about it. I just accepted it, as if I knew deep down, you'd leave. You'd find some way to escape me, to run from all of this. I know now that you didn't, but it set off something inside me. I became the monster I always knew was there. I have a darkness within me, Harper. I can't get rid of it. I've done a lot of bad things, and I wish I could change them, but I can't. Especially when it comes to you. You've now got scars on your back because of me."

"Don't think about it. We've all done a lot of bad things. I've done a lot I'm not proud of."

"I'll never forget what I did. It'll always be my punishment."

She licked her dry lips. Her wine no longer held any appeal to her. "What happened?"

"Tillie's dead. So are all the people you saw around the table and their witnesses as well. They're all gone."

"You killed Tillie?"

"Yes. I also released those women as well. They're back home."

"Oh."

"I've also sent some information to a group of men, an MC that I know deals with women who are being trafficked or have been. I believe they'll find the women who have already been sold and will try to locate them."

"Really? They can do that?"

"Yes. From my understanding, they can do anything."

"Wow," she said.

"Yeah, I know."

"I can't believe you killed Tillie." She had wanted to. Hitting that bitch had given her immense satisfaction that had lasted for days, far longer than anything else.

"It was easy. She was my first stop. Once I took care of her, it was easier to work my way up the chain."

"I thought Tillie was connected to someone bigger?"

"She was. Tillie was a first-class bitch, and she liked money. She loved power, and once I showed her owner what she'd actually been doing all this time, he was more than happy to have a deal. The information she had to trade with, for my life and Axel's."

"Information?"

"Tillie had been gathering evidence and money. She intended to either blackmail her owner, or sell it to the highest bidder for protection. With killing her, I got the details and also made sure there were no repercussions, which helped to wrap everything up quite nicely. Axel took care of the rest. He handled the negotiations, and helped get us out."

"Is that the end of it?"

"Not quite."

"Each fight came with risks, but I realized I wanted out completely and so, I'd take any fight that meant certain death. I no longer wanted to be the man my father had created, but my own person. I didn't want this life. It's not my legacy to keep on fighting for. It's his."

He told her how he and Axel fought each opponent, selling off information for a once in a lifetime offer of getting out. They used Alan's information that he'd kept hidden to help set them free. It had never been done before, but he and Axel had done the impossible. There were men who had stuck by his side, and who were loyal to him and him alone. Men who were ready to see him into any venture he saw fit.

"Where is Axel?" she asked. "You keep talking about him and how you both risked your life, and I'm trying not to freak out because he's nowhere to be seen?"

Draven smiled. "He took off about three days ago. When we finished it and we finally had our freedom, he told me he was done. That he had some things of his own to take care of, and that if we ever saw each other again, it would be a pleasure but not to hold my breath. We both made a great deal of sacrifices, and I'm not saying there won't be backlash later on, but for now, we're free men. I have no doubt we're being watched though, to make sure we're out for good. I'm not a rat though. That's how I got out. I didn't go to the cops. I went to the source. Information for freedom with the right people."

She reached out, touching his cheek. "You're sad about Axel."

"He's my best friend. There's no way I can be anything else but sad about that. He's the only one I have left."

Seeing Draven upset cut her up inside.

Putting her glass down, she moved across his lap, straddling him. He grabbed her ass, but she only wrapped her arms around his neck, holding him.

Draven ran his hands up and down.

"I'm so sorry for all that you lost."

He wrapped her hair around his fist and tugged on the strands, pulling her head back. "No, I'm sorry for everything I did to you. For wasting all this time. For believing him."

"It's fine."

"No, Harper, it's not fine. It's never going to be fine."

She traced a finger across his lips. She felt the evidence of his arousal pressing to her core. Harper stayed perfectly still as he stroked the line of her back and stared at him.

"I've got a question," she said.

There was really nothing else for her to say about the other thing. She couldn't change what happened, nor did she want to sit and think about it all the damn time.

It happened. They both made mistakes.

"Ask me."

"How are you able to afford this?" she asked. "It's not that I have a problem with it. I don't. Honestly. Money has always made me uncomfortable, but if you're no longer in the business, what about this place? What are you going to do from now on?"

"I wasn't just in the illegal shady business practices, Harper. I had invested a lot of time already into small ventures. I own a couple of coffee shops, a vineyard out in Italy, and I also love playing with the stock market as well. I'm not as rich as I once was. I made more dirty money, but I don't have it anymore. It's gone. I only have what is legal."

"A man of many talents."

"Yes."

His hands ran down to her ass, and Harper tensed up. Climbing off his lap, she took a seat beside him, and sipped at her drink.

"I make you uncomfortable?"

"It's not you. I mean, it is, but not directly you, does that make sense?"

"Not at all."

"Fine. I ... you hurt me. Kicking me out of your house and after everything we've been through. I don't want to rush this. If you're planning to stay, and I don't know, live here, then I'd like the chance for us to date each other. To actually spend time as a couple and not as friends or just as friends. To experience the right kind of stuff we should have all those years ago."

He stroked a finger across her cheek, tucking her hair behind her ear. "I'll happily date you, Harper."

She smiled. "I didn't expect you to relent so quickly. We don't have to get to know each other, but I'd like to date you. To see what it's like."

He laughed. "I happen to have a spare bedroom. You can sleep there tonight."

"Thank you, Draven." She stared at him. Her gaze dropped to his lips and she knew it was going to be hard to do this, but she would.

****

Dating wasn't so bad.

It was like being friends, just without the sex and knowing the sex was going to come eventually. In between work, Draven took her out to meals, to movies, and they did everything couples did. He finally met Stephanie. Like Axel said, he'd helped her to break out of her conservative skin and to learn to party.

Harper always had a new story to tell.

Every time he picked her up, she always looked ready to tell him not to bother. That was one of his biggest fears. Harper telling him she'd had enough, that she no longer wanted to be with him, and they were through.

He'd only just gotten her back, and already he was fucking nervous about everything he did or said, and it was killing him.

But he kept on dating her, even when he got nervous picking her up and with each phone call.

One night, after taking her to the opera, which was new for her, they were heading to dinner, and Draven stopped.

"What is it?" Harper asked.

"Do you enjoy spending time with me?" he asked.

"Yes, why? Have I given you a reason to think I don't?"

"You always look—forget it," he said, taking her hand.

She wouldn't budge.

"Harper, I don't want to do this."

"You can't just start something like that, cut off, and that be the end of it. That's not how this works."

"It's fine. We've got reservations."

"Draven, I don't care how many reservations you make. You clearly need to talk to me, and we can either cause a scene right now, with minimal people here, or we can scream the roof down and let a whole load of people know our business inside a restaurant." She pulled her hand away from his and folded it beneath her breasts.

He couldn't help but notice the curve of her tits. The dress she wore enhanced her breasts, her waist, and hips, and it made him ache to touch her. To hold her. To take her. To have her all to himself so he could just fucking enjoy her.

"You want to do this out here?"

"I don't see we have much of a choice."

"Do you want to end this with me?"

"What the hell are you talking about?" she asked.

"This. You and me. Are you building up to kick me to the curb, or what? I'm not wasting any more time."

"What made you even think that I was considering that?" she asked. She also glared as well.

"The way you look at me."

She laughed. "Seriously? You're going to cause this because I happen to look at you the wrong way?"

"I've killed men for a lot less."

She rolled her eyes, only this time he didn't see it as sexy, not even a little bit.

"Look, I don't know what is going on with you right now, Draven. I'm not wanting to end this. If I did, I wouldn't have gone home with you. Is this about sex?"

"No."

"Then what is it about?"

"I need to know that you're not fucking afraid of me. That you're not thinking of ways of getting out of this. I need to know you're in it as long as I am. For a lifetime."

"Draven—"

He held his hand out. "No, I need you to hear me out with this. I know you've got to say something, but I really need for you to hear me out first."

"Fine. Then let's hear it," she said.

"I'm in love with Harper Miller. I have been for a

long time. It has never changed. The time apart, it was … hard. I didn't want to kick you out of my house, but I had to. There is no place for me at Stonewall. I burned it to the ground, along with all of our legacies. They're gone. I'll never see them again. I'll never go back there either. There's nothing for me there. You reminded me of what it was that I wanted in life. What I had hoped to achieve and the only way I can get that, is with you. I see this look in your eye, and it scares me. I don't want you to be afraid of me, or to hate me. I can handle everything else that is thrown at me, but when it comes to you, I can't. There's only so much I'm willing to take, and I love you."

"I'm not lovable, Draven. I don't deserve it."

"Harper?"

"No! I don't want this to end. That's the furthest thing from what I want."

"I love you."

"You keep saying that," she said.

"It's true, and I've not spent nearly enough time telling you exactly how much."

She blew out a breath. "This is all … this is so sudden," she said.

"No, it's not."

"Draven?"

"No. You think about it. This is not sudden. This is very fucking late, and we've known this for a long time."

He saw the tears in Harper's eyes.

"You have all of me, Harper. Every single little bit of me. It belongs to you. No one else."

She moved toward him and pushed him hard. "First, I'm not afraid of you." She pushed him again, and this time the car behind his back stopped him. "I'll never be afraid of you. Second, I'm nervous because this is all new for me. I've been on dates with Ethan, but this is so much more. I can't think straight. I'm nervous I'm going to screw up and say the wrong thing and you'll realize I don't belong in this world. I'm not a good person, Draven. I've done so much stuff. I lost ten good years with you all because ... I didn't ask you to come to the bathroom with me. There are times I can't even look in the mirror because it hurts that much to know what I've done." She shoved him again, only he had nowhere to go. "I'm not just the girl from the poor area of Stonewall, regardless of where my father is now, Draven. I'm the girl who worked for your father. The one who he forced to help take girls. I should be in prison. Behind bars. I can't stand to think about what I've done. I close my eyes and see them. I know the mess I've caused, and I'm ashamed of myself, of what I did. Eighteen-year-old Harper, she's not here anymore. I'm me. I'm not used to getting what I want. I want you, nothing more. I'm the woman that ran away because she thought her best friends would be killed. I'm the person that continued to work for a man I despised because I was scared. I didn't fight enough, not then. I just took everything he told me to do, and I fucked up. *That's* the kind of person I am. I've been so scared because you'd see the truth of who I am, and all that I've done. I'm nothing. I wanted these dates with you, to make me ... feel something else. I don't need fancy cars, or jewelry." She chuckled. "I don't even need these dates, but they were fun to be with you after all this time, and I want to be that girl again. I don't get the opera. I'm not a fancy girl. I'm just me. I work in a florist, and I don't care what we went through. I'm not afraid of you." She placed her hands flat on his chest. "I'll never be afraid of you. This is all just new, and I'm a girl. Let me be a girl about all of this, about everything."

"Fine," he said, cupping her face. "You're not nothing. You're everything to me. I don't care what Alan did. It wasn't you. It'll never be you. I'll never turn my back on you. Never. I can wait for you to be ready. So long as you agree that if at any time you're scared or nervous, you come to me."

"Agreed," she said. "Don't forget this is all new to me too."

"I hate the opera."

She burst out laughing. "Why did you take me?"

"I thought you'd like it."

She kept on laughing. "That makes no sense to me at all. You're a crazy person, Draven Barries. Take me home." She pressed her lips to his, and he held her close, deepening the kiss.

Chapter Seventeen

Two months later

Dating Draven was ... strange.

Especially as Harper was the one to hold back. After everything they'd been through, she didn't want to rush their time together. This was a first for them, after ten years apart. They were taking their time and enjoying each other, and of course, to get to know one another without the threat of his father or anyone else in their life.

In the beginning, she was nervous in case there were repercussions from his past. There were times she'd see him gazing out over the city, and she was sure he was waiting for something. He was always careful, and she knew he carried a gun. She had also seen a guard was close by her at all times. Day by day, week by week, even as nothing happened, he was still cautious.

He'd been able to start a life with his businesses and become part of it. He worked from his laptop and often stopped by the florist shop and talked with Stephanie about ways to expand.

In fact, Draven had taken Stephanie out to look at another property across town while she was taking care of the shop.

He'd become such a sweet and tender ... boyfriend.

It seemed odd to call him that. She was arranging the delivery of some fresh roses when the doorbell sounded.

"Just a moment," she said.

Harper turned and froze. Standing before her was Axel. She'd not seen him in so long.

"Axel," she said.

"Hello, Harper. You've missed Draven."

"I know. I saw him with Stephanie. You're looking good."

"Thank you."

He looked a little scary.

"What's going on?"

"I wanted to come and see you. I know you'd tell Draven that you had, and so I can rely on you."

"What's going on?"

"Nothing. Not a damn thing. I've got a thing going on right now. It's kind of important. Your boyfriend has been looking for me, and I grow tired of it. Tell him to keep his distance or I'll make his life hell."

"Axel?"

"Tell him that, Harper. He'll get the message."

"Are you and him fighting?"

"No. What we are is moving on, and Draven won't let me. You make him leave or I will hurt him."

"I'll get him to leave you alone."

"Good. You look amazing. When he proposes, accept it."

"What?"

Axel turned on his heel about to walk away, but she rushed ahead of him, throwing herself in front of the door.

"Harper, please." He looked bored.

"I know you don't like me or anything right now, but there's no way you can tell a woman that and just walk away."

"I intend to."

"Axel, I mean it."

"Fine, fine. I saw he bought the ring. It's a brand new one. Not the family heirloom that was on his dad's side. It's pretty. It was always supposed to be you and Draven. You both make one hell of a couple."

"And you know how to spoil surprises."

He reached behind her to open the door. He held the door and slowly moved her without even breaking into a sweat.

"At least tell me you're all right," she said.

"I'm all right, Harper. Don't worry about me."

Harper watched him leave. Her heart pounded, and as Stephanie and Draven arrived hours later, all she wanted to do was ask him about it.

She didn't bring it up in front of Stephanie even though she wanted to so damn badly. Forcing a smile to her lips, she got through it. Closing time was a welcome relief to her.

"Are you going to tell me about what happened with Axel?" she asked as soon as they got in the car.

"Axel?"

"Yeah, he came to the shop while you were out."

Draven got out of the car, looking around.

"He's not there. He left. He said to leave him alone and to stop looking for him or he's going to make your life hell. I don't even know what that means."

"It's not important."

"He wants to be left alone."

"He's my best friend."

"So do as he asks and leave him alone."

"Is that all that he said?" Draven asked.

"No, he said something else, and I don't want to repeat it."

"Harper!"

"No, because what if he was lying and then I just look silly, you know? I'm not going to say what it was."

"Really?"

She pushed some hair out of her face and turned toward him. "Fine. Axel told me you were going to propose. There. I said it."

Draven snorted. "Leave it to him to spoil absolutely everything."

"Everything?"

She watched as he reached into his jacket and pulled out a velvet box.

"Is that what I think it is?"

"I've been wanting to give you this for some time now. I've tried to find the right moment, and now that Axel's fucked it up, I may as well. I want you to marry me, Harper. I want us to make this official. Real. To stop wasting time."

"You really want to go through with this?"

"Yes. You, me, this, us." He took the ring from the box. "I want to bind you to me forever so you know there's no one else in the world that I could ever want."

"I know there's no one else in the world."

"And now the rest of the world know who you belong to."

She stared down at the ring, then into the eyes of the man she loved. "You changed everything for me. You turned your back on all that you'd known, for me."

"Yes. I want you, Harper. More than anything else in the world. I love you more than anything. You're mine. You know you're mine."

She stared at the ring and knew there was no one else she could ever want.

Harper loved him, and scars and all, she would have stuck by him through everything. "Yes."

"Yes?"

"Yes." She nodded her head and laughed. "A million times yes."

He took the ring and slid it onto her finger. For Harper, it felt right. He took her hand, running his thumb across the diamond. "You're never going to regret this. Not now. Not ever."

When his lips pressed against hers, after all they'd been through, the heartache, the pain, the loss, all of it, they still had each other, and with that, nothing could take that away from them.

****

Six months later

Much to Draven's disappointment, Harper wanted a proper wedding, one for them to remember. Even though she hated being the main subject of conversation where people stared at her, she still went through with the wedding.

Of course, for Draven, he didn't have a best man.

He sent Axel one message. He wanted him, and no one else would be good enough for him.

Draven never got a response, and now as he stood in his changing room in the church, he had to wonder if Axel was even alive.

The only way he knew was from Harper seeing him six months ago, but now, was he dead? Was he lying in a ditch somewhere? He worried about his friend, but he took Axel's threat seriously and he'd backed off. He'd called off his men. Axel's threat was simple, if he didn't leave him alone, he'd take Harper.

It was well played, and seeing as the only person Draven really loved was Harper, he knew it was a real risk.

Staring at his reflection, he had Ian on his team, making sure Harper didn't do a runner. Not today.

He was running his hands down his suit, removing any wrinkles when the door opened and in stepped Axel.

His best friend looked like he'd been in a war zone. Neither of them had come out of their war unscathed. Behind closed doors, Draven still had to deal with certain … problems that arose from his past. He didn't discuss any problems with Harper as he didn't want her to worry. He wasn't back in the lifestyle; he simply helped certain men and women find the right contacts.

"You made it."

"You think I was going to let my best friend get married all on his own?" Axel stepped forward and started to fix his tie. "You got the rings?"

"Yes."

"Good. I'll have them."

"Where you been?"

"Draven, don't even start with the third degree right now. Not in the mood. Are you sure about this wedding?"

"I love Harper. I want to marry her."

Axel held up his hands. "I'm just giving you an opportunity to run if you need to."

"Not going to happen."

"Good. Right, let's get this show on the road."

"Are you sticking around?" Draven asked.

"I'll stay for the party, but once you and Harper go, I've got things I want to do. A life to get back to. You've got Harper now, Draven. We've done what we set out to do all those years ago."

"I miss Buck and Jett," he said.

"They should be here."

"They are," Axel said. "As corny as this shit sounds, they're right here, with us."

"You're right, that is corny."

"One last chance to ditch."

"I'm not ditching." Draven smiled. "I've waited for this moment for far too long."

He followed Axel out of the room, and they took their positions at the altar. The priest stood silent, and the guests talked amongst themselves.

Stephanie, Hannah, and Harper's little sister walked down the aisle, and then the song changed.

He saw Harper with Ian.

Her father had agreed to give her away, and seeing her right now, Draven's heart raced.

"You did good, buddy," Axel said.

Step by step, Harper walked toward him. This was how it was supposed to be all those years ago, and now finally after all this time, it was finally happening.

Harper was going to be his wife.

****

"I'll have this dance, Mrs. Barries," Axel said, taking hold of Harper's arm and leading her onto the dance floor.

"It's good to have you today."

"I'm not sticking around, Harper. Don't get used to me."

"Why not?"

"I've got shit I want to do. I know Buck and Jett would have wanted me here."

"So that's the only reason you decided to stop by?"

"That and to finally see you two tied town. You've always been Draven's queen. It's good to see you in your place."

She rolled her eyes. "What is going on with you?" she asked.

"Nothing. I've got my own life to lead, and now that Draven's out of the life, Draven and I, we can live it how we see fit. He's going more legit. He's even moved in with you. That has to be an experience."

Harper chuckled. "He doesn't like how small my apartment is. I love it."

"Good. He likes it when you fight him. When you don't bow down to what he wants. He's afraid that you fear him."

"Axel, why don't you stick around?"

"Can't do it. I'm afraid I've got someone waiting for me."

"You're seeing someone?"

"Without a doubt."

"Why didn't you bring her to the wedding?"

"It wasn't appropriate." Axel kissed her hand. "I've got to leave now. If you ever break his heart again, Harper, I will fucking kill you. I want you to understand that." He stepped close, his hand so near her neck as he held her tight. He could be choking her right now, and no one could stop it.

She saw Draven past his shoulder, walking toward them. She turned her head and kissed Axel's cheek.

"You'll never have to."

"Good. I'm glad we've got this understanding." Axel stepped back. "As always, Harper. You look stunning."

"What's going on here?" Draven said.

Axel let go of her hand. "I've got to head out. I think I can leave you two not to fuck this up for yourselves."

Before either of them could stop him, Axel was gone.

"Fuck!"

"What is it?"

"Nothing. I didn't want him to leave."

"I'm sorry."

"It's not your fault." Draven pulled her into his arms. "Hello, Mrs. Barries. What was he talking about before I came over?"

She didn't want to spoil the wedding. "Not a lot. Just wished us both a good future together. You know, one filled with love and babies."

He smiled. "Babies. You want them?"

She groaned. "I'm not sure. Maybe one day."

Draven kissed her temple. "You can count on it."

Harper rested her head against Draven's chest and closed her eyes. There's no way she was leaving Draven, not unless it was in a wooden casket. He owned her heart just as she possessed his.

Epilogue

Five years later

"Buck, Jett, get your asses in the house now. It's cold, and I won't have you ill for Christmas."

Draven folded his arms and watched as his twin boys rushed into the house. Not long after the wedding, he knocked Harper up, and five years later, his sons were playing in the yard. Both of them were fierce little warriors.

True to his word, they had never gone back to Stonewall. That place was in their past.

His sons ran past him, both of them heading to the sink, washing their hands before going to the table.

He watched as Harper rushed into the kitchen, picking up the platter of food. She held it against her hip, rustling their hair as she passed.

"Mom!" They both cried out, and she laughed.

Draven was so fucking happy that there were moments when he could just stand and watch them. He had to. It helped for him to make sure they were still real. Still alive. Still his family.

With everything he put Harper through, he spent most nights watching her sleep, marveling at the fact she was still his. She was his wife of five years, and the mother of his two sons.

"Are you coming?" she asked, hand on hip as she smiled at him.

"They were playing ball."

"Like always." She moved toward him, her hands on his chest. "Are you okay?"

"Yeah, I'm fine."

"Are you thinking about Axel?"

"No. I'm thinking about you." He pushed some

hair off her shoulder. "I'm always thinking about you and how lucky I am that you didn't leave me."

"I couldn't leave you, not ever." She cupped his face, kissing his lips. "Even if you did stuff dirt into my locker."

He gripped the back of her head, holding her tight against him as he took over the kiss, deepening it, making her kiss him back until she moaned.

"Call your dad to come and pick them up. I want you all to myself tonight."

"We can't keep using him to babysit whenever we want to have sex."

"Yes, we can," he said, sliding a hand down to cup her ass. "What else would we use him for?"

He pressed his cock against her, and she moaned. "I'll call now."

Draven reluctantly let her go, taking his seat at the table where his boys were waiting, patiently.

"Buck, Jett, Grandpa is coming by to pick you guys up for some fun," Harper said, taking a seat. "Doesn't that sound good?"

He smiled as they cheered.

Ian had been an awful dad, but he was proving to be a much better grandparent. It was the least he could do for them.

Draven watched Harper, anticipating the night to come.

She'd run from him, and he'd catch her. When he did, he'd fuck her hard, and then make love to her, showing her who she belonged to once again.

The End

www.samcrescent.com

SAM CRESCENT

Printed in Great Britain
by Amazon